WIDOWS OF MEDINA

FBI TASK FORCE S.W.O.R.D.
BOOK 3

D.D. BLACK

Medina
Lake
Washington
Bellevue
90
Beaux Arts
Village
Mercer
Island
Mercer
Island
Seward Park
405

"I have yet to meet one widow who hasn't changed in monumental ways as she has coped with her loss. Most of us have gotten to the point where we are not the "pleasers" we once were. We say what we think, we realize that life is precious, and we don't have time to be anything less than who we really are."

— Catherine Tidd

"Widowhood is a singular journey, but one need not walk it alone."

– Unknown

"Too many people spend money they earned to buy things they don't want to impress people that they don't like."

– Will Rogers

PART 1

WEALTH BEYOND BELIEF

CHAPTER ONE

Medina, Washington

July 8

"SHALL I OPEN IT, SIR?" Geoffrey presented the rare whiskey on an intricately designed display platter in front of Vincent Blackwood.

Amber and gold shadows streamed from the liquid showpiece, dancing across the sterling silver tray as Vincent lifted the bottle, cradling it like a newborn. "Macallan Valerio Adami, sixty years old. Let's give it a bit longer, shall we?"

Geoffrey nodded.

"Paid two-point-seven million at Sotheby's for it. They say only ten bottles like this are left in the world." Hearing a roar of laughter from guests walking outside his office, Vincent looked up. "Did everyone get to see the bottle?"

"Absolutely, sir." Geoffrey had spent much of the evening parading the bottle through the crowd, carrying it on its own silver tray and leaving it on display in various rooms. "And we have the glasses ready for tastings after you've completed your ritual."

Vincent held the bottle at arm's length, taking in the label. "It's supposed to be unreal—dark fruits, antique oak, treacle, ginger. Like drinking a piece of history, if history came in a glass."

"Sounds incredible, sir."

"We'll make sure you get your sip at the end of the night, Geoffrey." Vincent smiled. "Do you know, I come from whiskey stock?"

"I've heard bits and pieces." Geoffrey placed his hands behind his back, ready for the story.

"I do." Vincent chuckled, gently placing the bottle in the center of the tray. "My old man worked the line in some no-name whiskey factory in Kentucky his whole life, bottling cheap stuff they'd sell by the gallon. My grandad came over from Scotland, landed in Kentucky looking for work, and found it in coal. My father said my grandad always talked about wanting to go home, but he never made it out of the mines."

"Did your father ever visit?"

"Never had the money," Vincent said. "And I didn't make my fortune in time to take him. Now he's too far gone to enjoy it. I doubt he would remember it had once been a dream of his to go."

"That may be the saddest thing I've ever heard."

"Plenty of people never get back to their nesting grounds."

"Not that." Geoffrey looked down at his feet. "It's one thing to never reach your dreams, but it's crushing that it's possible to forget them altogether."

"Dementia is like that." Vincent took in a deep breath and let out a long exhale. "Guess I'm completing the circle for them now—bringing Scotland home in the rarest way possible."

"Good for you, sir."

"Thank you." Vincent nodded, as though settling an internal debate. "I think this year, I'll open the bottle myself."

"Very well, then." Geoffrey waited to be excused.

Vincent nodded to dismiss him. "Thank you."

"Oh, one more thing." Geoffrey reached into his pocket. "Of course, you'll be needing this, sir." He placed a foil cutter on the desk.

"Yes, thank you again." Vincent reached for the cutter. "It's been a hell of a year, Geoffrey."

"Happy birthday, sir." Geoffrey wasn't sure if Vincent was going to say more. After a beat, he sensed their conversation had ended. "Well, I'll leave you to it."

Vincent smiled and nodded. "Please tell my wife I'll be joining her soon."

"Of course." Geoffrey walked to the doorway and turned.

The study was a masterpiece of modern luxury, with floor-to-ceiling glass walls offering views of Lake Washington. Polished walnut shelves lined with first editions and rare artifacts framed the room, while a sleek, minimalist desk dominated the center, its surface aglow with embedded touchscreens.

"Open or closed, sir?"

"Closed," Vincent said, not looking up.

From the study, Geoffrey moved into the main section of the mansion. The grand entryway led into a sprawling, open-concept living space with soaring ceilings and walls of glass that framed an uninterrupted view of the water. Stone accents added natural gravitas to the sleek design, while recessed lighting bathed the room in a flattering glow. Every detail, from the polished concrete floors to the custom-built staircase with floating glass steps, spoke of understated elegance and cutting-edge technology.

Geoffrey moved efficiently, his eyes taking in everything. As he passed a server carrying a tray of canapés, he made a barely detectable gesture, giving a look that called the young man to attention. "Fingertips for finessing fancy foods, Brandon," he murmured, barely breaking stride. From the corner of his vision, Geoffrey watched Brandon discreetly correct his positioning.

Geoffrey's path carried him through the great room, where soft jazz played from a state-of-the-art sound system, and into the kitchen—an expanse of stainless steel and black stone countertops where the catering team worked like a well-oiled machine.

He paused briefly to inspect a platter of crab cakes being prepared for the next round of hors d'oeuvres. Spotting a garnish that was slightly off-center, he stared at it disapprovingly. In a flash, the expeditor adjusted it with a chef's tweezer, using a flick of his wrist. Satisfied, Geoffrey nodded to the sous chef and moved on, gliding through the mansion like a conductor orchestrating an invisible symphony.

Every door he passed slid open with a soft hiss, activated by sensors embedded discreetly in the walls. Touchscreens mounted in inconspicuous locations allowed staff to adjust lighting, music, or temperature with a whisper, but Geoffrey hardly needed them. The mansion's design might have been futuristic, but it was his presence that brought it to life, ensuring every element worked in perfect harmony.

Geoffrey stopped near the living room. Hailey Blackwood, Vincent's only daughter, was crouched in front of one of Vincent's more ridiculous purchases—a white robot dog with smooth, articulated limbs and glowing digital eyes. The thing stood motionless, its mechanical legs stiff, as Hailey, in a black cocktail dress, jabbed at her phone.

"Winston, fetch the champagne!" she demanded. The robot's head twitched to the right, the mechanical dog trying to understand the words. "I'm sorry—Princess Hailstorm—I haven't learned that trick. Would you like to teach me?"

Hailey groaned, looking up at Geoffrey.

Geoffrey shrugged. He knew that Suzanne, Hailey's stepmother, had taught the dog to call her that. It was a secret he was willing to take to the grave.

The dog turned its head to a neutral position, its eyes blinking as though scanning for further command. Then it stood there frozen with a distant stare on its face.

"Totally useless," Hailey groaned. The young woman had perfected that entitled groan.

"Perhaps, Miss Blackwood," Geoffrey said dryly, "fetching champagne is better left to the professionals."

Hailey was twenty-two and, after living for a year in an ashram in India, she had returned home to live with her father while simultaneously criticizing him for his wealth and the deals his company made selling technology solutions to the U.S. military. She had not yet earned herself a DQ rating, but he was quite sure it would be low when he got around to it.

He'd first come up with the idea of the Decorum Quotient, or *DQ*, during his early days working in private service, when he realized that wealth alone did not equate to refinement. The DQ was his private metric, a blend of factors he meticulously observed: the subtlety of a guest's attire, their tone when addressing staff, the balance of their generosity against their vanity, and the ease with which they navigated social situations. To Geoffrey, it was a measure of true class—something no amount of money could buy and no title could bestow. Over the years, he'd honed his scoring system to an art, quietly calculating each guest's DQ within moments of their arrival, combining every aspect of their appearance and presentation with the meticulous research he did before they arrived.

Most of the guests were outside, so, after completing a slow lap around the edge of the patio, Geoffrey took a position along the side of the house where he could see the party unfold.

He couldn't be certain, but he believed the men and women before him represented the single wealthiest gathering ever to take place in the state of Washington. What he was sure of was that there was more opportunity than ever to work on his DQ ratings.

He looked up at the sky, breathing a sigh of relief. After reports of possible rain, the weather had cooperated.

A small army of waiters moved in and out of the waterfront mansion like shadows, balancing silver trays with hors d'oeuvres and crystal glasses that caught the fading sunlight. Their destinations were the CEOs, politicians, celebrities, and others who managed to get on the list for the most important party of the summer.

A warm breeze drifted in, carrying the scent of freshly cut grass and the tang of the water. The lawn rolled gently toward the lake, the surface of which was golden and glassy, mirroring the distant Seattle skyline and making the Space Needle appear to stand tall in two directions.

"Geoffrey, Mrs. Cuttle is out of Dom Perignon."

Geoffrey turned and looked up the wide stone staircase that descended from the upper level of the patio. The queen of the mansion, Suzanne Blackwood, was making her way down.

"Not to worry, Mrs. Blackwood." Geoffrey moved his eyes from Suzanne to Mrs. Cuttle. The rail-thin woman in her mid-eighties consumed only vintage champagne, oysters, and the occasional side salad—'Hold the onions, they're *much* too offensive.' Her DQ was a solid seventy out of a hundred.

Though she drank lavishly, her charitable efforts around Seattle were legendary, and he'd never once heard of her mistreating a staff member. One and a half inches of champagne remained in her glass.

Like clockwork, a waiter approached her with a tray carrying a single empty glass and a new bottle of champagne.

"She'll soon be enjoying the 2002 Rosé," Geoffrey added smoothly.

Suzanne nodded. "I apologize, Geoffrey. I should have known you would be on top of things. You always are."

"Thank you, Mrs. Blackwood." Without looking at them, he tilted his head subtly toward a small group gathered under a wooden gazebo at the edge of the patio. "For the Miller family, I've dipped into your single malt scotch collection. Nothing over the top—only the Macallan 40-year—but I know that Mr. Blackwood is trying to conclude a deal with them and wants them to have a good time."

"And Mrs. Miller? She won't tolerate the scotch."

"I took care of her personally," Geoffrey said. "As I'm sure you know, Mrs. Miller's tastes are not as refined." Geoffrey added the slightest touch of condescension to his voice. "She simply asked for a 'Chardonnay,' and that's what I gave her."

"American?"

"Worse, Spanish table wine."

Suzanne smiled. "Very good. And Mr. Blackwood is..."

"In his study, Mrs. Blackwood," Geoffrey replied. "He asked me to tell you that he'd be out soon. I delivered the bottle at precisely 8 PM, as instructed."

Mrs. Blackwood let out a soft sigh. "Him and his silly little ritual," she said, shaking her head. But there was fondness in her tone, not dismissal.

Every year on his birthday, Vincent Blackwood opened a bottle of the rarest whiskey he could find and drank a single glass. Always alone. Before today, Geoffrey hadn't known it was in homage to his father.

"Very good," Suzanne said. "What about *her*?"

Like Geoffrey himself, Suzanne Blackwood could look at a person or gesture toward them in the most discreet way imaginable. This time, she was referencing Helene Marquez, and Geoffrey knew he had to handle this delicately.

"As you know," he said, "she has not come around to the idea that America can make wine. We're pouring Screaming Eagle Cabernet and Sauvignon Blanc, plus Magnums of Harlan Estate. For her, I opened a bottle of 1982 Château Latour. She's on her second glass. So, she must be enjoying it."

Helene Marquez was a fabulously wealthy businesswoman and also the ex-wife of Vincent Blackwood. Geoffrey knew Suzanne didn't want her here, but he also knew that the last thing she'd want is to come across as anything less than gracious.

"Very good," she said.

Helene Marquez, who was also Geoffrey's former employer, had a DQ score of only twenty, one of the lowest at the party. Her score was well-earned, a result of years spent perfecting the art of graceless entitlement.

She had a habit of snapping her fingers at staff, speaking to them as though they were dim-witted children, once famously berating a housekeeper for failing to starch her napkins to the "correct crispness." Her wardrobe was an endless parade of ostentatious designer logos, worn more for the price tag than the style, and she flaunted them at every opportunity. Worse, she loved to name-drop, peppering her conversations with mentions of "my dear friend" the ambassador or "that summer" at the Monaco Grand Prix, always just loud enough for the room to hear. To Geoffrey, she embodied the worst of new money—a gaudy display of wealth with none of the refinement to back it up.

Geoffrey watched as Suzanne made eye contact with Daniel Blackwood, her brother-in-law. "I'll check in later." And with that, she moved elegantly across the patio.

Suzanne Blackwood was a 91/100 on his DQ scale. Humble, understated, polite, and always perfectly in control, she was about as good as they came in the world of unimaginable wealth.

Geoffrey's obsession with the Decorum Quotient could be traced back to his father, a man who had inherited modest wealth and squandered it in a desperate bid to drown his grief after Geoffrey's mother died. What began as a few lavish dinner parties soon spiraled into a series of ill-advised ventures—a failing vineyard, a fleet of antique cars he barely knew how to drive, and endless, expensive gestures meant to keep up appearances in a world that no longer cared about him. By the time Geoffrey was old enough to understand the concept of money, there was nothing left. His father's careless spending had reduced them to a life of quiet struggle.

That bitter lesson had seared itself into Geoffrey's mind: wealth was fleeting, but the perception of grace and control could endure, even when the coffers ran dry. Which, as far as Geoffrey was concerned, would never happen to his family again.

He had a plan.

Through wise investments and frugal living, Geoffrey planned to leave this world a wealthy man. This and his only ever transgression to the Blackwood house to date—would leave him very wealthy. Geoffrey had created a fictitious server he'd named Dorian Quinton. D.Q. was only "hired" for events where staff was abundant and his physical absence would go unnoticed. Geoffrey made sure he was only ever paid in checks made out to "Cash" sent to a P.O. Box in a neighboring town. Money he would never touch himself but instead would use to build wealth for his future generations —if he were to have any—to recreate the solid nest egg, replacing all that his father had undone and more. This event would push D.Q. into overtime, and Geoffrey was excited to get that money invested into crypto where he could wash it before adding it to his investment portfolio.

Leaving the patio, Geoffrey did another lap through the party. Then, checking his watch, he realized that Mr. Blackwood should have been out of his study by now. It was time to offer guests a thimble-sized taste of the $2.6 million dollar bottle of Scotch.

He walked down the long, marble-floored hallway, his footsteps muffled by the thick Persian runner. Reaching the study door at the end, his gentle knock was answered with silence.

Mr. Blackwood usually answered right away. Frowning, Geoffrey knocked again, louder this time.

Still nothing.

A third knock, firmer this time, followed by the faint click of the electronic mechanism that engaged the door to slowly roll open. "Pardon my intrusion, sir, it's Geoffrey."

A custom Fibonacci-inspired chandelier of LED filaments cast a soft, cool light across the room. But Geoffrey's attention locked on Vincent Blackwood, hunched over the desk. His salt-and-pepper hair was still held perfectly in place.

A glass of whiskey sat beside him, mostly empty.

Geoffrey rushed forward, leaned down over him. "Mr. Blackwood." He was eerily still. "Oh no," he whispered. "Mr. Blackwood. Oh God, no."

CHAPTER TWO

Four Days Later

CLAIRE WAS ALREADY on her third interview for a new forensic psychologist, and things had gone from bad to worse. The current interviewee, twenty-nine-year-old Chloe Daschel, was the youngest of the bunch and seemed convinced she knew it all. In fact, she'd just pointed out everything Claire and her team had done wrong on a recent case involving a killer the press had initially dubbed the Color Killer and later named the Luminist Killer.

"So," Claire said, her tone clipped, "tell me how you would have handled the case."

"I'm so glad you asked, Claire."

"Chloe, I'd prefer you call me Agent Anderson."

"Oh, yes, of course, Agent Anderson. *Classic.*" Chloe smiled. "Anyway, what I would have done is this—"

Chloe leaned forward, her expression radiating the smugness of someone certain they were the smartest person in the room. "The first mistake your team made was relying on traditional behavioral profiling. I would have employed a multi-modal psychochromatic analysis, cross-referencing the color spectrum of the killer's shrines with emotional triggers derived from predictive algorithms."

Chloe paused, as if expecting applause.

"I see." Claire glanced at her list of prospects, drawing a small bee next to Chloe's name—an ironic notation to remind her that this candidate was *just too sweet.*

"We all know the use of crimson in shrine number four wasn't just about passion or rage—it was a subconscious cry for validation tied to unresolved childhood trauma. Do you see?"

Chloe must have mistaken her silence for interest, thinking Claire was taking notes on her brilliant analysis.

"By inputting the colors into my AI-assisted profiling tool, E-GO," Chloe continued excitedly, "I could have pinpointed the killer's age, gender identity, and even occupational tendencies within hours. But I understand why your team missed that—it's a pretty advanced approach."

Claire fought the urge to roll her eyes. Advanced? More like over-engineered nonsense. She'd seen the Electronic Guidance and Optimization tool (E-GO) in action before, leading teams astray with overly complex data. Claire still placed her trust in human deduction over technology that promised too much. "Interesting," she managed. "And what does your intuition—"

"Oh, I wasn't finished yet," Chloe interrupted. "Let me tell you my thoughts on Fitz Pembroke. Jack, wouldn't you agree that—"

Before Chloe could launch into another monologue, Claire held up a hand. "You've given us all we need. We're impressed by your understanding of E-GO." Claire glanced at Jack, who stood in the corner with his arms crossed. "Thank you for coming," she added, her tone polite but firm. "Jack will see you out now."

Chloe took off her glasses, looking up at Jack. "So, I've got the job?"

Jack's face was expressionless. "We'll let you know."

As Jack showed her out, Claire checked her phone. She hadn't heard from Fitz in six weeks, and sometimes she felt like a teenager waiting for an important text. Conducting these interviews with his potential replacement made her miss him more than ever.

She had no *romantic* interest in Fitz, and that was part of the problem. He'd left her task force after declaring he was in love with her. His exact words—which Claire would never forget—were, "I know you won't ever love me, Claire, but I can't stand having to face that fact every single day."

She had tried to convince him to stay, that his feelings would pass, but he'd been gone long enough to make her think they hadn't. Perhaps he was right—they never would.

She'd moved on, focusing on rebuilding the team, but the absence of Fitz left a gap none of the young profilers could fill. If she had to deal with another arrogant profiler, she needed it to be someone the team could respect—or at least tolerate.

The next interview was with Sonya Ticker, only a few years older than Chloe. Claire glanced over the resume again, though she hardly needed to. Sonya was the kind of candidate who didn't just tick boxes—she shattered ceilings. A Harvard graduate, Sonya had made her first million in investment banking before the age of twenty-six, a fact Claire found both impressive and slightly intimidating. Then, for reasons Claire had yet to piece together, Sonya had left Wall Street for the grittier, less lucrative life of an FBI profiler.

When Jack led her in, Sonya was every bit as polished as Claire expected. She wore a tailored navy suit, with a crisp white shirt underneath. Her dark skin gleamed under the soft light, and her hair was swept back into a sleek bun. Her stride was confident but controlled, her posture impeccable. But it was her eyes that caught Claire's attention. Behind her composed exterior was a razor-sharp intelligence.

Sonya raised her hand in a crisp, almost military gesture, adjusting her thin-framed glasses. Claire could tell Sonya was already sizing up the room, and everyone in it.

"Welcome, and thank you for coming," Claire said.

Sonya smiled. "I'm sure you've read my resume. I have little tolerance for boredom. Can you appreciate that?"

"I can." Claire realized that Sonya was here to interview her as much as the other way around.

"Your biggest question about my resume is why I moved from investment banking to the FBI."

"Yes," Claire nodded. "It's certainly unusual."

"It is." Sonya tilted her head slightly, shifting into storytelling mode. "I'd always intended to go into criminology—my dad is a defense attorney, and I think it was my way of rebelling." She smiled. "But straight out of Harvard, I went into investment banking. It made sense at the time—dual degrees in psychology and math, and I was good at seeing patterns in data and connecting them to the real world. A Seattle firm made me an offer I couldn't refuse. Within a few years, I was making serious money."

"That must have been interesting," Claire said, picturing herself at that age—raising toddlers and juggling work. Sonya's story was a stark contrast.

"It wasn't what I thought it would be," Sonya admitted. "The work felt... empty. Just moving money around, maximizing portfolios. No matter how much I made, it didn't feel meaningful."

"So, what changed?"

"I realized I missed what drew me to psychology in the first place," Sonya said. "The *human* element. I wanted to do something meaningful. So, I walked away, went back to school, and got my master's in criminology. It was the perfect blend—using data and analysis to understand human behavior, but with real-world stakes."

"And the FBI?"

"It was the logical next step," Sonya said. "I wanted to apply everything I'd learned—about people, about numbers, about systems—and use it to make a difference."

Claire studied her for a moment, nodding slowly. "I can see why Jack liked your file." Out of the corner of her eye, she saw Jack nodding emphatically, giving a thumbs-up.

Sonya adjusted her glasses.

The woman was deeply impressive, but Claire couldn't help comparing her to Fitz. As much as she'd complained about his wrinkled clothes and occasional scent of lager, there was something she missed about his wildness, his unpredictability. Fitz had been maddening, but he brought a spark to the work that no resume could replicate. Still, her boss, Gerald Hightower, had put together the candidate list himself, and Sonya was the last interview. Claire couldn't deny that she seemed more than capable.

Over the next twenty minutes, Claire outlined the mission of FBI Task Force S.W.O.R.D. Sonya asked sharp, intelligent questions about the team dynamics, investigative strategies, and challenges. By the end, Claire felt certain—this was the woman to replace Fitz.

Before Claire could proceed, Jack's phone dinged, breaking the moment. Claire shot him an annoyed look. "Jack, we turn phones off during interviews. You know that."

"Sorry," Jack said, pulling it out to silence it. His expression shifted as he read the notification. "Holy crap."

"What is it?" Claire asked sharply.

Jack hesitated, glancing between Claire and Sonya. "Nothing. It can wait."

Claire crossed her arms. "You've interrupted the interview twice. Share your news."

Jack exhaled. "Vincent Blackwood is dead."

Claire frowned. "He's been dead for four days. Story has been everywhere."

Jack shook his head. "The story that he died of a heart attack, yeah. But new evidence came in. He was *poisoned.*"

Claire had read all about Blackwood's death. Early reports had pointed to a heart attack—somewhat surprising for a rich, healthy man in his fifties, but not impossible. "What's the evidence?"

"It's from a news article, not an inside source," Jack said, reading quickly. "The autopsy showed *aconitine*, whatever the hell that is. Enough to kill him fast but look like a sudden cardiac event. The poison was delivered through his drink—an insanely rare Scotch. That's what they're saying, anyway."

Claire noticed Sonya's expression pique with interest. "*The Gilded Widow of Medina* strikes again."

"What do you mean?" Claire asked.

Sonya sat back in her chair. "I know nothing about this case, but I know quite a bit about that world. And about his wife, Suzanne Blackwood—the Gilded Widow. I wonder who the next lucky billionaire will be." She put her hands behind her head. "Blackwood is the *third* wealthy husband she's buried."

"How do you know about her?" Claire asked.

"I come from that world—sort of," Sonya replied. "I was raised in Medina. My mom was an accountant. Dad was a lawyer. They made over a quarter-million a year, but in Medina, we were considered poor."

"Sounds like you have a love-hate relationship with Medina," Jack said.

She smiled. "Only with everyone living in it."

Jack chuckled.

Claire stood, extending a hand to Sonya. "Excellent interview. You'll be hearing from us soon."

"Sounds good." Sonya smiled at Jack, who opened the door for her. She hesitated, surveying their basement office—the so-called Boiler Room, where the S.W.O.R.D. team operated. Her gaze lingered on the exposed pipes and scuffed desks. "My last office was on the forty-first floor—glass walls overlooking Seattle. This will be an interesting change of pace."

Claire nodded. "This is us."

"What makes you so sure you're going to be hired?" Jack gestured for her to pass him.

"If I didn't know before, your enthusiastic thumbs-up erased any doubt."

Claire mimicked Sonya's idiosyncratic glasses adjustment, and Jack nodded.

Sonya looked over her shoulder at Jack before leaving. "Two thumbs-up, no less."

CHAPTER THREE

"HOW DID THE INTERVIEWS GO?" Hightower straightened a stack of papers on his desk.

"They went all right," Claire said. "Definitely some characters."

"What did you decide?"

"I think we're going to go with the last interviewee, Sonya Ticker."

Hightower leaned back in his chair, placing his hands on the gleaming desk. "Really?" He seemed genuinely surprised.

"Who did you think I would choose?" Claire asked. "Jack likes her. Not that I'd let what he thinks weigh heavily on my decision. And I'm not sure how she'll fit in with the rest of the team, but she's definitely smart."

Hightower ran a hand over his bald head. "Honestly, I didn't think you'd like any of them."

Claire frowned. "Well, I don't love any of them. But wait—why didn't you think I'd like any of them? And why did you set me up to interview a whole slew of applicants you didn't think I'd like?"

"Because I want you to take Fitz back."

This took Claire by surprise. "Seriously?"

"Seriously," Hightower said.

"You've never exactly been his biggest fan," Claire pointed out.

Hightower picked up a pen from his desk and passed it from hand to hand. He didn't seem nervous, but he wasn't his usual buttoned-up, straightforward self. "I'm still not his biggest fan," he admitted. "But I can't deny results. With Fitz on board, your team brought in two pretty massive cases in short order, and his work on the Interstate Reaper case—well, unconventional maybe, but it speaks for itself. That case is already being written about in psychological journals. The way he pried what he pried from the mind of that man..." Hightower shook his head, impressed. "Sometimes I wish I could live like that, you know? Pound a few lagers, not bother to get my jacket pressed, wear dirty socks, and roll out of bed hungover only to solve one of the most significant unsolved serial killer cases in American history."

Claire hadn't quite thought about it like that. "It was a *team* effort," she pointed out. "It took all of us to bring that case home."

"I know," Hightower said. "But there's also the fact that Fitz works for half as much money as all these new people will accept."

"Do we even know what he's doing now?" Claire asked. "I haven't heard from him."

"He's doing some freelance consulting for various lower-profile departments, working from home where he can keep his nose clean. He's also teaching part-time."

"University of Washington?" Claire asked.

Hightower chuckled. "You think they'd hire him? Not in his wildest dreams. He's teaching at a community college."

Claire leaned forward, eager to change the subject.

"Before we go any further on the new profiler thing—Vincent Blackwood. Did you see what came out today?"

"I heard," Hightower said.

"We want the case," Claire said.

"It's not our jurisdiction," Hightower replied.

"It *could* be," Claire countered. "Suzanne Blackwood has had three husbands die. That's not just tragic—that's statistically insane. We already know she killed the first one."

"Self-defense," Hightower said. "Wasn't that one ruled self-defense?"

"It was, but now that we know the latest one was murdered—well, if nothing else, the pattern alone warrants federal attention."

Hightower shook his head. "Patterns are one thing, Claire. Jurisdiction is another. Medina PD and the state are handling this. We're talking about a private citizen, not a criminal empire or an interstate operation. It's not our wheelhouse. Not to mention, Suzanne Blackwood happens to be one of the wealthiest women in the state."

"Three dead billionaires," Claire said, leaning forward. "Self-defense, boating accident, poisoning. C'mon, Gerald. We bring this case in, and how good will it look for you, for the department?" When he didn't reply, she continued. "Self-defense, boating accident, poisoning. Tell me you don't see a killer."

"Maybe," Hightower countered, "or I might see a widow with bad luck and a case that's not our problem."

"You don't believe that," Claire shot back. "Come on, Gerald. If this were just a one-off poisoning, I'd agree with you. But three dead husbands? The FBI doesn't ignore things like that, and you know it."

Hightower sighed. "Even if I gave you the green light, the Bureau's not going to pour resources into a case that doesn't scream federal. And you're already understaffed."

"We won't need extra resources. Just the S.W.O.R.D. team and Sonya. We'll take Sonya."

Hightower studied her for a moment. "You'd have to make a real argument. Medina PD isn't going to hand it over."

"They won't have a choice," Claire said. "If we find even a hint that this could involve fraud, tax evasion, or anything crossing state lines—hell, Suzanne Blackwood probably has assets scattered across the country—we can justify federal jurisdiction."

Hightower let out a long breath, then nodded reluctantly. "Fine. But there's one condition."

Claire raised an eyebrow. "What's that?"

"You take Fitz back, too," Hightower said.

"Seriously?"

"Dead serious," he said. "If I'm going to let you stretch our jurisdiction and drag us into this mess, I want the best profiler we've got. And that's still Fitz. Like him or not."

Claire hesitated, then nodded. "Okay. But if he comes back smelling like stale beer, you're dealing with him."

"Fair enough," Hightower said, a rare smile crossing his face.

"And I still get Sonya, right? If she's willing to work with us, that is."

Hightower nodded.

Claire stood and walked to the door, then turned. "One more condition."

"Are you really in a position to make demands?"

"A request, then?"

"What is it?"

"If Fitz comes back, can he bring back Ranger?"

Even though the golden retriever had been the S.W.O.R.D. team's unofficial mascot, technically he belonged to Fitz, and the dog had left when Fitz did.

Hightower didn't say a word. Claire read his silence as permission.

Claire sat alone in the Boiler Room, watching a YouTube video on her laptop. Fitz stood at the front of a modest lecture hall, gesturing with his hands as he spoke, his voice steady and captivating. The title of the lecture read: *The Grey Divide: Where is the Line? AI Biases vs. Human Intuition and Empathy*.

"An algorithm doesn't form goosebumps. You can feed it every case file, every psychological study, every behavioral trend ever documented, and it can tell you a lot." Fitz paced slowly. "But what it can't do is *feel* anything. It can't sit across from a suspect and notice the way they tap their foot when you mention their mother, or the slight hitch in their voice when they're lying. It doesn't feel the energy in a room shift when you've touched on something real. AI can't decode humanity because it's not human."

Fitz paused, leaning against the lectern. The room, which was packed, seemed to hang on his words. "Profiles are not just about data points. They're about context. Experience. And, most importantly, feeling and empathy. Knowing when to push and when to pull back. When to treat someone like a puzzle to be solved, and when to treat them like a person. Machines can't do that. Maybe someday, but not yet. And maybe, not ever."

Claire's gaze lingered on the screen. Fitz looked sharper than she remembered. The faint puffiness in his face was gone, replaced with a leaner, more rested appearance. He looked like he'd been sleeping regularly for the first time in years. Even though he'd only been gone for six weeks, for a fleeting moment she wondered if the Fitz she'd known and the one on her screen were still the same person.

She'd called him and left a voicemail after the meeting with Hightower. And she expected that he'd jump at the chance to work this particular case. Fitz, among his many traits, *hated* rich people, possibly because he came from a wealthy family in England that had largely cut ties with him. Or possibly because he'd personally squandered his share of that wealth before being cut off. As he was fond of saying, he put the *broke* in Pembroke.

But, in any case, the chance to investigate a wealthy widow who may or may not have poisoned one of the richest tech CEOs in America would certainly entice him. Especially since she may have murdered two other husbands as well.

She shook her head, picked up the phone, and dialed. Claire heard two rings before she was funneled to his voicemail.

She braced herself while waiting for the beep. "Fitz, it's Claire again. Come on, man. Hightower wants you back on the taskforce. Give me a call."

CHAPTER FOUR

The Next Morning

WHEN CLAIRE REACHED THE BASEMENT, the first person she saw was Sonya Ticker, who was standing at the door to the Boiler Room. She was wearing the same style as her interview outfit, but today the linen-blend suit was solid red.

"So, you're taking the job." Claire couldn't hide the surprise in her voice.

"I like a challenge." Sonya shrugged.

"Challenging cases or co-workers?" Claire asked as she unlocked the door with her badge.

"I was hoping to find a position where I'd come across both."

Claire smiled. "Then I can guarantee you'll like working with us."

Sonya walked past Claire into the Boiler Room. "Let's get to work."

Hearing Jack and Kiko, Claire held the door open and watched as they came around the corner. Their voices indicated they were in the middle of a heated debate. A crescendoing pitter-patter overtook the sound of their argument, and Violet emerged from behind.

"I can't stand to listen to those two," Violet said as she passed through the door.

"Jack." Claire interrupted the monologue he was giving Kiko. "I want you to show Sonya around today."

"She took the job?" he asked.

"She did." Claire imagined if Jack had a tail, he'd be wagging it like a puppy. "Let's hope she doesn't regret it."

"She will," Kiko said, rolling her eyes at Jack behind his back as he rushed in to find Sonya.

Claire gave everyone a moment to get settled, then walked to the front of the room. "I have some news about the makeup of our team."

Violet was in her usual spot in the back at her desk, facing her wall of monitors. Jack left Sonya's side and took a seat across from Kiko, and Sonya sat where Fitz always had. Claire felt a pang of nostalgia seeing Sonya in Fitz's old seat—a reminder of the gap his absence left, and how much things had changed since he'd walked away.

"So, what's the news?" Jack asked.

"Hightower says we can have the Blackwood case, but we have to take Fitz back."

"What does he—" Jack began, but Claire cut him off.

"Jack, this isn't going to be a discussion." Claire knew Jack would be the first to make a stink. "I've already invited him."

She paused, looking from person to person. Jack's face, usually fairly stoic, showed a slight bit of disappointment, which he masked with a raised eyebrow. Claire could tell Sonya was trying hard not to react, but there was no way she wouldn't feel something hearing on her first day that the person she was replacing might be coming back to join them.

"With that said," Claire continued, "let's move on. Violet?"

The large screen on the wall lit up as Violet did her thing.

"Three dead husbands," Violet said as a photo of a forty-something man in a tuxedo popped up. "The first was self-defense. David Radcliffe. A documented abuser," Violet said as she pulled up the next slide. "There were police reports from neighbors about domestic disturbances, and Suzanne herself had filed a restraining order two years before the incident. Then rescinded it. The night of his death, David came home intoxicated and started a physical altercation. Witnesses reported hearing shouting, and Suzanne claimed he attacked her in the kitchen. She pushed him away, and he fell down the stairs, breaking his neck on impact. The police investigation was thorough—she had bruises and injuries consistent with her account of physical abuse, and there were no signs of premeditation. The case was ruled self-defense, and she was cleared of all charges. Pretty open and shut."

"Any chance it *wasn't*, though?" Kiko asked.

"We'll get to that," Claire interjected. "No evidence yet, but we can go back, see if anything was missed."

"The second husband—Michael St. Pierre—fell off a boat in the Pacific on a fishing trip," Violet said, switching the slide to a handsome man in his fifties with bright white hair and a deep tan. He stood on a boat proudly holding up some sort of fish. "He was eaten by sharks. This was all that was left of him."

She clicked again, and Claire recoiled slightly at the photo. It showed a bloated, half-eaten corpse tangled in the frayed lines of a fishing net. The man's torso was largely intact, but his lower body was missing, torn away in ragged chunks, leaving jagged edges of exposed bone jutting from putrid meat. The flesh that remained was pallid and swollen, mottled with the telltale blue-gray of time spent in the water. Deep gouges ran across his torso, unmistakably the work of a predator's teeth. In the background, the deck of the police boat was slick with seawater, and two officers in rubber gloves stood by, faces grim.

"Any drugs found in his system?" Jack asked.

"No," Violet replied.

"How long between when he fell in the water and when they discovered the body?" Claire asked.

"Police report says the captain called in the accident right away, but the body wasn't found for forty-eight hours," Violet said.

Jack leaned back in his chair. "So it's definitely possible he was drugged and pushed over the side, and those drugs had dissipated in his system by the time they found him."

"Possible," Violet said, "though we have no evidence of that."

"We have no evidence of *anything*," Claire said. "Let's get to the third case."

"Vincent Blackwood, age fifty," Violet said.

The picture on the screen showed a handsome man, one Claire recognized immediately. She wasn't the type to follow business and tech news closely, but Vincent Blackwood had become more than just a businessman, more than a tech CEO. With frequent appearances on the news, massive political contributions to both parties, and a portfolio of philanthropic endeavors, he had transitioned into celebrity status. His PR team had ensured his face was everywhere, from glossy magazine covers to talk show interviews, presenting him as a larger-than-life figure—one who seemed untouchable until now.

Violet clicked to the next slide. "The method was... subtle," she began. "Someone injected a small amount of aconitine directly through the cork of his prized Scotch."

"Did it have a metal or wax seal over the cork?" Jack asked.

"Metal," Violet said. "But the needle used was so fine that it left no trace noticeable to the naked eye. Could have been a Coravin, one of those high-end wine gadgets that let you extract a glass of wine without pulling the cork. The toxin infused the booze, and when Blackwood poured his drink that night, it was a fatal dose. What makes this particularly insidious is that there was no sign of tampering until the cork and seal were examined under a microscope."

Claire frowned. "So no fingerprints? Nothing left behind?"

"That's one of the problems," Violet said. "The bottle was *covered* in fingerprints. According to the butler, it had been passed around and left out for display. Dozens of people handled it that night. So that's no help."

"And most likely," Jack said, "the poison had been deposited well in advance."

"Why do you say that?" Kiko asked.

"Kinda obvious," Jack said, "who would risk poisoning the bottle at the party?"

"Lots of people." She said it like Jack was a fool. "Maybe that's the only time they had access to it."

"If it was poisoned before," Jack countered, "that cuts down the number of possible suspects significantly."

"We're getting ahead of ourselves," she said, cutting through the tension.

Jack and Kiko's back-and-forth had grown more heated than the topic seemed to call for. Recently, Claire had found out they'd been having an interoffice relationship. They'd ended it voluntarily, but she sensed some lingering bitterness between them—or possibly, an ember. Her own romantic life lacked anything resembling a spark these days, so she wasn't entirely sure which.

Jack and Kiko both leaned back, as though on cue.

"What exactly is aconitine?" Sonya asked. "And how does one get it?"

"Alkaloid derived from the monkshood plant," Violet said, "also known as Aconitum. Extraction of aconitine is complex and requires a sound understanding of chemistry—likely using solvents to isolate the toxin from the plant's roots or flowers. Given the potency of aconitine, the suspect would only need a few plants to produce a lethal dose, as just 5 milligrams can be fatal for an adult. For a 750 ml bottle of alcohol, dispersing roughly 20 to 25 milligrams would ensure each shot could be deadly, given the liquor's volume and the toxin's solubility. The bitterness would be hard to mask, but a strong liquor could conceal it long enough for the victim to consume a dangerous amount before noticing anything unusual."

"Didn't he have some ritual with his whiskey?" Sonya asked.

Violet nodded, then displayed an article from *Whiskey Monthly* on the screen. "This is a quote from an interview Blackwood did. 'If you experience turbulence on an airplane, and the oxygen masks drop, you're supposed to secure your own mask before helping those around you. Money is like oxygen in that way. My father taught me to be of service to the world. First, believe it or not, you have to be a little bit selfish to do that. If you're going to give what you can give to the world, you have to take what you need first. So every birthday, I open up a bottle of whiskey and have the first glass by myself as a toast to my dad. After that, the rest of it I give away. When I was twenty-five, it was a 375-milliliter bottle of Wild Turkey. Now I can afford whatever I want, but the sentiment is still the same.'" Violet glanced around the room. "The ritual wasn't just something he did—it was a philosophy. In the articles about him, it's mentioned *constantly*, just like the fact that he was claustrophobic, which apparently was his only flaw. Like kryptonite to Superman."

"And that means," Sonya said, "that anyone with a passing interest in Blackwood could have known exactly what he was going to do with that bottle."

"Exactly," Violet agreed.

Claire's phone buzzed in her pocket, and she pulled it out. "Sorry," she said. "I meant to turn this off." She glanced at the screen and saw Fitz's name.

Unable to resist, she swiped open the text.

I've a whole new life now. Stronger. Healthier. Down to two beers a day. Going to give it a miss, but cheers.

She read it twice, her expression tightening, then looked up at the group. "Apparently," she said, "Fitz has no interest in coming back."

"Terrible," Jack said, his voice full of a sarcasm only Fitz could bring out of him.

"I like Fitz," Violet said. "Reminds me of my drunk uncle who used to ruin Thanksgiving, but kinda in a good way."

Claire squinted at her phone, again reading his text. "I'm gonna call him again."

If he'd actually gotten himself a new life, actually cleaned up his act, his presence could only strengthen her taskforce.

CHAPTER FIVE

FITZ WAS SWEATING, the dampness soaking through the back of his T-shirt as he set the twenty-five-pound dumbbells onto the yoga mat. They landed with a dull thud. His breathing was labored, his arms burning—but it was the good kind of pain, the kind that made him feel like he was shedding parts of his old self. He wiped his hands on his shorts and sat cross-legged, staring at the mat.

Margaret had bought it for him a month ago, hopeful about introducing him to yoga. He hadn't made it to that stage yet, though he'd promised her he would. Someday. For now, it kept the dumbbells from marking up the hardwood floor.

His phone rang, cutting through the faint hum of the portable fan. He lumbered over to the small desk crammed into the corner of the room and checked the screen.

Claire. *Again.*

A familiar tension coiled in his stomach. He took a deep swig from the sleek, overpriced water bottle Margaret had insisted he needed to fill and drink six times a day.

If it were filled with beer, you could do it, she'd teased.

Margie, water isn't beer, was his only defense.

So far, he was consistently drinking four.

"Claire," he said, leaning back in his chair, trying to sound relaxed. "To what do I owe the pleasure?" He knew exactly why she was calling.

"Fitz," Claire replied, her tone brisk. "I'll get straight to it. We need you back on the task force."

He rubbed the back of his neck, feeling the sweat. "Kinda got that sense from your first two calls. But as I said in my text, I've moved on. Got a whole new life now. Going to give it a miss."

"Your new life," Claire said, skepticism evident even through the phone. "And what does that entail, exactly?"

Fitz hesitated. He hated this question—hated trying to explain his messy combination of genuine attempts at self-improvement and half-hearted avoidance. "I'm dating a lovely young woman named Margaret. She's grounded. Has me drinking water. *Water*, Claire, can you believe that? Keeps me out of trouble."

"Margaret?" Claire asked, her tone somehow digging under his skin. "Drinking water? Is that what's keeping you out of trouble, Fitz?"

"Let's just say I've been focusing on character-building," he said with a faint laugh, though it sounded forced even to his own ears. "Margie has me looking at the future."

There was a pause, a hesitation from Claire that made him shift uncomfortably in his chair. "Fitz, about before you left..."

He stiffened, gripping the arm of the chair. "We don't need to talk about that," he said quickly.

"I wasn't saying we *should*," she replied. "I just... I know it's why you left, and I—"

"Claire," Fitz interrupted, his voice tight. "Please. Just

leave it. I made a mistake saying what I said, and I'm not proud of it. But it's done. I'm done."

The silence on the other end stretched too long, and Fitz felt the weight of it pressing down on him. He wanted to hang up, but that would be worse.

"So, you're not even tempted?" Claire finally asked, her voice colder now, shifting back to professional mode. "Suzanne Blackwood. The Gilded Widow. Three dead husbands. Vincent Blackwood poisoned in the middle of his birthday party. Sounds like exactly the kind of case you'd want to sink your teeth into."

"It does sound riveting," he admitted, leaning forward to rest his elbows on his knees. "But no, Claire. I'm not coming back. Not this time."

"We can't take the case without you," she pressed. "Hightower said so himself."

"Then don't take it," Fitz said. "Anyway, weren't you going to look into your parents' case?"

Another pause, and he could practically hear the frustration radiating through the phone.

"Don't bring *that* up," Claire said, anger creeping into her voice. "Enjoy your new life, Fitz."

"I will," he said quietly. "Good luck with the case. Or, whatever." He hung up before she could say anything else, staring at his phone for a moment before setting it face down.

He glanced at the yoga mat, then at the dumbbells, and finally sank back into his chair, both physically and emotionally drained. He took a long chug of room-temperature water, hoping to replenish himself.

It tasted like nothing and did nothing to fill him back up.

CHAPTER SIX

CLAIRE LEANED over Benny's shoulder, watching as his nimble fingers flew across the keyboard. The screen was alive with lines of code and a small window showing a blank canvas bordered by colorful icons. A header at the top read *Scribble Sight* in bold, playful lettering.

"What are you working on?" Claire asked, resting her chin lightly on his head.

"An app," Benny said, his tone nonchalant, but she caught the flicker of pride in his voice. "It's called *Scribble Sight*. You draw something—whatever you want—and then it uses AI to analyze it, like a reverse-Rorschach test. You make a drawing, and it tells you what you're thinking. It gives you a sort of psychic reading using psychological analysis based on what you drew."

Claire raised an eyebrow. "Sounds... ambitious. So, what does it do? I scribble a cat, and it tells me I've got nine lives?"

Benny laughed, tilting his head to look up at her. "No, Mom, it's not that literal. It looks at patterns—like, do you draw smooth lines or jagged ones? Do you press hard on the mouse or barely touch it? Do you fill in all the space or leave a lot blank? It interprets that through a bunch of psychological theories I've been reading about. It's kinda like a fun horoscope."

Although he'd been born with Down syndrome, neither she nor Benny had ever let that stand in the way of him living his life. Sure, he had his unique struggles, but his enthusiasm and his apparent gift for gaming and computers were something Claire was determined to support, even if she couldn't understand half of what he said about it.

Claire grinned. "And where exactly did you get these psychological theories?"

"The internet," Benny said with exaggerated confidence. "I trained the AI model myself using a database of drawings and their associated personality traits."

"Of course you did," Claire said, ruffling his hair. "So, what does your app think of *your* personality? And what does it tell you about your future?"

Benny shrugged. "I drew a tree earlier. I'll read you what it said: *You have an expansive imagination but struggle to ground yourself in reality. Will you grow roots before the next storm to remain strong? The choice is yours alone.*"

"Sounds accurate," Claire teased. "What happens if I draw, say, a tornado?"

Benny's face lit up as he spun back to his screen. "Draw it! Here—use the mouse." He clicked into the canvas and passed her the mouse.

Claire scribbled an untidy swirl, watching as the app processed her drawing. After a few seconds, a box popped up with text.

"*Your creative flair is a wild force, straining against control,*" Benny read aloud, laughing. "*You are capable of brilliance under pressure. But will you let overthinking cloud your decisions when the wind picks up? The choice is yours alone.*"

Claire snorted. "It says I'm *capable of brilliance*? I'll take it."

Benny looked up at her, a sly smile on his face. "It also says you should get me a chocolate cake and take me on a vacation."

"That app is too smart for its own good," Claire said, nudging his shoulder. "But seriously, Benny, this is impressive. You're thirteen, and you're building apps like this? When I was your age, I was still figuring out how to program a VCR. I once tried to start and stop the recording to cut out all the commercial breaks. When I played the video back, I learned I'd done the exact opposite. The entire video was just commercials."

He shrugged, but the pride in his smile was unmistakable. "Yeah, well, wait until I add the feature where it tells you what line of work you're best suited for. That'll be cool."

"Uh, I won't be pursuing that prediction." Claire shook her head, grinning. "I don't think I could take it if it tells me I should be in law enforcement."

"Glad you told me, Mom." Benny raised an index finger, thinking. Then, breaking his own silence, spoke as he typed. "I'm adding some personalization code logic. I won't let it pigeonhole you like that, Mom."

"You're a genius, kid. One more thing—don't start analyzing my work doodles. I don't need to know what they say about my stress levels, and neither do you."

Benny laughed, turning back to his screen, already lost in his code again.

"I'm gonna head down to the kitchen," Claire said. "You want anything? Chocolate cake?"

"I'm good," he said, not looking up.

As much as she enjoyed spending time with Benny, Claire's mind kept flashing back to her conversation with Fitz. He always had a way of bringing up something that got under her skin. And these days, her skin wasn't that thick.

The tragedy of her early childhood was never far from her mind. With Benny, she didn't share anything worse than her disappointment over not being able to re-watch a commercial-free *Wizard of Oz*. But lately, devastating memories and feelings were taking up more and more of her mental and emotional space.

She found a half-full bottle of cabernet on the counter, left over from the night before, and grabbed a glass from the cupboard. Pouring it, she allowed the case to ease into the front of her mind.

Roughly six weeks earlier, Claire had learned from her friend Simone Aoki that there might have been more to the story of the cult her parents had been a part of than she knew. That wasn't exactly a surprise—she didn't know much to begin with.

At the time, shortly after the mass suicide, a joint FBI-ATF-Homeland Security Task Force investigation had concluded that the story was as simple as it was horrific. Charismatic cult leader Thomson Flaggler had convinced three dozen of his followers that divine intervention would soon freeze time, leaving everyone on earth stuck in a state of eternal punishment for the sins of humanity. To escape this fate and guarantee an endless communion with the divine, followers drank diluted wine mixed with Valium and cyanide.

Everyone on the commune died. Everyone except Claire, who was only a baby at the time.

Claire took a sip of the wine and walked to her little office. She stared up at the name on a small slip of paper pinned to the corkboard: *Diego Vega*.

Simone had told her that she'd spoken with one of the agents on that task force, a man who had been very young at the time and was now retired. He'd told Simone there was much more to the story—facts that hadn't made it into the official report. For the past month, Claire had kept the name of that agent, along with his phone number, pinned next to a map of her tiny hometown.

But she still hadn't made the call.

Fitz didn't know what it was about Claire, but she always managed to say something that got under his skin.

This time, it wasn't what Claire had said, it was what she'd done. The fact that Claire had hired someone to take his spot was a lot, but choosing Sonya Ticker was just too much. Sonya Ticker was now under Fitz's skin like a botfly.

He told himself he was happy—he didn't need the task force, didn't need the rush of chasing leads with the S.W.O.R.D. team. But Fitz knew himself too well to believe that. Flawed as he was, he liked to think he didn't lie to himself. And the truth was simple and sharp: he desperately wanted to be back working with S.W.O.R.D. And he desperately wanted this case in particular.

As he made his way down the stairs of his duplex, he shook off the lingering thoughts of their conversation.

About halfway down, a strange smell hit his nose. It wasn't unpleasant, just... unfamiliar—earthy, herbal, with a sharp undertone of something medicinal.

In the kitchen, he found Margaret standing at the stove, stirring a bubbling pot of brownish liquid. The surface of the brew was littered with what looked like leaves and bits of bark, the steam curling up and filling the room with the strange aroma. Fitz walked over, slipping an arm around her waist as he leaned to peer into the pot.

"What is that?" he asked.

"An herbal concoction," Margaret said, her tone breezy. "A remedy. Good for longevity. Full of antioxidants, adaptogens, and all that good stuff."

"Longevity?" Fitz repeated, arching an eyebrow. "Looks more like you're brewing a potion to ward off evil spirits. Or maybe it's a love potion?"

"You think I *need* to use one of those on you?"

"Point taken."

Margaret laughed, nudging him with her elbow. "You fell for me on night one."

"True, although the smell of this concoction has me questioning my judgment."

"Oh, ye of little faith. This is ancient wisdom, Fitz." She turned back to her brew and pointed out the contents of the pot. "There's reishi mushroom, ashwagandha root, and a bit of cinnamon bark for flavor. And over there—" she pointed to a small bowl of ingredients on the counter, "—that's holy basil and a pinch of ginseng. I'll add those at the finish."

Fitz leaned against the counter, watching Margaret at the stove. Her long black hair fell loose down her back, the ends curling slightly in the humidity of the kitchen. She had that unhurried, deliberate way about her, stirring the pot like she had all the time in the world. The faintest hint of lavender lingered in the air around her, mixing with the sharp, herbal scent of her brew.

"Right," Fitz said, giving her a dubious look. "And what exactly is all this supposed to do for me? Make me immortal? Give me superpowers?" He kissed his bicep and winked at her.

Margaret rolled her eyes, grinning. "Nothing quite so dramatic. Plus, I thought you already had superpowers. It's just meant to keep your body balanced. Lower stress, support your immune system, maybe help you live longer. Live better."

"Because drinking a steaming cauldron of leaves and twigs sounds exactly like the key to a long life," he quipped. "I'll spend more time trying to choke that poison down than I'll gain from drinking it."

"Mock all you want, like it or not," Margaret said, giving the pot one final stir, "I'm making you drink it."

Fitz groaned in mock protest. "Does it at least come with a chaser? Or do I have to chew on bark to mask the aftertaste?"

Fitz enjoyed the back and forth, and he was under no illusion about Margaret: he was falling in love with her. And yet, his mind kept returning to the case.

Vincent and Suzanne Blackwood.

He had to admit that he wanted it, and not just for the chance to take apart billionaire lives—which, honestly, he would have done for free. It was something deeper. He didn't know Sonya Ticker personally, but he knew her type: young, well-off, brimming with theories and confidence, armed with algorithms and charts to back up every psychological analysis she pulled out of thin air. The kind of person who lied to herself as smoothly as she recited data. The kind of person the team would end up needing to save from herself.

Yes, Fitz wanted the case. But more than that, he wanted to save the team from Sonya Ticker.

Margaret turned toward him. "Come back to me. Where are you?"

"I'm here." Fitz returned to the present and re-engaged with Margaret. He looked at the lines around her eyes—soft, but hinting at something deeper—maybe exhaustion, maybe wisdom.

"You're impossible, you know that?" She carried herself with the easy confidence of someone who could convince a stranger of almost anything, which made sense given her work.

She was a psychic for rich people. It was a third-date revelation that she'd been intentionally obscuring. She wasn't wrong to do so. Fitz might have bailed before giving her a chance if she'd been upfront with him about her profession.

Fitz knew psychics were just doing cold reads, playing off subtle cues and probabilities to craft what seemed like profound insights. It was a scam—he was certain of it—but he couldn't get Margaret to admit it. Strangely, it became part of her allure—the one suspect he couldn't crack. Sometimes, he wasn't even sure *she* knew it was a scam. He didn't believe in any of it, not for a second, but somehow that only made her more fascinating. After all, opposites attract, as the cliche went. They'd met on a dating app the night he quit the S.W.O.R.D. team, hit it off immediately, and she'd begun to move in only a month into the relationship.

Fitz smiled, leaning closer to peer into the pot again. After a moment, his expression softened, and he placed a hand gently on Margaret's belly. "You're sure this snake oil won't affect the baby?"

They'd found out only yesterday that Margaret was pregnant. This was Fitz's new life.

Margaret's eyes softened, and she rested her hand over his. "It's *for* the baby," she said quietly. "To help make them as smart as you."

Fitz chuckled. "Well, in that case, I'm not so sure you should drink it."

CHAPTER SEVEN

BY 8 AM, everyone had gathered in the conference room. Claire had made peace with the fact that Fitz wasn't joining the team—at least, that's what she kept telling herself. She'd told Hightower that Fitz was still considering it, buying them at least one more day with the case. Maybe by then, they'd have enough to convince him to let them continue.

Claire held up both hands to silence the chatter. "It looks like Fitz won't be joining us after all. Sonya, I wanted you from the start, and I know we have everyone we need in this room to bring any guilty party to justice." She made eye contact with Sonya, who offered a slight, polite smile.

"You know I'm going to do my best—and I've already started," Sonya said.

"Good. Sonya, we have every confidence in you," Claire replied. "We'll get to your thoughts in just a moment. As you might already know—if you were online, watching television, or literally standing around being alive on this planet—this case has already made national news."

Claire held up a copy of *The Seattle Times*. The large headline across the front page read: *Black Widow Strikes Again?*

She tossed the newspaper to Jack, who frowned, his lips tightening as he read. He glanced at Kiko, who raised an eyebrow and let out a low whistle before passing it on.

"The public pressure around this case will be immense," Claire said. "The sheer amount of information as well as disinformation is already staggering, and I—"

She paused, her eyes darting to the door as a strange scratching sound interrupted her.

Kiko turned around to look toward the sound as well. "What the hell is that?"

The sound continued—claws scraping against metal.

Suddenly, the door swung open, but there was no one there. Claire frowned, then glanced down. A pale golden coat filled her view, and she sighed with a mix of amusement and resignation. It was Ranger, Fitz's dog. And if Ranger was back, Fitz couldn't be far behind.

Kiko leapt from her chair and scrambled to the center of the table, pulling her knees tight to her chest. She was terrified of animals of all kinds—even Ranger, who was one of the least threatening dogs Claire had ever known.

Jack let out a booming laugh. "It's all right," he said, hurrying over to the door, then dropping down on one knee. He greeted Ranger with a hearty pat.

Just as suddenly as Ranger had burst into the room, Fitz swung the door the rest of the way open and stepped inside, grinning.

Jack turned towards him, still on one knee.

Fitz laughed loudly at the scene before him. "Oh, Jackie boy, you're a catch, and I do love you—but I'll have to turn down your proposal."

"I'd sooner marry *you*," Jack whispered loudly, speaking to Ranger, who was leaning his head back and forth to put pressure against Jack's hands as he continued to receive scratches behind the ears.

"Fair enough. I'm quite sure I'd be hard-pressed to find someone who didn't feel the same." Fitz laughed as he looked around the room. "Oy, you lot. Here I am." He spread his arms wide, his grin infectious. "I'm back."

"But how did Ranger...?" Violet didn't finish her question aloud. Claire knew that any question Violet voiced—even when stated in a complete sentence—was rhetorical. According to Violet, if she didn't know how to solve a puzzle, the answer was unknowable. She sat there silently on her half-revealed question, studying the dog for answers, leaving the rest of them wondering if she would finish asking it.

"How did Ranger open the door, you might ask?" Fitz gave a whistle. Immediately, Ranger came to his side and sat. "Good boy." Fitz patted the dog and swung his collar to the front. "Check out this bling. Ranger and I stopped by security on our way in."

"What?" Violet ran up and went into a squat next to Ranger, opposite Jack. She inspected the dog's tag, then looked up at Fitz. "Aw, they made him an electronic badge. Wait a second, Fitz, you put a big sticker over your own badge, didn't you? It has his picture on it. Aw, Kiko, come see it—come see Ranger's cute little badge picture."

Kiko craned her neck to look over the side of the desk and then slowly brought her feet to the floor one at a time, all the while monitoring the dog's response to her movement closely.

"If nothing else can get you over your distaste for animals, this mug shot would." Jack pointed at the badge and looked up at Kiko. "He's wearing a bow tie!"

"I see." Kiko nodded, looking at the picture from a safe distance.

"I tried getting him a real badge," Fitz said. "Hightower wouldn't budge, so I had to get creative." Fitz kept talking, unaware that everyone was focused on the dog. "How does he expect me to get into this room when my hands are full of burritos?"

"You're late, Fitz." Claire placed her fists on her hips, but she didn't think anyone bought that she wasn't just as amused as the rest of the team.

"Ranger made us stop for burritos." Fitz looked toward the dog accusatorily and shrugged.

Hearing his name, Ranger's eyes snapped sidelong, his eyebrows tenting in quizzical inquiry.

"I'm not sure which is more irresponsible, Fitz," Claire continued, "giving Ranger a counterfeit keycard, or giving him keys to your car."

"That dog is probably a safer driver," Jack said, standing to shake Fitz's hand.

Fitz returned the gesture, and they engaged in the ritual with masculine fervor. "I hate to admit when Jack's right, so I'll just say this—he's not wrong."

Ten minutes later, after introducing Fitz to Sonya and allowing everyone to catch up briefly, Claire retook her spot at the front of the room.

"As I was saying before Ranger burst through the door with his partner in crime..." She paused, letting the room settle before continuing. "This case has already gone national—and it's not really even a case yet." Claire glanced around the room, reading the tension on each face. "On the one hand, we definitely have a murdered victim: Vincent Blackwood. On the other hand, we have the recently thrice-widowed Suzanne Blackwood. A billionaire widow bereft of three dead husbands is not evidence enough."

"And yet," Fitz added, leaning back in his chair, "the press has already decided she's guilty. Along with most of the country."

"And she probably *is*," Jack said, leaning forward.

"Exactly," Sonya agreed.

"So, what's the plan?" Kiko asked, her arms crossed.

"Sonya and I are going to interview Suzanne this morning," Claire said. "I've already spoken with the Medina Police Department and have gotten a transcript of their first interview. It was very preliminary—just about the night itself—and nothing we don't already know. Fitz and Jack, I want you to go interview Geoffrey. He's the butler, household manager, estate manager, or something like that. I want you to dig into everything he knows—the gossip about the family, the people at the party, anything he saw, thought, or did."

"It's a great tradition," Fitz said, smirking. "The domestic staff always know all the gossip about the rich people."

"Downton Abbey?" Kiko asked, raising an eyebrow.

"The tradition goes back long before *Downton Abbey*, in both literature and film," Fitz replied. "But yes, I'll be happy to talk with Geoffrey."

"What should I do?" Kiko asked.

"You stay here with Violet," Claire said. "I have a feeling we might need you later."

Kiko looked confused. "What do you mean?"

Before Claire could reply, Jack chimed in. "You did such a good job pretending to be a rich snob during the Color Killer case," he said, glancing at Claire. "At least, from what Claire told me. My guess is she wants to hold you back in case we need another similar performance."

Kiko smiled. "Got it. Violet and I will stay here and look into Suzanne's past. See if we can dig up anything else about the first two husbands."

"First *three* husbands, actually," Violet said, tapping a few keys on her keyboard. "I just got this."

A picture popped up on the large screen: a young couple, maybe nineteen or twenty, standing in front of a cornfield. The man, a bit stocky but handsome, with a youthful face, sandy hair, and an easy grin, had his arm slung around a striking young woman with dark curls cascading over her shoulders. She wore a formal dress that seemed at odds with the rustic backdrop, her smile wide but not quite reaching her eyes.

"Is that Suzanne Blackwood?" Jack asked.

"It is," Violet confirmed. "She first got married in 1984 to a man named Delvin O'Reilly."

"And how did she kill *him*?" Jack asked, leaning back in his chair.

Violet tapped on her keyboard again, and a new photo appeared. This one was much more recent. A man stood in front of a sleek auto dealership, graying but still recognizable, his build a bit softer now. He wore a crisp navy polo shirt with the words *O'Reilly Ford* embroidered on the chest, the same name emblazoned in bold letters on the sign behind him. Rows of shining trucks and SUVs stretched out into the background. His expression radiated contentment, the smile of a man who had built a life he was proud of.

"Actually, this one looks to be alive and well," Violet said. "Still living in Ohio. He owns three Ford dealerships, got remarried in 1991, has three kids, and seems to have lived happily ever after."

"If he wasn't then, I bet he's glad she left him now," Jack said.

"After we talk with Suzanne, we need to talk to O'Reilly," Claire said, her voice definitive. "This guy's our only shot at hearing the other side of the story."

CHAPTER EIGHT

CLAIRE PULLED up to the entry gate, shielding her face from the half-dozen photographers who had chased their SUV down the street. They passed television vans, random people with phones, and a few dozen others who just seemed to want to be part of the story.

Flashing her badge at an overly smiley security guard, she said, "Claire Anderson, FBI. I spoke with Mrs. Blackwood earlier." Claire wondered if Suzanne would be as composed as she sounded over the phone, or if the reality of her situation would reveal cracks in her demeanor.

The guard examined her badge. "I'll need to see one from her, too."

Sonya, in the passenger seat, handed Claire her ID, which Claire then passed to the guard.

"She's not on the list," the guard said.

"She's with me," Claire replied.

"Sorry, Agent Anderson, only those on the list can enter." The guard's smile disappeared. "With or without you, she's not on the list. I'll have to call Mrs. Blackwood." He slid the window closed and picked up a white, old-fashioned landline.

Claire turned to Sonya. "I didn't tell Suzanne about you on purpose. I wanted to see if bringing a profiler would unsettle her, maybe make her slip up. People often think they can fool an FBI agent, but they believe profilers have almost psychic abilities."

Sonya chuckled. "I wish I did."

The guard returned, opening the window and handing back Sonya's ID. "You're both cleared."

"Thanks," Claire said, passing the card to Sonya.

"No problem." The gate swung open slowly. "Apologies for the delay. We're told to stick to the list."

Claire nodded and drove through, following the road in a wide arc toward the mansion. She eased the SUV into a brick circular driveway that surrounded a fountain.

"Pretty nice place," Claire said, pulling to a stop behind a red Porsche 911 with a custom license plate that read: *1LOSTGRL*.

Sonya cocked her head, smiling wryly. "Pretty nice?" she said. "I looked it up on Zillow. This place is worth ninety million."

"Like I said," Claire replied, "pretty nice." She approached the grand oak door, glancing at Sonya. "Ready for anything?" she asked, only half-joking.

"Always," Sonya replied, straightening her blazer.

Before Claire could knock, the door opened slightly, and a white poodle erupted in a frenzy of barking. Next to it stood an impeccably still robot dog—similar in size but metallic, with glowing blue eyes.

The AI dog's head tilted slightly, and it spoke in a cheerful British accent. "Welcome to Blackwood. I am Sir Waggington, but you may call me Waggs, and this," it gestured toward the poodle with a mechanical paw, "is Piper. Please place your belongings on our sniffing station. Here you will find treats for Piper. You may need these if you wish for her to obey you. We both know a number of tricks."

Piper barked between each of Waggs' sentences, as if adding her own commentary.

Sonya's eyes lit up as she leaned closer to Waggs. "This is incredible! No fur, no drool, no vet bills. And look—no treats needed for obedience." She pointed at Waggs. "Sit."

Waggs immediately obeyed, lowering itself smoothly.

"But no actual *bond*," Claire said. "Who wants a dog without emotional intelligence? It's just following commands."

"Honestly, Claire, I'm not sure Piper has much in the way of emotional intelligence either." Sonya pointed at the poodle, still barking and dancing on the spot. "Piper, sit."

The poodle ignored her.

Claire sighed, grabbed a treat from the sniffing station, and crouched down. "Piper, sit."

Piper stopped barking, plopped onto her haunches, and eagerly accepted the treat.

"Good girl," Claire said, standing up. "So, you'd take Waggs over Ranger?"

"Why not?" Sonya asked.

Claire turned to the AI dog. "Play dead."

Waggs immediately flopped onto its side, emitting an exaggerated whirring noise, its tongue-like sensor dangling from its mouth.

Sonya clapped her hands. "Amazing!"

"Now watch this." Claire held another treat above Piper. "Piper, play dead."

Piper tilted her head as if considering the request. Then, with dramatic flair, she flopped onto her side, landing with an audible huff, her eyes fixed on the treat. Claire straightened, placing the treat back on the sniffing station.

"What now?" Sonya asked.

"Now, we wait." Claire smiled, shrugging.

"Wait? For what?"

"You'll see." Claire crossed her arms.

Piper lay still for several moments, her chest rising and falling rapidly. Eventually, her nose twitched, and she hopped up, sniffing at Claire's pockets. Finding no more treats, Piper gave an indignant huff and trotted off to bark at something in another room.

Sonya raised an eyebrow. "What was the point of that?"

Claire gestured at Waggs, still lying perfectly still. "Fitz once taught me something about AI."

"Okay, I'll bite," Sonya said, skeptical. "What did Fitz teach you?"

"When you tell AI to do something, it does it. And that's the problem."

"A problem? That sounds like a dream come true." Sonya adjusted her glasses. "That's like if I woke up and actually was psychic. Every case closed, all problems solved."

"It's different. You'd stop using your psychic powers at some point. Let's say you tell AI to make cogs. It doesn't need a treat or a reminder. It'll keep making cogs, tearing apart buildings, countries—maybe even planets—until the entire universe is nothing but cogs."

Sonya laughed. "That's one terrifying apocalypse."

"Piper will get tired and move on. An AI won't stop." Claire leaned down toward Waggs. "Waggs, how long will you play dead?"

Waggs's voice responded cheerfully from the floor. "As long as you wish, Claire."

"Good to know." Claire frowned, an unsettling realization hitting her. She looked at Sonya, who seemed to be thinking the same thing.

"How do you know Claire's name?" Sonya asked the AI dog.

"I'm always listening, ma'am. You told me earlier."

"Do you know *my* name?" Sonya asked.

"No, ma'am, I do not."

"When did I tell you Claire's name?"

"*Honestly, Claire, I'm not sure Piper has much in the way of emotional intelligence*." Waggs read back Sonya's earlier words, mirroring her tone precisely.

"That's what's disturbing," Sonya said, shaking her head. "AI's constant surveillance."

Claire agreed, but was eager to get to the interview. "Waggs, where's the mistress of the house?"

"The mistress is in the solarium, ma'am," Waggs replied.

Claire nodded at Sonya. "Let's go."

They left Waggs's lifeless metal body in the entryway and followed the sound of Piper's persistent barking toward the solarium.

"I see you've met my little friends," a voice called as they passed through a vestibule connecting to the solarium.

Claire looked up to see Suzanne Blackwood descending a marble spiral staircase. The living art space around her featured plants growing in every direction—an intricate balance of order and chaos, forming a multidimensional canopy. The air was warm and humid, carrying the faint, earthy scent of fresh leaves and damp soil, making it feel as though they were stepping into a living, breathing ecosystem.

But Suzanne herself seemed to be the focal point—rootless and floating, much like the air plants that surrounded her, taking each step with grace.

"It's lovely here," Sonya said, mesmerized. "Are those air plants?"

"Yes, Tillandsia xerographica," Suzanne replied. "Vincent had dozens of these flown in from Central America every year for his birthday. When they'd finish blooming, he'd have them flown back. He didn't want to disrupt conservation efforts."

"May we ask what his connection to this plant was?" Claire felt a growing curiosity—was this just another eccentricity of a wealthy man, or did it hold a deeper significance to the case?

"Of course. You're here to ask questions, and I'm prepared to answer." Suzanne gestured at the plants. "Vincent went on a shamanic retreat in the late eighties—said this plant spoke to him. It takes years to mature, sometimes decades. It has no roots, just air, water, and sunlight. And when it blooms, it's spectacular. I think he saw himself in it—an awkward kid who took time to bloom, who thrived without much, and who planned to bloom for a long time." Suzanne took a deep breath, her eyes misting slightly. "He left out the parts about ayahuasca and plants speaking to him. Funny, though."

"What's funny?" Claire asked, following Suzanne's gaze.

"He never mentioned that once it blooms, the plant begins to die. It's true, though. After the bloom, it starts fading—but not before sending out new growth, offspring to continue the cycle." Suzanne looked from Claire to Sonya, her energy shifting. "You're right; it's lovely here. But right now, it's making me sad. Could we speak outside instead?"

"Of course," Claire said. "We're grateful you're willing to speak with us." Even though Suzanne was a primary suspect in Vincent Blackwood's murder, Claire decided to ease into the conversation so as not to frighten her or cause her to close down.

"Actually, I was relieved when you reached out," Suzanne replied. "No offense to the local officers, but I hoped more experienced investigators might look into Vincent's death. Follow me—or, more accurately, follow Piper."

Claire noticed the dog had stopped barking. Maybe Piper

only carried on when strangers were around, settling once they were acknowledged by her owner—much like the man at the gate.

"Was that your Porsche out front?" Sonya asked. "Are you the One Lost Girl?"

Suzanne glanced back, smiling slightly. "The Porsche is Hailey's. I drive a Subaru. Vince always told me to get a nicer car, but, well, I'm happy with it." She looked at Claire, her expression sad.

Claire offered a polite nod, but inwardly, she felt a twinge of discomfort. She realized she had made a mistake. She'd let herself form an image of Suzanne Blackwood before meeting her—the cold, unfeeling widow who wasn't grieving enough. But now, standing before Suzanne, Claire saw something different. The woman's poise, her careful words, the genuine sadness in her eyes.

Suzanne was striking, but not because of wealth. Her silvery hair was pulled into a bun, her eyes were bright and expressive. She wore an elegant yet casual outfit—a linen blouse, tailored slacks, and leather sandals. For someone whose fortune could buy anything, Suzanne seemed remarkably humble.

This realization forced Claire to reassess her approach; she needed to remain open to the complexities of Suzanne's character rather than fitting her into a preconceived narrative—the easy suspect, the black widow.

As they made their way back to the entrance, Suzanne gestured for Claire and Sonya to exit while she grabbed a treat from the sniff station. She threw it for Piper before closing the door behind her. Piper barked once, but seemed content to stay indoors.

Waggs, of course, remained lifeless where it had fallen, still playing dead.

CHAPTER NINE

"LETTING you drive is my first olive branch, Jack." Fitz used both hands to grip the chest strap of his seatbelt like it might save his life.

Jack shook his head, his eyes never leaving the road. Fitz could sense Jack's silent amusement without needing to see his expression.

"Fitz, you and I both know—if you'd insisted on driving, peace wouldn't matter—we'd never live long enough to need it."

"Indeed, it wouldn't." Fitz gave a hearty laugh, then closed his eyes tight as Jack swiftly pulled out into dense, fast-paced traffic. Jack drove a little too aggressively for his taste, but between the two of them, Jack was undoubtedly the safer driver.

Fitz decided to offer Jack a different olive branch—a genuine question about his life. "So, Jack, are you dating these days?"

During Fitz's time with Margaret, she'd taught him that other people enjoyed talking about themselves, too. On more than one occasion she'd finished listening to Fitz ramble, then asked, "So, do you have any questions about *me*, Fitz?" This time, he didn't need her to remind him to act like he cared about the other person in his presence.

Fitz noticed Jack's raised eyebrow, a clear sign that Jack was skeptical about Fitz's sudden interest. "Uh, yes. I am actually seeing someone."

"*Outside* the office, I hope." Fitz couldn't help himself. Any tower built, even if he'd skillfully constructed it himself, Fitz always found a way to topple.

Jack swiftly turned the steering wheel with one hand, making a sharp maneuver that made Fitz tense. "As a matter of fact, yes."

To Fitz's relief, Jack sounded less defensive than he feared.

"And you?" Jack continued. "Anyone who isn't your direct superior catching your fancy?"

"*Touché*," Fitz said. "It appears that both of our olive branches are plagued with thorns."

"Indeed," Jack said.

"Her name is Margie," Fitz said. "I think I'm falling for her."

"What's she into?" Jack asked. "I mean, besides pompous Englishmen with inflated egos."

"Ego, yes, but belly?" Fitz sucked in his gut, which was less robust than the last time Jack had seen him. "You've got to at least give me some credit."

Jack glanced over and gave him a slight, approving nod. "You're right, you're right. I can tell you've been working on yourself. Well done, Fitz."

"Anyway," Fitz said, steering the conversation back. "She's a psychic for rich people."

"You're kidding," Jack said.

Fitz shook his head. "I wish I was. If you'd asked me who

I'd be least likely to date, a psychic would've made the top ten."

"Weren't you the one who told me about opposites attracting?" Jack asked.

"Why yes." Fitz nodded. "But until now, my psychological theories never applied to *me*. I guess in this case, they do."

Jack laughed, his eyes still on the road.

The silence between them grew, and Fitz reminded himself to be polite. "What about you, Jack? What's your girlfriend like?"

Jack pulled into the driveway of what Fitz assumed was the worst house in Medina, Washington, then cut the engine of the SUV. "She's a personal shopper. After the whole thing with Violet and Kiko..." He trailed off, leaving Fitz to fill in the blank.

"I heard about that," Fitz said. He gave Jack a nod, trying to convey genuine interest. "Well, I'll be interested to hear more about your personal life, Jack."

Fitz got out of the SUV and looked up at the house. It was at least three times larger and much nicer than the duplex he was renting, but still—for Medina, Washington—it wasn't much. It wasn't on the water, and it was far from a mansion. Fitz deduced it must be part of a neighboring mansion's estate, a rental.

As they strolled up to the front door, Fitz kept his observations light. "It occurs to me—your girlfriend being a shopper for rich people and mine being a psychic for rich people—both jobs require psychology and cold reading to a certain extent."

Jack stopped, turning to give Fitz a considering look. "That's actually correct."

"Don't sound so surprised," Fitz replied, knocking loudly on the old door.

Jack shook his head. "No, I mean that's *exactly* what she told me. When she first meets a potential client, she reads everything about them. Shoes. Whether they've had plastic surgery. The car they drive up in. The house and everything in it, if they're meeting at a house. Or the restaurant they choose, if they're meeting at a restaurant. She reads everything, so before her clients even start speaking, she knows what kind of items she'll be buying. She doesn't only take care of their wardrobe; she shops for holiday gifts, birthday presents, that kind of thing."

Fitz barely listened, just nodding at the appropriate moments. He was more focused on the door, hoping someone would answer quickly and save him from hearing more about Jack's girlfriend.

His prayers were answered. The door swung open to reveal Geoffrey Osgood, a man in his early sixties with a neatly trimmed beard and a tired expression. He was dressed casually, in a plaid shirt and dark jeans. Fitz thought he looked more like a retired schoolteacher than a house manager.

"Geoffrey Osgood?" Fitz held up his badge.

"Yes," Geoffrey said, his voice tinged with curiosity. "So, you're FBI?"

Fitz offered a brief nod. "I'm Fitz. And this is Agent Russo. We're here to figure out who killed your boss. Might we come in?"

CHAPTER TEN

"HOW ABOUT WE START," Claire said, "with you telling us a little about the night your husband died."

Suzanne slowed, allowing Claire and Sonya Ticker to catch up. "I can do that."

In the distance, beyond the sprawling emerald lawn and scattered fir trees, Claire glimpsed the bright blue of Lake Washington. The water sparkled in the morning sunlight, its surface rippling gently in the breeze. She couldn't remember ever being at a house this extravagant, but she could understand the appeal. It was close to Seattle, yet the grounds felt like a secluded European estate, the house itself an ultra-modern techno-castle.

Suzanne led Claire and Sonya past Hailey's Porsche, parked on the circular driveway. Claire took note of the bumper sticker: '*There is no away…*' She made a mental note to ask Hailey about it later.

They walked alongside Suzanne down a cobblestone path bordered by meticulously pruned boxwoods. The scent of fresh-cut grass mingled with the faint floral sweetness of nearby lavender bushes.

"We always made a big deal about his birthday," Suzanne said. "Everyone was there—politicians, celebrities, businesspeople, mostly men."

A pair of robins darted from a nearby birch tree, chirping as they disappeared into the distance. Claire glanced at Sonya, who had taken out her notepad, her eyes watchful. They'd reviewed the guest list during the ride over. No names had jumped out as obvious suspects, which only meant that *everyone* was a suspect. And Suzanne was still the primary.

"Was your husband having trouble with anyone at the party?" Sonya asked, stepping over a patch of dewy grass.

"He was well-liked. At his level, everyone has a few enemies, but no one stands out. He was at the peak of his life." Suzanne paused, her gaze shifting to the shimmering lake. "Wealth, fame. His health was good, as far as we knew. I have no idea why someone would do this." She hesitated, brushing a strand of silver hair from her face. "Then again, I wasn't deeply involved in his businesses, so it's possible there was some rivalry I didn't know about."

Claire glanced at Sonya, who studied Suzanne carefully, her pen hovering above her notepad.

They continued walking, their footsteps scuffing on the stone pathway. To their left, an expansive rose garden stretched out, blossoms ranging from pale blush and golden amber to deep crimson and rich purples. A gardener in a wide-brimmed hat worked silently, his pruning shears clicking rhythmically.

"The party," Claire said. "How about you walk us through it?"

For the next ten minutes, Suzanne described the party in vivid detail—how guests arrived, the catering setup, and the plans for later that night. The wind carried the sound of a boat engine from the lake, and Claire glanced toward the water, where a lone kayaker glided past the property's edge.

"At eight, Vince went to his office. Geoffrey brought him the bottle, and you know what happened next. He was so proud of that bottle—you know the story about his dad and his humble beginnings."

"The bourbon factory?" Sonya asked, her tone carrying a slight edge of skepticism.

Suzanne caught it immediately. "I know, I know," she said with a light laugh. "He embellished it a bit. They were middle class, not living in a trailer or anything. But yes, his dad worked his whole life at the bourbon factory. That part's true. They lived modestly—maybe not as modestly as Vincent made it sound—but they weren't well-off."

The path led them alongside a patch of deciduous trees. A gust of wind rustled the leaves overhead, sending dappled light across Suzanne's face. Her tone remained warm, not defensive, despite Sonya's subtle attempts to provoke a reaction.

"In any case, you've probably heard about the ritual he had with his whiskey," Suzanne continued. "He'd open the bottle, drink a shot, and..." Her voice faltered, cracking as she looked toward the lake. "When Geoffrey came back ten or fifteen minutes later..." Her shoulders slumped slightly. "He was dead."

"How are you coping?" Sonya asked.

Suzanne's gaze lingered on the lake for a moment before she answered. "I'm managing as best as I can." She adjusted the cuff of her blouse, smoothing it methodically, as if the act helped her ground herself.

"It can't be easy," Sonya said. "Losing someone so suddenly. It must make life feel... chaotic."

Suzanne turned back to them, her expression calm. "I've had my moments, of course. But I've learned to focus on what I can control."

Claire noticed Sonya give a faint nod, as if agreeing, though Claire recognized it as something more calculated.

Sonya wasn't finished. "That's admirable," she said. "But surely you must have questions. About why someone would do this. Whether they were targeting Vincent... or you."

Suzanne straightened, shifting her weight to one foot. "Me? Why would anyone target *me*?"

Sonya tilted her head slightly, her stance shifting almost imperceptibly, like a shadow moving closer. "You're a public figure in your own right. Wealth, status—they come with their own dangers. Jealousy. Resentment. Maybe even secrets. Not to mention, well, I'm sure you've seen the papers, the news. I'm sure you knew that your past husbands would be brought up."

Suzanne's hand moved to her necklace, fingers brushing the small gold pendant before falling away. "*Of course* I knew that," she said. "The black widow thing is a sexist stereotype, and my life has been thoroughly examined in the public eye. I don't *have* any secrets."

"No?" Sonya replied, her lips curling just enough to suggest curiosity rather than challenge. "Suzanne, forgive me for saying this, but let's not play the sexism card, okay? You're thrice-widowed. You expect people to believe it's a coincidence?"

"What?" Suzanne's brow furrowed.

"Honestly, Suzanne, you expect us to believe you've buried three husbands and have no secrets?"

Sonya glanced at Claire for support, but Claire kept her expression neutral.

Suzanne snapped a furious look at Claire. "Who does this woman think she is?" She stopped walking and turned to Sonya. "I don't expect anyone to believe anything. But if I'm asked a question and I bother to answer, I answer truthfully. When you ask if I have secrets and I say I don't, I don't."

"That's good to hear." Sonya's tone was unconvinced. "Because secrets have a way of surfacing, don't they?"

Suzanne stepped closer to Sonya, her intensity palpable. "Let me remind you, I'm not the only one with a past, Sonya." Tears slipped down Suzanne's cheeks. "Vincent was also married before me. Look through *his* life before you start swatting at the cobwebs in mine."

"I'd think you'd want to clear out those cobwebs yourself, given your situation. People talk. Friends, family, staff... even pets, in a way."

"Excuse me?" Suzanne snapped, wiping her tears with the back of her hand.

"People leave trails," Sonya said with a faint smile. "A pattern here, a habit there. It's what makes uncovering the truth possible. You strike me as someone who would appreciate that kind of clarity."

"Of course," Suzanne said, breathing differently now, subtly trying to control her emotions. "Clarity is important. And I know you're just doing your job."

Claire noticed the shift in Suzanne's posture. Sonya had turned the power dynamic. She was doing everything she could to get a reaction out of Suzanne, and it had worked.

And yet, it wasn't doing anything to convince Claire of her guilt. In fact, it was doing the opposite.

"We're sorry for your loss," Claire said, offering a look of condolence that Suzanne seemed to absorb. "I imagine Vincent's death has disrupted everything for you." She gestured briefly toward the lake. "The life you shared, the plans you made. What happens now?"

"I'm... I'm," Suzanne hesitated, then continued down the path, leading them back toward the mansion. "I'm taking things one step at a time."

"Of course," Claire replied.

"But surely you've thought about what's next," Sonya

added, her voice now gentler. "Your home, your businesses, your travels... any long-term plans?"

The question lingered, the soft rustle of leaves overhead filling the silence. Claire watched Suzanne closely, noting the subtle tension in her hands as they clasped, then released.

"Just taking it day by day," Suzanne said finally, her voice quieter now.

At the end of the lawn, a stone pathway meandered toward the water and what appeared to be twin guest houses, each of which was larger than Claire's own home—easily four thousand square feet. Modern marvels of glass and steel, their sleek lines softened by cedar accents. Large, floor-to-ceiling windows reflected the sunlight, offering sweeping views of the lake.

"Is that where Hailey lives?" Claire asked.

"For *now*," Suzanne replied, her tone hinting at more than just a simple report of circumstances.

"Mind if we leave you here, Suzanne?" Claire asked. "Since she was at the party, Sonya and I need to question her as well."

"I don't mind coming with you," Suzanne offered.

"Actually, we'll need to speak with her alone," Sonya said, her tone authoritative.

"Fine," Suzanne said. "And if you find her less cooperative than me, don't read too much into it, okay? She's, well... you'll see for yourselves."

Claire reached for the doorbell beside the minimalist glass and steel front door, which was flanked by native plants. Before she could press it, the door flung open. The rush of air pushed past her, followed by the cool blast of air conditioning.

"Don't touch it!" A young woman Claire assumed to be Hailey grabbed her arm, stopping her before she could press the button. "Do you even know how much noise pollution modern humans have to deal with?"

Hailey frowned as Claire withdrew her arm and shot a look at Sonya, who had her head cocked like she was taking mental notes.

Hailey, around twenty-two, stood framed in the doorway, her style a curious blend of '60s hippie and '70s punk. Her wavy, unkempt hair fell around her shoulders. She wore a loose tie-dye shirt tucked into ripped black jeans, paired with well-worn combat boots. A small nose ring glinted in the sunlight, and an intricate, tribal-style tattoo curled along her wrist. What struck Claire most was her expression—a mix of defiance and disdain that dared anyone to challenge her.

Claire held out her badge.

Hailey opened her eyes slowly, anger washing over her face as realization struck. "Oh my goddess!" Hailey's voice was sharp. "I should've known when I saw *her* walking you here. It's not my fault Daddy loved my mother more than her."

"Are you Hailey Blackwood?" Claire asked calmly.

Hailey crossed her arms, leaning into the doorjamb. "Look, lady, I didn't kill my father. It's bad enough I have to deal with Suzanne's AI dogs, and now she's sicced the FBI on me? That utter bitch!"

CHAPTER ELEVEN

"WOULD NOW BE a good time for us to chat?" Fitz asked Geoffrey.

"No, of course it's fine." He stepped back, opened the door wide, gesturing for them to come in. "I assume this is about Mr. Blackwood?"

It was always useful to assess a suspect's willingness to meet when you were already at their doorstep. So far Geoffrey hadn't exhibited any incriminating behaviors.

"Yes, we'd like to ask some more questions about Mr. Blackwood." Jack came up beside Fitz, edging his shoulder slightly in front of him.

Fitz stepped into the tidy, modest house. His gaze swept across the room, catching on a sleek, white and silver robot dog sitting motionless in the corner.

"What's with the dog?" Fitz asked.

Geoffrey glanced at it and let out a short laugh. "Ah, that. Suzanne gave it to me last Christmas. She and Mr. Blackwood got a pack of three, apparently. It was... very generous. But I still don't know how to use the thing."

"You don't seem like much of a tech guy," Fitz said, watching Geoffrey carefully.

Geoffrey shook his head. "Not in the slightest. I've got the manual somewhere, but I haven't had the time to figure it out. It's been sitting there since I got it."

Fitz smirked. "With a name like Geoffrey Osgood and a job like house manager, I half expected you to be British, too."

Geoffrey laughed. "Nope, born and raised in Tacoma. Sorry to disappoint."

They followed Geoffrey through the house into the kitchen, which was small by Medina standards but well-kept. Fitz took in every detail: the way Geoffrey moved—calm but slightly stiff—and the way his hands lingered on the back of a chair as he gestured for them to sit.

"Can I offer you some coffee?" Geoffrey asked.

"No thanks," Fitz said, choosing to remain standing. Jack leaned against the counter, arms crossed, his casual stance at odds with the intense focus on his face.

Geoffrey clasped his hands together. "How can I help you gentlemen?"

"How about we start with the night of the party," Jack said. "You were in charge of it, correct?"

"Every detail," Geoffrey replied, and for the next fifteen minutes, he walked them through the basics of the party as Jack and Fitz peppered him with questions. Mostly he just confirmed what they already knew. When he got to the part where he'd left Mr. Blackwood with the poisoned whiskey, Jack wasted no time getting to the point.

"We're looking at everyone close to Mr. Blackwood. Can you think of anyone at all who might have wanted to hurt him?"

Geoffrey let out a slow breath. "I've seen the news so, before you ask, Suzanne had nothing to do with it. She loved

Vincent. I know people like to whisper about her, but she's a kind woman. Tough, sure, but not capable of murder. The trauma she went through with her last husbands, too. I can't imagine what she's having to go through now."

Fitz studied Geoffrey's face closely. His words sounded sincere, but there was a slight hesitation before he spoke, as if he was choosing his words carefully.

"And why are you so sure?" Fitz asked.

"I've worked for her for years. She's just a good person."

Fitz let the silence that followed stretch out, watching how Geoffrey shifted his weight from one foot to the other.

Finally, Geoffrey cleared his throat and continued. "That said, you're looking for potential suspects. And there are a few people who *do* come to mind."

"Go on," Jack said.

"Well, there's Daniel Blackwood, Vincent's brother. They weren't exactly close, though they kept up appearances well enough. If you'll forgive the *Godfather* reference, Daniel strikes me as a Fredo, whereas Vincent was like Michael and Sonny combined."

"Smart and tough?" Fitz asked.

"Exactly, while Daniel... he's well-meaning, but he's no Vincent Blackwood."

"Who else?" Jack asked.

"Then there's Helene Marquez, his ex-wife. They are still business partners—well, they were until Mr. Blackwood was murdered. Their relationship... was *contentious*, to say the least."

"How so?"

"Please excuse me. I'm still in shock talking about Mr. Blackwood in the past tense. Anyway, Mrs. Marquez felt she deserved more control in their shared app business, more credit for its successes. They argued about it often. It wasn't a secret. She often talked about it publicly."

Geoffrey paused, glancing toward the window. Fitz noticed the movement and wondered if it was a habit or a subtle check for onlookers.

"Then there's Hailey, Vincent's daughter. Unfortunately, as much as Mr. Blackwood did his best to cover for her screwups, she's obviously... troubled." He shook his head. "My advice, keep a short rein on your daughters." Geoffrey spoke like he was reporting from experience. "I watched Mrs. Marquez raise Hailey—and it wasn't how Mr. Blackwood wanted things. That girl was given a new silver spoon for every day of the week. She's already on her *third* red Porsche. The last one she traded in wasn't even a year old. She said she couldn't drive it anymore because it smelled like her ex-boyfriend."

"She sounds pretty delicate," Jack said.

"You don't know the half of it. The rumor is, she'd cheated on her boyfriend with a guy who'd spilled his fries on the passenger seat floor. He didn't clean them up, and neither did she. This young, privileged girl, nearly an adult, told her then-boyfriend she'd spilled the fries then asked him to clean them up. Can you imagine the audacity?"

Fitz said nothing.

Jack just frowned.

"She insisted they'd been hers," Geoffrey continued. "But her ex knew she wasn't eating those fries herself. No self-respecting female socialite living in—or even adjacent to—Medina would be caught dead consuming something like that. Anyway, the boyfriend left, and the fries stayed. If the rumors are wrong, her ex-boyfriend smelled like rancid, rotting French fries. That girl wanted a new car so she wouldn't have to clean up her own disgusting mess. She is ridiculous."

"Women can be like that," Jack said.

Fitz knew that Jack didn't mean what he was saying. He

was taking on a role, warming up the suspect. Garnering favor like this might prove useful to the case in the future, even if Geoffrey only turned out to be a witness.

"Right." Geoffrey shook his head contemptuously. "My take is, if Mrs. Marquez hadn't spoiled that girl so badly, she wouldn't be the entitled, lazy brat that we're left having to endure the presence of today."

"A shame," Jack agreed.

"Anyway, enough about Hailey," Geoffrey continued. "There's also Lena Quan."

"And what's her angle?" Fitz asked.

"It's not long or complicated." Geoffrey adjusted a picture on the wall that hadn't even looked off-kilter to Fitz. "Same old story. A woman with a grudge takes on a billionaire mark, looking for an easy payday. She's a former employee. She didn't leave on good terms and made some threats after she was let go."

Fitz nodded, jotting down notes. "And Suzanne herself? You've said you'd heard the rumors about her other husbands, right? I know you said she's a good person, but..."

Geoffrey frowned. "I'll tell you the same thing I told the police two days ago: those were tragic accidents, not crimes. Well, the first one was actually self defence, but that bastard had it coming after what he'd done to her. Suzanne wouldn't hurt anyone. Vincent was a gentleman and he was her knight in classy armour. She told that to people all the time."

Fitz tilted his head slightly, observing the way Geoffrey's hands clenched behind his back.

He decided to test the man's composure. "You know, in all the mystery novels I've read, there's one cliché that always seems to pop up."

"What's that?" Geoffrey raised an eyebrow.

Fitz smiled faintly. "The butler did it."

Geoffrey gave a reluctant chuckle. "Well, I'm not a butler, and I didn't do it."

Fitz's smile faded as he locked eyes with Geoffrey. He held the stare a moment too long, watching for any flicker of discomfort. Geoffrey didn't flinch.

"Well, if you think of anything else," Fitz said, breaking the tension. "You have our contact information."

"I'll let you know." Geoffrey nodded. He jumped at the cue, moving—a bit too eagerly, Fitz thought—to show them to the door.

"One more thing," Jack said. "The party. Both Lena and Helene were there that night, despite the fact that Helene was Vincent's ex and Lena was a disgruntled employee. Why?"

"I don't make the list; I just ensure that those who are on it have gotten their invites." Geoffrey let out a small laugh. "But I do have a *system*."

"What is it?" Jack asked.

"DQ scores." Geoffrey smiled.

Jack looked to Fitz, who could offer no insight. They were both stumped.

"It's their Decorum Quotient." Geoffrey looked at them excitedly. "I call it their DQ. It's a calculation system I made."

Fitz and Jack returned blank stares.

Geoffrey's face fell. "It's just a scale. I use it to rate how well people carry their wealth."

"How do the characters on your list rate?" Fitz asked.

"Suzanne Blackwood is fabulously rich, but treats her staff well and is gracious beyond belief, so she scores very high. And she was always gracious with Hailey and Helene. Helene, though, she's terrible, well below average. But Mr. Blackwood had already suffered the kind of earthly hell his ex-wife was capable of putting him through and wanted no part in stoking that fire."

Jack nodded. "And Lena Quan?"

"She and Hailey haven't earned their DQs yet. I do understand why Lena would have been invited to the party. What better way to show everyone you're not worried about what a person might say publicly than to have them in attendance at your birthday party? *Keep your enemies closer*, and all."

Fitz could understand that.

"But Suzanne didn't have any enemies," Geoffrey continued." She and Helene, they spend time together. They've been meeting regularly for at least the last year. Medina Tennis and Country Club. They brunch there, take lessons. Every other week. These women and a few other widows meet there regularly."

Fitz considered this. "Helene is a widow, too?"

"Her second husband, the one after Vincent, died of cancer. Two years ago."

Jack seemed amused. "Bunch of rich widows, having brunch and playing tennis?"

"A cliché, I know," Geoffrey said.

"Do you know when their next meeting is?" Jack asked.

"Of course I do," Geoffrey said. "I always know Mr. and Mrs. Blackwood's itinerary. I keep their calendars. Well, now I keep Mrs. Blackwood's."

Geoffrey took his cell phone out of his pocket and tapped at the screen. "Let's see... here it is." Geoffrey held out the phone with the calendar displayed on the screen. "If you can stick around, you're in luck. Their next meeting is today. Two o'clock at the country club restaurant for brunch."

"Brunch at two?" Fitz frowned.

"When you wake up between eleven and noon every day," Jack pointed out, "two is the perfect time for brunch."

"Maybe we will pay them a visit." Fitz nodded and began moving toward the door.

"No one can possibly feel worse about the circumstances around Mr. Blackwood's death than I do," Geoffery said, walking them out. "*I* was the one who brought him that bottle. *I* was in charge of every aspect of the party where he was poisoned to death. And I hope you catch whoever did this."

As they left, Fitz glanced back at the robot dog, its sleek body catching the light. "What a thing."

Jack nodded. "That's the most well-behaved dog I've ever met."

"He would be a bit more impressive if I'd powered him up. Shall I?" Geoffrey asked.

"That won't be necessary," Fitz said. "A dog like that will never be a best friend of mine."

"I can't imagine that dog would want to be *your* best friend either, Fitz," Jack said.

"I don't think it cares who its best friend is," Geoffrey added. "I threw out the box, but it said, *Guaranteed to never byte*—and by byte I mean it read B-Y-T-E—*the hand that powers it up*."

"Cute," Jack said.

"Also, bloody awful," Fitz added.

CHAPTER TWELVE

"SO, what does 'There is no away' mean?" Claire asked Hailey.

"Pssh. How can you *not* know?" Hailey rolled her eyes. "I'm constantly having to explain this to people." She sighed. "We think the things we throw away just vanish. But there is no 'Away.' Do you know the address for the place we call *Away*?"

Claire wished she'd just Googled the meaning of the bumper sticker instead of bringing it up. "I don't," she said, reflecting on how hypocritical Hailey's rant sounded, considering the Porsche likely cost more than Claire's first house. At seventeen miles per gallon, Hailey wasn't doing the environment any favors of her own.

Hailey closed her eyes, taking a breath like she was in deep meditation. "You and Me, Planet Earth—that's the address. *Away* is inside each and every living thing. All of that biohazard lands in the air we breathe, on the food we eat, in the water we drink. We're literally poisoning our home. And I don't mean the planet. I mean our *true* home."

Hailey traced a line from her head to her toes with both index fingers. "This flesh and blood home."

Sonya brushed her hair out of her face as the wind picked up. "May we come in?"

"No." Hailey returned to her wide-legged stance, arms crossed. "I'd prefer we take this to my father's house. My boyfriend's asleep."

"We'll be quiet," Sonya promised, squeezing past her and into the house.

Claire followed quickly, ignoring Hailey's mumbled objections.

Inside, the house resembled a luxury design magazine. High ceilings and an open floor plan added grandeur, while marble floors, bespoke furniture, and abstract art gave it a modern but impersonal feel. Every detail was curated for aesthetics over comfort, from geometric chandeliers to the pristine, unused stainless-steel kitchen, which was littered with empty take-out containers.

"Nice place," Sonya said.

Hailey snorted, crossing her arms as she perched on the edge of the couch. "You think? It's fake. All of it. My dad loved appearances more than anything else."

Claire ignored the comment, taking the armchair across from her while Sonya leaned casually against the wall. "Let's talk about your relationship with your dad, Hailey. Just to clarify—Helene Marquez is your mother?"

"Yeah," Hailey said, her tone clipped. "My *real* mom. Not Suzanne."

Sonya tilted her head. "That must have been... complicated. Your biological mom nearby, your dad remarried to Suzanne, and they were all tied up in the business together?"

Hailey shrugged, but didn't meet Sonya's eyes. "It wasn't that complicated. My mom was his ex and one of his business partners. Basically, he bought an app she created. Was gonna be the next big thing. Suzanne was his wife. Everyone had their roles, and no one ever overstepped. Except for me, I guess."

Claire leaned forward slightly. "How so?"

"Let's just say I wasn't Daddy's perfect little girl," Hailey said. "I didn't worship him like everyone else did. My dad had consumer stuff, but he also sold tech to the Pentagon, okay? He was a warmonger, building gadgets to help people kill each other. And you're here trying to figure out who killed him? Maybe start with the people he helped kill."

Claire noticed Sonya's expression change, but she stayed quiet.

Hailey continued, "He spent money on stupid crap, like those robot AI dogs. He bought three of them from some South Korean company—said the 'Three-Pack Pup-Pack' was the deal of the century. How is spending a million bucks on hunks of ephemeral waste that pretend to be dogs a 'good deal'?"

"Didn't he buy you that Porsche in the driveway as well?" Claire asked. "I'm assuming he did."

"I *need* that to get to school," Hailey snapped.

"What are you studying?" Sonya was quick to defuse Hailey's energy.

"You know, I'm not just some spoiled rich kid." Hailey's tone was defensive. "I'm getting my degree in Interactive Social Justice Dynamics and Ludonarrative Dismantling."

Claire blinked. "Come again?"

"It's a self-designed major," Hailey said. "I'm using games to challenge power structures. My thesis is a tabletop RPG that teaches players to dismantle hierarchies in real-time."

Claire stifled a laugh, but Sonya said, "Good for you," in a tone that sounded sincere enough.

"People don't realize we're living in the future," Hailey explained as though standing in front of the class. "Those who control gaming are the new shepherds, and we haven't realized yet that *we're* their sheep. I want to dismantle their narratives and give a platform to gamebuilders who are leading people toward the good."

"That's all fine, Hailey," Claire said firmly. "I know you might not have agreed with what your dad did with his life. But we're not here to debate his business ethics. We're here to find out who murdered him. If you know something, now's the time to speak up."

Hailey's jaw tightened, her fingers twisting the edge of her tie-dye shirt. "I don't know anything, okay? But I can tell you this—he had enemies. Real ones. Not just disgruntled family members like me."

"Enemies like who?" Sonya asked.

Hailey sighed, exasperated. "You've got the usual suspects, right? My stepmom. Suzanne. You probably know about Lena, his former employee—don't bother going there—she's innocent. And I *never* trusted Geoffrey. Then again, my art therapist tells me I have trust issues with *all* men." She cleared her throat. "So if you're asking me if I know who killed him, I don't. And honestly, I don't care."

Claire's expression hardened. "I think you *do* care. You wouldn't be this defensive if you didn't."

"Oh, is that your FBI profiling expertise talking?" Hailey's eyes narrowed. "You people think you're so smart, don't you? I've read enough to know the FBI screws up as many cases as it solves. More, probably."

"This isn't a game, Hailey." Sonya straightened, her expression sharpening. "Your dad is dead, and someone's responsible. If you want us to believe you're not involved, maybe stop trying so hard to throw us off."

Hailey's face flushed red, and for a moment, Claire thought she might snap. Instead, she stood abruptly, pacing the living room.

"You don't get it," Hailey said, her voice cracking. "You think because he was my dad, I'm supposed to defend him? Pretend like he was this great guy? He wasn't. He was controlling and arrogant, and yeah, he pissed off a lot of people. Ask me, it was probably one of his business associates who killed my father."

A knock at the door stopped her mid-sentence. Hailey sighed and walked over, opening the door to let in a man Claire assumed was her uncle Daniel. He bore a striking resemblance to his deceased brother, Vincent—same sharp jawline and piercing eyes. But where Vincent had radiated authority, Daniel seemed softer, almost weary. His salt-and-pepper hair was neatly combed, and he wore a tailored blazer over a crisp shirt and slacks. He held a sleek cell phone in one hand, which he slid into his pocket as he reached the bottom step.

"Agents," Daniel said, offering a polite nod. "I couldn't help but notice you on the porch a few minutes ago. Suzanne told me you were coming, but I had to finish up a call."

Hailey, now ignoring all of them, plopped down cross-legged on the floor, picked up a controller, and began playing a video game on the massive TV. The sound of leveling up and electronic chatter filled the room as she clicked furiously at the buttons.

"Really, Hailey?" Daniel sighed. "Games are for kids."

"What?" she muttered without looking up. "You're the one butting into my conversation."

Claire gestured toward one of the chairs. "Mr. Blackwood, would you mind sitting down? We'd like to ask you a few questions."

"Of course." Daniel took a seat on the edge of the couch, his posture relaxed.

Sonya stepped forward, her arms loosely crossed. "Can

you tell us a little about your role in your brother's company?"

Daniel sighed and leaned back slightly. "Advisor. That's what he called me, anyway. Truth is, I didn't know nearly as much as Vincent—not about business, not about technology, not about... well, anything, really. He was the genius. I was just the guy he called when he wanted a second opinion or someone to bounce ideas off. Part of me thinks he only put me on the payroll because he felt bad for me."

Sonya tilted her head. "That doesn't bother you? Knowing you were... less involved?"

Daniel met her gaze evenly, unruffled. "No, it didn't. Vincent was brilliant, and he built something extraordinary. I didn't envy him. I was happy to help however I could."

"But isn't it possible," Sonya pressed, "that somewhere, deep down, you might have been jealous? Wishing you had his influence, his power?"

Daniel chuckled, shaking his head. "No, absolutely not." He paused, then his expression grew thoughtful. "You know, it's like... imagine you're standing in a garden. And there's this tree—this massive, magnificent tree—that towers over everything. You could be jealous of how tall it is, how much sunlight it takes for itself. Or you could stand in its shade and just enjoy the coolness it offers."

Claire studied him carefully, noting the ease with which he spoke. He wasn't defensive, didn't bristle under Sonya's question. If he was hiding something, he was a master at it.

"So, you were content to be in Vincent's shadow?" Claire asked.

Daniel nodded. "*More* than content. I admired him. He was my brother, and I was proud of what he accomplished. That's why his death..." He trailed off, running a hand through his hair. "It's a loss not just for me but for everyone who depended on him. He held the world together for so many people."

As he spoke, Hailey muttered something under her breath, her fingers mashing the controller.

"What was that, Hailey?" Claire asked.

"Nothing," Hailey said, not looking up. "Just... people always think he was so great. They didn't live with him."

Daniel frowned but didn't respond, his gaze softening as he looked at his niece.

Claire turned back to Daniel. "Thank you for your honesty, Mr. Blackwood. We may have more questions later."

Daniel nodded, his expression somber. "Anything I can do to help."

As they left the guest house, Claire whispered to Sonya, "What do you think?"

Sonya shrugged. "He seems sincere. But sincere doesn't always mean innocent."

Claire glanced back at the house one last time. "No, it doesn't."

"That said, I think Suzanne isn't telling us everything."

"Really?" Claire asked. "She seemed deeply honest to me."

"Nah, she was too polished by half," Sonya said.

"Hmm, maybe," Claire said. To her surprise, she found herself wishing Fitz had been with them to break the tie.

CHAPTER THIRTEEN

AS JACK DROVE, Fitz called Claire to get her approval to head over to the country club. The thinking was that, now that Claire and Sonya had interviewed Suzanne, Jack and Fitz could speak with her from a different angle, and then they could gather again to compare notes. After making him promise not to let Jack do any "cowboy stuff," she'd agreed.

She'd also passed along more information about Suzanne's first husband, which Violet had pulled up from various public records and a few phone calls around Suzanne's old hometown. The strangest thing was that he seemed to be a normal person—apparently happily married with a family, running his car dealerships, and living the kind of life that was the opposite of everything Suzanne had moved to Seattle to find.

Fitz had stashed this away, figuring he might be able to use it later.

Jack parked in front and led the way, flashing his badge to the attendant at the door.

"We're here to speak with Suzanne Blackwood," Jack said. "I believe she's having brunch."

The man looked confused, walked a few paces away, and

spoke hurriedly into his walkie-talkie. A moment later, he returned.

"Absolutely," he said, leading them into the dining room. "Suzanne and her friends are right through here."

The dining room exuded quiet opulence, the kind of understated elegance that whispered rather than shouted its price tag. Polished mahogany tables gleamed beneath soft, gold-toned chandeliers, their light diffused through intricate crystal shades. The walls were paneled in cherry wood, adorned with oil paintings of pastoral landscapes, each in gilded frames that likely cost more than a year of Fitz's salary. Waitstaff moved silently through the room, their uniforms crisp, their postures impeccable. The scents of freshly brewed coffee and truffle oil wafted through the air. Fitz let his gaze wander, taking it all in, but Jack walked with purpose, leading the way as they neared Suzanne's table.

Around the table sat Suzanne Blackwood, as well as a slightly younger woman, likely in her early fifties, whom Fitz assumed was Helene Marquez. A smarmy, overly tanned man crouched next to them, chatting conspiratorially.

As the agents approached, the man stood. "Brentley Flemming," he said, holding out a hand and shaking Jack's, then Fitz's. "You two need a tennis coach?"

He laughed, but Fitz just stared at him. "Is your name *really* Brentley Flemming?"

Flemming nodded, then casually placed a hand on both Helene and Suzanne's shoulders. "Work on those backhands, ladies. See you in a couple weeks." He strolled across the dining room, stopping to greet various patrons—mostly women—on his way out.

Helene spoke first, addressing Jack. "Aren't you just the buttoned-up FBI agent we all dream of?"

Jack reached out and shook her hand. "Jack Russo. You must be Helene Marquez?"

Suzanne stood as well. "Thank you both for coming. I spoke with your colleagues earlier, but I wasn't expecting a follow-up so soon. I appreciate your thoroughness. What can I do to help?"

A third woman joined them, returning from the restroom, Fitz assumed, seeing her tuck a lipstick into her purse. She had curly brown hair and a sadder look than the other two. Suzanne introduced her.

"This is Samantha Matri," Suzanne said. "The third member of our little widows' club." She held up both hands and smiled ruefully. "Yes, I know how dark that must sound. But until you've lost a husband, you can't understand how much you need the support of the women in your life."

"I'm going to take off," Samantha said. "It's been lovely, ladies."

"Now, how can I help you?" Suzanne asked.

"Well, there is something I wanted to talk about," Fitz said. "We spoke with your— well, house helper, butler, whatever he's called—Geoffrey."

"I know," Suzanne said. "He gave me a call and let me know you might be coming. I hope that's all right. He and I share everything. I count on him for *everything*."

"Fine," Fitz said. "I know you already covered the basics with my colleagues, but here's my question. The biggest party of the year, and you invite one of your husband's public enemies, Lena Quan? I—"

Fitz stopped when Helene burst out laughing.

"You really don't know much about rich people, do you?" she said.

Jack scowled, but Fitz only smiled. He didn't mind this sort of confrontation at all, and he genuinely wondered what the hell she was talking about. "Go on," Fitz said.

Helene gestured toward the bar, where a youngish Asian woman sat sipping what looked like a Bloody Mary. "Lena

Quan is right over there," Helene said. "Don't you understand that what shows up in the newspapers and what is real are very different things?"

Fitz folded his arms. "Enlighten me."

Helene wrapped an arm around Suzanne's shoulders. "I was married to Vincent Blackwood for nine years. We got divorced and didn't speak for two years. But we shared a daughter, Hailey, and we got over it. I got remarried, he got remarried. I got very rich, he got even richer. It's not like on TV, where I have to hate his new wife, and she has to hate me." She paused, considering her next words carefully. "Wealth beyond belief softens a lot of hard feelings."

"And with Lena," Suzanne interjected. "That was all performative, for the lawyers and the newspapers. Yes, she was pissed off that she got fired, and yes, she talked about it in the press. She was suing my husband's company to try to get more severance. It's just business."

"Just business?" Jack asked.

"I could teach *you* a thing or two about business," Helene said, a sick kind of seduction twisting across her face. "But I don't have time for that right now. Lena and I have our spa treatments coming up."

Helene had that overconfidence Fitz had seen in a dozen criminals who figured they were smarter than the officers investigating them. She was too comfortable, too self-assured, and it made Fitz suspicious. Unlike Suzanne, who seemed genuinely cooperative, Helene's attitude suggested she believed she had nothing to fear. Fitz wasn't buying it for a minute. She seemed far more likely to have secrets worth hiding. And the thing he wanted most was to listen in on whatever those two women were going to talk about during their spa treatment.

He glanced over at Jack, wondering if he was thinking the same thing. Jack was either pretending to be seduced by

Helene or *actually* being seduced by her. Fitz couldn't tell. But the way the two were staring at each other left him concerned.

"Could you point me toward the little boys' room?" Fitz asked Suzanne. "I'll be right back—would love to continue speaking with you. But for now, Jack"—he punched Jack lightly in the arm—"why don't you begin asking her about her very first husband?"

Jack broke eye contact with Helene. "Will do, boss," he said.

Fitz hurried toward the bathroom, already plotting his next move.

PART 2

MEN VERSUS WOMEN

CHAPTER FOURTEEN

FITZ FOLLOWED the signs toward the bathrooms, but as soon as he passed the door marked "Gentlemen," he veered left, his eyes catching a sleek metal sign that read "Spa & Wellness Center."

The hall widened, lined with soft recessed lighting and paintings of abstract landscapes. He kept his pace normal, trying to appear like any other member who belonged at the club. He wasn't sneaking—he was far too large to *sneak*—but he wasn't exactly on official business either.

The entrance to the spa was marked by tall frosted glass doors, etched with a delicate floral design. Inside, the air was cooler, scented with eucalyptus and lavender. Soft instrumental music played in the background, and the entire space was designed to soothe. A marble reception desk stood at the center of the lobby, flanked by shelves of neatly arranged products—fancy oils, creams, and candles with names he'd never heard. Overhead, a massive chandelier hung, its design mimicking cascading water droplets. Everything here screamed quiet luxury.

A well-groomed man in a tailored vest and tie greeted

him from behind the desk. “Good afternoon, sir. Welcome to the Wellness Center. How may I assist you today?”

Fitz put on his most affable smile, one he’d seen plenty of rich blokes use. “Good afternoon. I was wondering about your couple’s treatments. My wife and I have an anniversary coming up, and I’d love to surprise her with something special.”

“Of course, sir. We offer a range of dual treatments, including massages, facials, and aromatherapy experiences. Would you like a brochure, or shall I explain them in detail?”

“Well, perhaps you could show me the room where it happens?” Fitz said, adding a feigned curiosity to his tone. “You know how it is—want to make sure it’s just right for her.”

The spa attendant hesitated for the briefest moment, then smiled again. “Certainly, sir. This way.”

The attendant led Fitz down a hallway painted in a calming shade of sage green, accented by gold sconces. He opened a door at the end of the corridor, gesturing for Fitz to step inside.

The couples’ treatment room was spacious, almost absurdly so, with two massage tables draped in pristine white linens. A fireplace flickered in the corner, its mantle adorned with fresh orchids. A seating area with overstuffed armchairs and a small table held an arrangement of teas and infused water. The lighting was warm and the hum of a hidden sound system played what sounded like distant waves and whale songs.

“As you can see,” the attendant said, “we aim for an atmosphere of complete relaxation and intimacy. This is one of our most popular rooms.”

Fitz nodded, hands in his pockets as he scanned the space. “Calming, indeed,” he said. “My wife will love it.” He turned toward the attendant, offering a polite smile. "Thank you for showing me."

"Not at all, sir. Shall I reserve it for you?"

"Not just yet," Fitz said. "Still working out the surprise, you see. I'll be in touch."

The man led Fitz back out, but Fitz stopped at the door. "I hate to ask, but might I take a photo or two? I'd like to have my florist plan a few arrangements to customize the room for the special day."

"Absolutely," the man said, "though we also have a club florist who can help you with that."

"I'm pretty set on my own florist," Fitz said, a phrase more ridiculous than any he'd ever heard himself say.

"Very well then. I'll leave you to it."

"So," Jack said, "your first husband. Back in Ohio." He folded his arms and watched her facial expression.

Suzanne seemed far away for a moment, her gaze drifting, but then her eyes shot back to him. "That was a long time ago. I know what's in the papers, and I suppose you want to know what happened. Why is *he* still alive?"

"It crossed my mind," Jack said.

"Well, we married very young. And although I loved him, and he loved me, we just wanted different things. These days they call it..." she raised her hands into air quotes... "A 'starter marriage.' When two people marry in their late teens or early twenties before they really know what they want. Then they part ways fairly amicably later on, once they've grown into themselves a little. He's a good man, but..." She gestured vaguely around her. "Well, look around you. I just wanted more. *Deserved* more. Do I look like the kind of person who was meant to spend her life in Dayton, Ohio?"

Jack frowned. Her tone wasn't quite as arrogant as her words, but it wasn't humble either.

"I know, I know," Suzanne said quickly. "I know how that sounds. I have nothing against him. He wanted that small-town life—a car dealership, a house with a picket fence. I just wanted more, and there's nothing wrong with that. I don't apologize for that."

"And you shouldn't," Jack said.

Suzanne picked up her phone. "Oh, I have to get to yoga!" She stood and handed Jack a business card from her purse. "Please don't hesitate to be in touch if you need any more information."

As Suzanne hurried away, Jack glanced across the room and caught sight of Helene and Lena Quan meeting up, their heads close as they exchanged a few words before heading toward the spa.

Jack wasn't entirely sure what Fitz was up to, but the way he'd hurried off earlier had him wondering.

~

When the spa attendant left him alone in the treatment room, Fitz pulled his phone from his pocket and quickly dialed Jack.

"Hey," Jack answered, "Fitz?"

"Don't hang up," Fitz said. "Just leave the line open."

Without waiting for a response, Fitz set his phone to speaker mode, turning the volume all the way down. He glanced around the room, weighing his options. Finally, he saw the perfect spot—a narrow gap between the two massage tables draped in pristine white linens.

He crouched down, slid his phone into the space, and adjusted it until it was hidden but positioned well enough to pick up the sounds in the room. Standing, he gave one last glance to ensure nothing looked out of place, then turned toward the door.

He smoothed the front of his jacket, molding his expression into the same affable demeanor he'd worn when he arrived. As he walked by the attendant he said, "Have an excellent day, my good man!"

He was no Kiko, but he felt it was the finest acting performance of his career.

CHAPTER FIFTEEN

FITZ FOUND Jack back in the dining room. He leaned in, keeping his voice low. "Did you hang up the call?"

Jack gave him a disapproving look. "I didn't, but don't tell me you—"

"I did," Fitz cut in, glancing around. He gestured subtly toward the bar. Jack followed him over.

The bar was sleek, modern, with a polished marble countertop shimmering under the glow of pendant lights. Rows of top-shelf liquor lined the backlit glass shelf, arranged like trophies. A soft jazz tune played from a hidden speaker. The bartender, a middle-aged man in a tailored vest and bow tie, greeted them with a professional nod.

"What can I get you two gentlemen?" he asked.

"Are we eating?" Jack asked, turning to Fitz.

"I'll take a burger and a Bloody Mary," Fitz said, then pointed at Jack. "He'll take the lightest salad you've got, double grilled chicken, and an unsweetened iced tea. Right, Jack?"

Jack smirked. "You got it."

The bartender nodded and moved to put in their order.

"Got your AirPods?" Fitz asked, lowering his voice.

Jack frowned. "Yeah, but I thought Claire said 'No cowboy stuff.'"

"On the contrary, she said I needed to keep *you* from doing any cowboy stuff. Said nothing about *me*."

Jack frowned. "C'mon, that—"

"Just give me one of the airpods," Fitz said, cutting him off. "You take the other."

Jack shook his head.

"I know, I know," Fitz said quickly. "We won't tell Claire or use this unless we have to. But I don't trust Helene, and I don't think you do either. Something's up, and I want to know what it is."

Jack looked dubious but reached into his pocket and handed Fitz one AirPod. "Fine. But you owe me."

Fitz adjusted the AirPod in his ear as he leaned casually against the bar. Jack kept his expression neutral, swirling the ice in his tea. The jazz music blended with voices coming through their AirPods as the feed from Fitz's hidden phone began to pick up sounds.

At first, it was ambient noise—footsteps on carpet, the soft clink of glass, the quiet pop of a bottle of massage oil. A cart squeaked as it moved across the room, followed by murmurs between spa attendants.

Then, the voices of Lena Quan and Helene Marquez came through. As they entered, their tones were light and casual, punctuated by occasional laughter.

"God, my back is killing me from all that tennis yesterday," Lena said, her voice muffled as she moved closer.

"Maybe if you spent less time flirting with Brentley and more time on your serve, you'd be fine," Helene quipped, the amusement in her tone unmistakable.

Lena laughed. "Please, Brentley couldn't coach a pro, much less me. He's too busy tanning himself into leather."

The conversation meandered as they settled onto the massage tables. Fitz winced, enduring five minutes of chatter about their last doubles match and jokes at Brentley's expense, including a particularly unflattering comparison to a trophy husband. He glanced at Jack, who rolled his eyes but said nothing.

The tone shifted as Helene's voice softened. "So, how do you think Suzanne is holding up? I mean, with everything she's been through..."

"With great grace," Lena replied sincerely. "I honestly don't know how she does it."

Helene sighed. "She's a survivor. I'll give her that."

There was a pause, then the sound of oil being poured and hands moving across skin. A massage therapist's voice broke in: "A little more pressure here?"

"Perfect," Helene said. Her voice dropped, still audible but careful. "But you have to admit, it's been... an adjustment."

"You could say that," Lena agreed. "An adjustment for all of us."

"True." Helene hesitated. "It's... strange, isn't it? The way things are now."

"You mean with Vincent gone?" Lena's tone was conversational, but Fitz detected a hint of curiosity.

"Don't think of it that way," Helene said after a pause. "It's not about that."

"Isn't it?" Lena pressed. "You were still in business with him. Right?"

Helene's response was measured, almost too casual. "We had... some overlap."

"Come on, Helene. You and Vincent weren't just partners; you were competitors," Lena said, her voice tightening slightly. "The personal growth app? I heard you were trying to push him out."

Helene's laugh was soft, controlled. "Competition is just business. You know that as well as anyone. And anyway, *he* was trying to push *me* out."

"Sure," Lena said. "But now there's no competition, is there?"

Silence followed, broken only by the sound of kneading hands and the soft sound of waves and whales.

"Let's not think of it that way," Helene said after a long silence, her voice almost a whisper.

As the conversation waned, the bartender returned, placing their meals and drinks on the marble bar. Fitz immediately dug into his burger, the rich scent of truffle fries wafting up as he took a bite.

Jack frowned at his salad. "We're not really eating this, are we? We've got work to do."

"Damn right we are," Fitz said, waving a fry before popping it into his mouth.

Before Jack could respond, a faint beep chimed in Fitz's ear.

"Call waiting," Jack said, holding up his phone. "It's Claire."

He accepted the call and Claire's voice came through, sharp and urgent. "Get back here."

"Claire," Fitz said, "I'm about to dig into a burger. Probably the most expensive burger ever billed to the FBI, and—"

"Hailey Blackwood just drove her quarter-million-dollar Porsche into a temperature-controlled waterfront yoga studio. And Suzanne Blackwood was inside."

CHAPTER SIXTEEN

CLAIRE SIPPED her second capuccino of the day as Jack and Fitz hurried into the Boiler Room, finally joining the team just as Violet projected her research on Lena Quan onto the big screen on the wall.

Ranger trotted over to greet Fitz, tail wagging enthusiastically. Fitz smiled, but it quickly turned into a frown when he realized the dog was more interested in the doggy bag he was carrying than in him.

"You had time to stop for lunch?" Claire asked, raising an eyebrow.

"It was for work," Fitz said. "We had to blend in."

"And you still had time to eat three-quarters of your burger," Jack added, smirking as he took his seat.

Fitz ignored the jab, setting the doggy bag on the edge of the table as he and Jack joined the others.

Claire stood at the front of the room, hands clasped. "Before we get into the Lena Quan stuff," she began, trying to stay composed despite the overwhelm creeping into her mind, "here's what happened with Hailey. We can't talk to her yet, but I spoke with a local officer. We're likely to be the first to interview her, so we've got some leverage. Apparently, she drove her Porsche 911 straight into the glass wall of the yoga studio Suzanne was at."

Jack leaned forward. "Where's this yoga studio? You called us only maybe fifteen or twenty minutes after she left my sight."

"It's not far from the country club," Claire said. "Apparently, she goes there after her tennis brunch."

"Quite the fitness queen," Kiko muttered. "Wish I could eat brunch and do yoga all day."

"Don't we all," Claire continued. "We still don't know why she did it, what happened, or whether this has anything to do with the murder. Hailey is clearly troubled, and now we potentially have her on attempted murder with a vehicle, at most, and a whole list of other felonies, at least. But we're going to bracket this for now and get back to it later."

She turned to Violet. "Okay, Lena Quan. Go."

Violet tapped on her computer screen and a photo of a young Asian woman popped up next to her bio on the wall. "Lena Quan," Violet began, "is a highly sought-after app designer and engineer, known for her cutting-edge work in the personal growth and wellness tech space. She's been credited with developing some of the most advanced behavioral feedback algorithms on the market. Before her public fallout with Vincent Blackwood, she was the lead engineer at his company, spearheading their flagship project, an app called ManZone."

The screen flickered, and a series of bolded quotes from Quan's public statements replaced her bio.

"Vincent Blackwood is a tyrant who built his empire on the backs of his employees."

"Working for Blackwood isn't just a job—it's indentured servitude."

"He'll take credit for your work, grind you into the

ground, and toss you aside the moment you're no longer useful."

Violet glanced back at the team. "These were part of her media campaign last year, when she was suing Blackwood's company after being let go. She didn't hold back."

"Take this with a grain of salt," Jack said, "but both Helene and Suzanne seemed to think the animosity was for show, part of her lawsuit. They all seemed to be buddy-buddy."

"Noted," Claire said, though she had her doubts.

"I'm guessing I don't want to know what the ManZone app is," Fitz said, leaning back in his chair.

"You don't," Sonya said, crossing her arms. "No offense, but you would *not* enjoy this app, Mr. Pembroke."

"What's that supposed to mean?" Fitz asked.

"Hold on, you two," Claire cut in, her tone enough to halt their budding argument. She turned to Violet, who was still typing furiously at her laptop. "You have something on the app they'd worked on?"

Violet glanced up and nodded. "Yep, give me a second." She clicked a few more times, then cast the results onto the big screen, which lit up with the logo for the ManZone app: a sleek, black shield icon with a bold red "M" emblazoned across it.

The tagline underneath read, *ManZone: Reclaim Your Edge.*

"So here's what we're dealing with," Violet said, gesturing to the screen. "ManZone is a modern all-in-one app targeting young men—think Gen Z and younger Millennials. It's marketed as a way to counteract the ways they feel excluded in society."

She clicked, bringing up screenshots of the app's interface: sections for personal fitness plans, videos on intermittent fasting and cold plunges, and slick graphics promoting crypto trading. "It's a mashup of personal fitness and health routines, tips on 'taking back your power,' and even crypto trading strategies."

Fitz raised an eyebrow. "Sounds... balanced."

"That's the problem," Violet said. "On the surface, it's about self-improvement and confidence-building, but some parts of it border on straight-up toxicity. They're trying to walk a fine line, though. There's content from influencers, videos on Roman history—stuff meant to inspire discipline and strength."

Claire frowned. "And in reality?"

"In reality," Violet continued, "it's designed to suck in as much male attention as possible. Blackwood's company even courted a few minor celebrities to promote it—MMA fighters, YouTubers, TikTok influencers. You name it."

"And Lena Quan worked on this?" Jack asked.

"Exactly," Violet said, switching to another screen showing old design documents tied to Lena's name. "She was part of the team that built the original algorithm before she got canned. Which, if you ask me, means she had some serious skin in the game before the fallout with Vincent."

Claire watched as this sank into the room. "What about Helene? Wasn't she partnering with Vincent as well?"

"Helene Marquez created an early version of the app," Violet said, "and Vincent purchased it. For her, it was a 'labor of love,' and she intended it to be a collaborative platform for both men and women. However, after the acquisition, Vincent shut Helene out of its development entirely and rebranded it as a male-focused product, transforming it into a testosterone-driven tool that contradicted her original vision. The betrayal left Helene furious and humiliated."

"That sounds like a motive to me," Fitz said. "But where are you getting all that information? We just spoke with her and, well, she was not forthcoming."

"I combed the web for every mention of them. Actually

got most of this from Instagram live videos Hailey did when her dad shoved her mom, Helene, aside. She was pissed on her behalf. Called it part of the patriarchy she was going to tear down. And there's something else," Violet continued. "This took some digging."

She tapped on her screen, and a news article popped up. The headline read: *Tech Mogul Vincent Blackwood Buys $2.6 Million Bottle of Scotch at Private Auction.*

"The Scotch that killed him," Kiko added.

"The head auctioneer who sold it," Violet said, pointing at the screen, "was Byron Davidson. He went to Stanford with Lena Quan. Same age, and they even lived in the same dorm. Plus, they're friends on Facebook and connected on LinkedIn."

"So she had access to the bottle," Claire said, "or at least *could* have."

"It's circumstantial," Sonya said, "at best. I still think we need to keep our eye on the ball: Suzanne."

"Bollocks!" Fitz said.

"I agree with Fitz," Jack said. "Suzanne just didn't strike me as a cold-blooded killer. And the bottle—that's more than circumstantial. If we can prove Lena used that connection to tamper with the bottle, that's our case."

Claire folded her arms and stared at the screen. "We need to find out exactly how close Lena and Byron really are. And if this connection was more than just old college ties." Claire noticed Sonya's look, something like disappointment or exasperation. "Sonya, speak up."

"I just... I guess I just don't agree with any of this. Statistically speaking, Suzanne is *by far* the most likely suspect, even though, I admit, so far, the evidence doesn't point to her."

Fitz leaned back in his chair, his fingers tapping rhythmically on the edge of the table. "You're too hung up on statistics, Sonya." He leaned forward, his jaw clenched, eyes narrowing. "People don't live their lives like numbers on a spreadsheet. They follow their hearts. Their guts."

Sonya stood, smoothing her blazer as she walked to the small coffee station in the corner of the room. "You want a coffee, Fitz?"

"Sure," Fitz said.

She grabbed two paper cups, carefully measured out some grounds, and set the coffee machine humming. Turning her back to Fitz, she said, "Come on, Fitz. Be serious. Suzanne's first husband dies in self-defense because he's abusive. Her second husband conveniently dies in an accident. And her third? Dead on her watch? If you can look me in the eye and say that doesn't sound statistically improbable, I'll eat my badge."

Fitz smirked from his seat. "Well, you don't *have* a badge yet. And furthermore, her *first* husband is alive and well, as we've established. But I understand your point–I just don't agree with it. You've got your tidy little logic boxes, and you think everyone should fit into them. But people don't work that way. They're messy, unpredictable. They make choices that defy explanation, that laugh in the face of probability."

Sonya finished pouring the coffee, added a splash of milk to one mug, and grabbed both cups. "That's not what the evidence says," she said, returning to the table. "I don't need to believe in unicorns and fairy dust. I believe in patterns, probabilities, and—what's that thing called again? Oh, right—science."

Fitz chuckled as she handed him a cup. "You think your science is some unassailable truth, but it's just a tool. A blunt instrument at best. People are infinitely more complex than your algorithms can handle."

Sonya raised an eyebrow, sipping her coffee. "Really? Enlighten me, oh wise one."

Fitz shrugged. "Maybe you've got enough knowledge to impress your professors or your parents. But your understanding of psychology? Of humanity? It's rudimentary, at best."

Sonya's lips twitched into a tight smile as she stood again, took Fitz's coffee out of his hand, and walked toward the trash can. Holding Fitz's coffee above the bin, she tipped it over. A thin stream of brown liquid dribbled out through the sip hole.

"Oi!" Fitz protested, standing halfway out of his chair.

Sonya gave the cup a slow squeeze, forcing the lid to pop off. The remaining coffee gushed out in a dramatic splash before she dropped the empty cup into the trash can with a satisfying thunk. She turned back to him, her smile widening.

Claire sighed.

"Mic drop," Kiko said from across the room, smirking.

Fitz leaned back in his chair, shaking his head. "Well, that's one way to win an argument."

The phone in the center of the desk buzzed, and Kiko tapped it onto speakerphone. "Boiler Room, this is Kiko."

"It's Cathy. Boss wants to talk to Claire."

"I'll be right up," Claire said. "Anything I should prepare for?"

"Well," Cathy said. "Is there any chance Fitz was sneaking around a spa at the country club in Medina?"

Claire glanced at Fitz, who didn't look away. He simply cocked his head and nodded.

"I'll be right up," Claire said.

Kiko ended the call.

"She meant Jack, right?" Claire asked.

Fitz walked over to Ranger, who rubbed his chin into Fitz's leg. "Afraid not. Which reminds me: I gotta call them and find a way to get my phone back."

CHAPTER SEVENTEEN

"*YOU'RE* the one who told me to bring him back in," Claire said, raising both hands in a placating gesture as Hightower adjusted a stack of papers on his desk.

"I did," Hightower snapped, "but I expected you to be able to control him."

Claire stood. "I can't control that guy. No one can."

Hightower pulled a cellphone out of an envelope and slid it across the desk. "It's Fitz's. Manager sent it over by courier." He let out a long breath, running a hand over his face in exasperation. "What the hell made him think he was in a *Mission Impossible* movie? He knows they have security cameras everywhere." He shook his head, leaning back in his chair. "Do you think I want to get calls from the most expensive country club in Washington State? Do you know how many millionaires and billionaires go there?"

Claire shrugged. "I don't."

"I don't want to be beholden to these people, but in some respects, we are," Hightower continued. "For now, can you just keep that guy out of the field? He can still be his brilliant self—just keep him in the damn office." He stood up, as though about to dismiss her, but then stopped and kept going. "Seriously, I would have expected that kind of stunt from Jack. What the hell do you think got into Fitz?"

"He said he has a whole new life now. I think he's dating. He looks like he's lost a little weight, his clothes are cleaner... maybe he's on the straight and narrow. Thought he'd be an action hero."

Hightower grimaced. "He's lucky they don't have video cameras in the actual therapy rooms. If they did—" He shook his head. "Well, they seemed to have bought the story that he accidentally left his phone in that room. But you and I both know that's not what happened."

"My guess is Fitz knew they didn't have cameras in there," Claire said. "He's reckless, but he's not stupid."

Hightower walked Claire to the door. "Just remember. Most of our politicians answer to people in Medina, or people like them. They can get me transferred, get you shut down. We have power, sure. And you know I'm not afraid of a fight."

"Neither am I."

He waited until she met his eyes. "But this is a fight we don't want."

Fitz and Sonya appeared to be in the middle of an intense staring contest when Claire returned to the Boiler Room.

"I'll give you three-to-one odds that Suzanne is innocent," Fitz was saying.

"I'll take that bet," Sonya shot back, her eyes flashing. "Hundred bucks. And I'll do you one better. If it *wasn't* her, I'll resign from the team."

"I'll take that bet," Fitz replied, reaching out and shaking her hand.

"Enough," Claire said, stepping between them. "Violet, what did you find while I was getting read my rights by Hightower?"

Violet clicked a few keys, sending a flurry of documents to the screen. "We went through the divorce records of Vincent Blackwood and Helene Marquez. Nothing out of the ordinary. They were both rich; they both got richer after they divorced. We did confirm, though, that *she* started the app, and all her interviews about it were actually pretty compelling. At the time it was called *2gether*. As in, *numeral* two, *gether*"

"Clever," Jack said.

"The bottom line?" Violet continued. "She wanted to create a new type of social media that would integrate photos, videos, influencers, dating, even banking—like Facebook mixed with your local gym, mixed with a dating app, mixed with... everything else."

"It's the holy grail in tech," Jack said. "A single app that does everything. Social, financial, entertainment, and so on."

"First, she partnered with her ex-husband on some content," Violet continued. "Then he bought out the app, promised her a big role, and cut her out completely. Turned it into... well, you know what he turned it into. The man-o-sphere."

"And I believe that's a motive," Fitz said.

"And I believe motive isn't enough," Sonya countered.

"We also went over the footage from the party," Violet said, cutting in. "Well, actually, Kiko and I did—while our two shrinks argued. We don't have every room or every minute, but there were dozens of people with access to that bottle. Plus, it was left alone on display in several spots without cameras, as people came and went. It's going to take me hours to go over all of it, but so far, it's gotten us nowhere."

Claire noticed that her fists were clenched and she slowly released them. It seemed as though each new lead in the case opened up three more.

"I also spoke with the auction company and the delivery company that transported the bottle to the mansion," Kiko added. "It's all a bunch of nothing for now—a couple dozen names on paper, any of whom could have used a needle to poison the bottle. I'm guessing that's a dead end."

Claire pinched the bridge of her nose, her head pounding. She wished she had Benny's scribble app handy so she could take out her frustration on a picture and have her fortune read back to her. But she needed to stay professional.

"Here's the plan," Claire said, straightening up. "Sonya, Jack, and I are going to the hospital. Hailey has been cleared to speak with investigators, though she won't be released until later today. Her injuries are minor—hit with a few shards of broken glass, a couple of stitches on her arm. Suzanne is there as well."

She turned to Fitz, locking eyes with him. "You stay here with Violet and Kiko."

She paused, daring him to protest, but Fitz was smart enough to keep quiet.

CHAPTER EIGHTEEN

THE PRIVATE HOSPITAL room had an understated luxury. Soft cream walls, polished wood accents, and a large window with a view of the skyline gave the space a warmth that contrasted sharply with the tension in Claire's chest. Hailey Blackwood sat upright in the bed, her dark hair pulled into a loose ponytail, her left arm wrapped in a pristine white bandage. Despite her minor injuries, her face was pale, her lips pressed together in a cold scowl.

Claire entered first, Jack and Sonya flanking her like a set of bookends. Jack held his notebook loosely in one hand, while Sonya adjusted her blazer and scanned the room with a clinical detachment.

Hailey's brown eyes darted between them. "Am I being arrested?" she asked, her voice thin but sharp.

Claire pulled up a chair and sat at the side of the bed. "Not yet," she said calmly. "But we've got you on attempted murder, Hailey. You drove your Porsche into a building full of people. You could've killed someone—your stepmother included."

Hailey's jaw tightened. "It *wasn't* attempted murder," she muttered.

"Then what was it?" Claire leaned in, her tone measured. "Because if you don't get serious about helping us right now, you're going to leave this hospital in cuffs."

Hailey's gaze flickered to Jack, who was jotting something down, then to Sonya, who stood with her arms crossed, her head tilted slightly as she studied her.

"I snapped, okay?" Hailey said finally, her voice trembling.

Claire didn't let up. "Snapped how?"

Hailey took a shaky breath. "I've always been fine... or at least, I pretended to be. Pretended I didn't care that I wasn't in the will. My dad always said he'd cut me out, but I didn't think he *meant* it. I still got my allowance. I mean, twenty-five thousand a month is nothing compared to what he had, but it was something, right?"

"Go on," Claire urged, deciding not to comment on Hailey calling her twenty-five-thousand dollar monthly stipend an "allowance."

Hailey's eyes filled with tears, her voice breaking. "I found out this morning that he actually did it—cut me out of *everything*. Fully. The lawyers said Suzanne convinced him. She's the reason. She told him I didn't deserve a dime and that I wasn't serious about my life. She made sure I got nothing. Not even my allowance anymore. They were gonna cover the rest of the college, then cut me off."

Sonya stepped closer to Hailey. "How did you feel when you found out?"

Hailey looked at her as though the question were ridiculous. "How do you *think* I felt? Furious. Heartbroken. I couldn't believe he'd actually listen to Suzanne when it came to his own daughter."

"And that's when you 'snapped'?" Sonya asked, pressing just enough to dig deeper.

Hailey nodded, the tears spilling over. "I don't even remember deciding to do it. I just... I knew where she'd be. And when I got there and saw her standing there in her stupid Lululemon outfit, acting like she owned the world, I just—" She broke off, sobbing. "I hit the gas and crashed into it."

Jack finally spoke. "Were you trying to kill her?"

Hailey shook her head violently. "No! I don't know. I just wanted her to feel the way I felt. Destroyed."

Claire made her eyes hard, locking onto Hailey's tear-streaked face. "You're in a lot of trouble, Hailey. But right now, the only way out is the truth. All of it."

Hailey sniffled, wiping her nose with the back of her hand. "That's it. That's the truth. I lost it. I didn't want to kill her... I just wanted her to pay."

Sonya stepped forward. "You felt powerless, didn't you? Like you didn't matter to him anymore, like she'd taken everything from you?"

Hailey nodded, her sobs softening.

"Hailey," Sonya continued, "right now both your stepmother Suzanne and your mother Helene are being considered as suspects in your father's murder."

Hailey's head snapped up, her face tightening in disbelief. "What? No. Not my mom. She would never... And not me, either... I—"

"We know your mother and Vincent had significant business disagreements," Claire interrupted. "We know she had reason to be angry with him, largely because of videos you posted online."

Hailey gripped the edge of the blanket. "I was high when I made those videos. And so what? Business is business, but they still loved each other."

"*Loved* each other?" Sonya asked. "Even after he pushed her out of her app and turned it into something both you and she despised? A 'tool for the patriarchy' I think you called it."

"Yes!" Hailey said, her voice cracking. "I thought they were going to get back together. That he'd finally get sick of Suzanne." Hailey's hands balled into fists. "You don't understand! They had this... connection. Even when they fought, there was something between them. Suzanne ruined everything. My dad never should've married her."

Sonya studied her for a moment, then glanced at Claire, who gave a subtle nod. They had pushed Hailey far enough for now, but her defensive reaction about Helene raised as many questions as it answered.

"Stay put," Claire said. "I know you're getting out later today, but Medina PD will need a statement as well. They'll handle the charges against you." She walked to the door. "But for now, consider your driver's license *suspended*."

On the way out, they passed the room where Suzanne Blackwood was recuperating. Jack stopped at the door and turned to Claire. "You mind if I take this one alone? I think she... well, I think she kind of had a thing for me."

Claire raised an eyebrow. "You *can't* be serious."

"I'm just saying," Jack replied, running a hand over his bald head. "I've been known to have a certain effect on women. Helene, too. They were both flirty."

"Good grief," Sonya muttered. "Even more delusional than Fitz."

"Let me talk with her alone," Jack insisted, stepping closer to the door. "I promise it'll be worth it."

Sonya opened her mouth, clearly ready to object, but Claire put a hand on her shoulder. "He's got this," she said.

"And anyway, I want to get your read on that Hailey conversation."

Jack nodded, clearly satisfied, and slipped into the room, leaving the two women standing in the hallway.

CHAPTER NINETEEN

JACK STEPPED into Suzanne's hospital room, his expression softening as he saw her sitting upright in bed. Her left arm was bandaged, but the pristine white linens and the scent of antiseptic couldn't hide her elegance. Despite her injuries, she retained an impressive poise.

She offered him a faint smile as he approached.

"Mrs. Blackwood," Jack began, pulling up a chair beside her bed, "you're looking remarkably well, considering... everything."

Suzanne chuckled. "It's Suzanne, please. And I'm fine, Detective. Just a couple of stitches. You'd think I'd been through something far worse with the way everyone's fussing."

"Not a detective, technically," Jack said, "but I *am* here to ask some questions. And also, I was concerned. "

She tilted her head, a faint blush creeping into her cheeks. "You're very kind to say so. But I assure you, I'm tougher than I look."

Jack smiled. "I never doubted it for a second." He hesitated, then continued. "I wanted to ask about Hailey. What might have provoked her to drive her Porsche into that yoga studio? I mean, it's not exactly a minor tantrum."

Suzanne sighed, glancing down at her hands. "I assume you already know Vincent and I made some difficult decisions regarding Hailey... financial ones."

Jack nodded. "I'd like to hear it from you, though. What kind of decisions?"

"She's... troubled," Suzanne said, choosing her words carefully. "She has issues with drugs, and Vincent and I agreed that giving her millions of dollars would only enable her. So would continuing her allowance. So yes, I convinced him to tell his lawyers to cut her out of the will. We felt it was the responsible thing to do. You don't give a kid like that unlimited resources. It's dangerous."

To Jack, this sounded perfectly reasonable, but he kept his expression neutral. "Does Hailey know that's why she was cut off?"

"She didn't, not at first," Suzanne said. "But I suppose she found out recently. I'm sure she felt betrayed."

Jack leaned back slightly, studying her. "Do you think there's any chance she could have had something to do with Vincent's death?"

Suzanne shook her head. "I don't think so. She's impulsive, not calculated. Driving into that yoga studio? That's Hailey. But poisoning her father? No, that's... different."

Jack nodded, letting her words settle before asking, "What about Helene? Any chance she could've been involved?"

Suzanne stiffened. "Helene is my friend. At least, I considered her one."

"But?" Jack prompted.

Suzanne hesitated, then sighed. "Friendships often end where business begins. I know she was furious when Vincent rebranded her app and cut her out. They didn't agree on much, and she felt betrayed. I suppose... I suppose it's possible."

"What can you tell me about the app?" Jack asked, watching her closely. "Vincent and Helene were working on it together, but disagreed about the direction it should take?"

Suzanne shrugged. "I don't know much about it. Vincent said it was the future of his company, but he wasn't the type to share the details with me. All I know is that it was something he was obsessed with. He thought it could revolutionize the way people connect. Bring young men back to their full potential, or something."

Jack filed that away, his mind already spinning through possibilities. "Thank you, Suzanne. You've been quite helpful. And candid."

She smiled faintly, brushing a strand of hair behind her ear. "Honesty is all I have left, Agent Russo. And please, do let me know if there's anything else I can do to help. I'd hate for Hailey to suffer more than she already has."

Jack rose from his seat, giving her a nod. "We'll do our best to get to the truth."

CHAPTER TWENTY

THE TEAM WAS JUST FINISHING up dinner when Claire had an idea. She pushed the wrapper of her sub sandwich aside and turned to Kiko. "Kiko," she said, "let's see you do your thing."

Kiko, stationed in the corner of the room, was attempting to shove a pizza box into the overflowing garbage can while keeping one eye on Ranger. The dog stood poised, ears perked, clearly on high alert for any stray piece of pepperoni that might fall his way.

"What thing is that?" Kiko asked, glancing over her shoulder.

"The thing where you're both people at once," Claire said, leaning back in her chair.

Kiko straightened up, brushing her hands on her jeans. "Oh, *that* thing."

A couple of times lately, Kiko had done uncanny impressions of people having a conversation, moving seamlessly back and forth between two potential suspects—or even between members of the S.W.O.R.D. team. It was as though she could set her own personality aside entirely and step fully into someone else's, capturing not only their tone of voice or mannerisms but also inventing eerily accurate dialogues they might actually have. It was equal parts impressive and unsettling.

"So, who do you want me to be?" Kiko asked.

"Helene and Suzanne," Claire said.

"I've only watched a little video on each of them since you made me stay here and skip the interviews." Kiko folded her arms and gave Claire a pointed look. "Appearances at charity balls, that kind of thing."

"You've got this," Claire said. "And, like I said before, we may need you to go undercover at some point."

"All right. I'll give it a try." She walked to the front of the room and closed her eyes, her expression softening as she took a moment to focus. "I'm going over everything Violet's pulled up on them, everything I saw in videos, and... everything I heard Fitz and Sonya arguing about."

The team quieted, their attention shifting fully to Kiko as she began her transformation. For a moment, she stood perfectly still, then lifted her head, her posture shifting, and began. Within seconds her entire demeanor changed. Her posture straightened, her head tilted slightly, and a soft, composed expression spread across her face.

Her hands moved delicately, as if smoothing invisible wrinkles in her lap.

Claire took a sip of her Diet Coke, watching as Kiko transformed. The way Kiko held her head just so, the composed smile—every detail screamed Suzanne.

"Oh, *Helene*," Kiko began, her voice soft and polished, with a hint of condescension. "Do we really have to talk about Vincent again? Gossiping about the dead—it's just so... inelegant."

Kiko paused, then turned abruptly, her shoulders snapping back and her chin jutting forward. Her expression hardened, and her voice dropped, sharper and more biting.

"In the bedroom, he wouldn't even take his socks off," Kiko said, now fully embodying Helene. "And you want to talk about *elegance*?"

Fitz let out a burst of laughter. "Socks on?"

Suzanne reappeared with a delicate shrug and an amused smile. "That's, well, inappropriate, isn't it? And I didn't marry him for his charm—or his sense of adventure in the bedroom, clearly."

Claire laughed this time, too.

"Clearly," *Helene* agreed. "And yet you married him all the same. Barely waited for the ink to dry on the divorce papers."

"Helene, please," *Suzanne* said, brushing an imaginary strand of hair behind her ear. "It's not my fault you left him lying around like a pair of worn-out loafers."

Claire almost choked on her soda, and the room burst into laughter again.

Kiko's movements became smaller, her voice gentler as she embodied Suzanne's changing posture. "But you must have loved him once, Helene. That's why it must have hurt so much, when he..." she paused for effect, "...*took* your company. Your hard work. Your dream. I can't imagine what that was like."

Fitz's grin slowly faded, and Jack's posture straightened as Kiko shifted deeper into the performance.

Helene reappeared, her tone sharp. "Don't you dare pity me. You think you're better than me, don't you? Sitting there in your overpriced yoga pants and that ridiculous, holier-than-thou voice—"

"I don't think anything of the sort," *Suzanne* interrupted, her voice trembling. "I just... I think you must have been hurt."

"Hurt?" *Helene* spat. Kiko's entire body tensed, her hands

clenching into fists. "Hurt doesn't begin to cover it. He didn't just steal my company—he stole my life! And you—"

Kiko, as Helene, lunged forward suddenly, grabbing at her own throat. Her Suzanne voice came out, panicked and gasping. "Helene, please! Stop!"

Claire froze, her soda halfway to her lips, as Kiko mimicked strangling herself, her face reddening as she gripped her own neck.

"I gave him *everything*!" Helene screamed through Kiko's voice. "And you just took it, like the spoiled little princess you are!"

Suzanne's voice sputtered again, weak and desperate. "Helene, let go! Please."

Kiko's hands dropped suddenly, and she stepped back, shaking herself out of the moment. She blinked a few times, her expression returning to normal.

The room fell silent, everyone staring at her. Even Ranger, who had been pacing in the corner, stopped and let out a low whimper.

"Well," Kiko said, brushing her hands together, "that got *dark*."

Claire sometimes worried about Kiko. She remembered a time during a previous case when she'd stayed in character for hours, well after they'd left the interview. It had taken Claire and Jack both to snap her out of it. If someone could so convincingly become others, what did that mean about how connected she was to herself?

Claire set her soda down and exhaled. "Kiko, remind me never to piss you off."

The room burst into nervous laughter, but Claire couldn't shake the vividness of Kiko's performance. It wasn't just that Kiko had captured the women's voices and mannerisms. For a moment, it had felt like Helene and Suzanne were actually there—and like Helene's rage wasn't entirely fictional. There was something about the raw intensity in Kiko's eyes, the way her hands shook with fury, that made Claire wonder if Helene's hatred ran deeper than they had initially thought.

"Well," Fitz said, breaking the silence, "I've seen enough." He pointed at Kiko. "You're guilty! Helene. I mean, not Suzanne. You did a great job with both, by the way."

Claire had rarely heard Fitz sound so sincere.

"Really," he continued. "I like to think I can feel people's emotions, their motivations. Understand them deeply. You can *become* them. What do you Americans say, 'And the Oscar goes to...'"

"It's a gift," Kiko said. "And a curse."

Sonya rolled her eyes. "That's how guilt is decided on this crew? Improv theater?"

"No one's deciding guilt," Claire said. "This was just an exercise. My thinking is this: we've already talked to Suzanne. Sonya, you and I haven't had the chance yet to talk to Helene. I'd like to bring her in for a voluntary interview first thing in the morning."

She looked around the room, her eyes landing on Fitz. "You've gotten your read on her. I'd like Sonya to get hers as well. That sound fair?"

Fitz nodded reluctantly. "Fine."

"Good," Claire said. "Let's hope she agrees to come in."

CHAPTER TWENTY-ONE

THE WOMAN ADJUSTED her seatbelt as she turned onto another quiet street. The fabric always felt too close against her neck, rubbing just slightly, but tonight she didn't bother fixing it again. Maybe it was because she felt numb, or maybe she just didn't care anymore.

Tonight, there were bigger things on her mind. The air coming through the open window was cool but carried no real scent—Medina's streets were too carefully maintained for any bad smells to linger. The curbs were clean, the streetlights evenly spaced and glowing with a warmth that illuminated the shapely hedges that lined the sidewalks.

Her phone buzzed on the passenger seat, rattling against the smooth leather. She ignored it, her eyes scanning the road.

A gas station came into view, sleek and understated. The pumps gleamed under bright LED lights, their screens free of grime or scratches. There was no trash strewn about, only a discreet receptacle near the entrance, its silver lid spotless. She pulled into a pump on the far side, away from the handful of luxury cars that were idling nearby.

The phone buzzed again as she stepped out, and she snatched it with a swipe. Clicking it shut, she stared at the cheap plastic shell for a moment before placing her thumbs against the hinge and pressing. The phone cracked cleanly in two, the sound sharp and satisfying in the quiet. She walked to the trash can by the pump and slid the broken pieces beneath a folded magazine and a half-empty bottle of sparkling water.

At the pump, she swiped her card, watching the numbers climb on the digital screen. Her gaze flicked to the cameras mounted high on the canopy, their lenses angled perfectly to capture the pump and the lot beyond.

As the tank filled, her thoughts wandered, unbidden, to middle school.

She'd *hated* middle school. Every day, she would come home, throw her backpack into the corner of the mudroom, and then stand frozen in the kitchen, staring at the fridge.

She wouldn't cry at first. Not until her mother asked how her day had gone. That was the signal—the dam would break, and the tears would flow hot and endless, staining her mother's blouse as she sobbed.

The boys at school hadn't just ignored her. They went out of their way to be cruel, finding new ways to underline the fact that she wasn't one of the girls they wanted. Once, she had worn a bright pink sweater to school. Her mother had picked it out, saying it made her look beautiful.

The boys had noticed. "Barbie!" one of them had shouted as she stepped off the bus. "Where's Ken?" The laughter followed her down the hall, ringing in her ears all day.

The pump clicked off. She replaced the nozzle and folded the receipt neatly before sliding it into her pocket.

Her next stop was a nearby ATM tucked into the side of a gleaming, all-glass bank. The parking lot was nearly empty, save for a Range Rover idling near the entrance. She parked directly in front of the machine, leaving her engine running. The ATM's screen glowed faintly green as she slid in her card, and moments later, $500 in twenties spilled into the tray. She folded the bills neatly, tucking them into her wallet before driving off. She'd barely used cash over the last few years, but now she might need it for escape. Better safe than sorry.

As she headed to the next ATM, her mind drifted to high school. She'd expected things to change then, to improve. They didn't. The boys were crueler, their mockery more refined. They would whisper insults just loud enough for her to hear, pointing out every flaw—the way her hair never seemed to lie flat, the braces that made her smile awkward, the way she wore her skirts a little too long. Each jab was calculated, meant to leave a mark.

Her senior year, she had asked a boy to prom. He sat behind her in calculus and always borrowed her notes. He smiled at her sometimes, leaned in close enough that she could catch the scent of his deodorant. She thought maybe he liked her—or at least respected her enough to say yes.

When he laughed at her, the sound had filled the room. "Me? With you?" he'd said, loud enough for half the class to hear. "Sorry, I don't think so."

The second ATM was on the edge of a shopping plaza, nestled between a wine boutique and a designer dog grooming salon. She parked, got out, and repeated the process. Another $500, neatly folded into her wallet. The receipt she crumpled in her hand, glancing at the spotless trash can near the ATM before tossing it inside.

The streets of Medina were quiet as she drove on, the cash tucked securely in her bag. Her mind flickered to those memories again, but she forced them away.

They didn't matter now.

She had more work to do.

CHAPTER TWENTY-TWO

THE NEXT MORNING, Claire stepped out of the car and took in the estate before her. They hadn't reached Helene, so they'd decided to make a surprise visit.

Jack and Sonya got out after her, followed by Kiko, who'd convinced Claire to let her come just this once.

To Claire, the house looked like a relic from another era, its cedar shingles aged to a silvery gray. It was nothing like Vincent Blackwood's modern fortress of glass and steel. This place had weight, history, the kind of presence that didn't need to impress you but still made you feel small.

The roof sloped down to meet deep eaves, and ivy curled up one corner of the house, clinging as if it might eventually swallow the entire structure. Tall, dark green shutters framed the windows, which seemed too small compared to the sprawling façade. She noticed the porch—wide, with a pair of heavy columns that looked like they could have held up the world in their prime. Now, one had a faint crack running through its base, barely noticeable unless you were looking closely. The air smelled clean, sharper than the Seattle suburbs, with an undercurrent of wet cedar.

They were only a quarter mile from Vincent and Suzanne's estate, but whereas their home screamed *new* and *modern*, this home was all about classic elegance. "Looks like old money," Claire murmured, glancing at Jack and Sonya.

"Definitely not Vincent's style," Jack said, craning his neck to take in the steep gables and the heavy stone chimney.

"I like it," Kiko said. "Sure beats my five hundred square foot studio."

Sonya was already scanning the front door, painted an almost-black green that matched the shutters. The brass knocker was polished to a mirror shine, but the door itself looked weathered, its edges warped.

Claire approached first and rang the bell. Its chime wasn't a normal ding-dong but something deeper, richer, like a note from a church organ. She waited, her eyes flicking to the stained-glass transom above the door. Pale light filtered through it, throwing patches of green and gold onto the porch's dark wood.

After a long moment, nothing happened. Claire rapped the knocker once, a sharp, purposeful sound. "Helene Marquez? FBI."

No answer.

Jack leaned over and gave the door a push. It creaked open an inch.

Claire exchanged a glance with Sonya, who was already pulling on gloves.

Jack muttered, "Doors don't just open themselves. You think she's expecting us?"

"Could be a wellness check," Claire said, pushing the door open all the way. The entryway stretched ahead, wood-paneled walls absorbing what little light spilled inside.

"That's what we're calling this?" Jack asked, but he

followed her lead, his hand drifting toward his holster as he stepped inside.

The grand staircase in the foyer curved up to a second floor, its balusters painted the same deep green as the shutters. A stained-glass window on the landing threw jagged splinters of light onto the risers, but it wasn't enough to brighten the space.

"Split up," Claire said. "Kiko, stay with me. Jack and Sonya, you two stay together."

Claire stepped away from the others, heading toward the kitchen. The open-plan design was at odds with the rest of the house—a newer remodel, with sleek quartz counters and minimalist cabinetry that jarred against the heavy wooden beams running along the ceiling. The room was spotless, the stainless-steel appliances gleaming. But something about its perfection made her uneasy. No coffee cup left on the counter, no mail piled up by the sink. Nothing that said someone had been here recently.

Her eyes swept the space until she spotted a door tucked into the far corner. It was partially ajar, revealing a narrow staircase descending into darkness.

"Basement," Claire murmured. She pushed the door open further, revealing steep wooden steps that creaked under her weight as she descended, Kiko right behind her. The air grew cooler with each step, damp and heavy, carrying the scent of earth. Her hand brushed the unfinished wall as she moved, the rough texture gritty against her gloves.

At the bottom of the stairs, the well-lit basement was cluttered but orderly—boxes neatly stacked, a wine rack filled with dusty bottles, and an old workbench covered with tools that looked like they'd been untouched for decades.

She almost missed it at first: the faint whisper of a draft against her face. She turned toward its source, her eyes landing on the far wall. A section of shelving jutted out slightly at an odd angle, the edge of a door barely visible behind it. The air here smelled different—not just damp but ancient, like stone left untouched for centuries.

"Stay with me, Kiko."

"Right behind you, boss."

Jack and Sonya moved through the house, their boots echoing off the glimmering hardwood floors. The living room was expansive, filled with oversized furniture that somehow still managed to feel formal. A grand piano sat in one corner, its black lacquered surface free of dust, and the fireplace was framed by a pair of matching armchairs.

Jack checked behind the heavy velvet curtains, then glanced back at Sonya, who was rifling through the stack of coffee table books. "What is it about you and Fitz, anyway?"

Sonya didn't look up, flipping through a book on early 20th-century architecture. "What do you mean?"

"I mean, there's some serious tension there. You look at him like he personally insulted your thesis."

She closed the book with a quiet snap and set it back down. "We just have different approaches to psychological profiling. Plus, I've heard you two used to *hate* each other."

"Hate each other like brothers, I guess."

Sonya moved to the fireplace, running her hand along the ornate mantel. "He's insecure."

Jack snorted. "No argument there." He knelt to peer behind the sofa, then straightened, glancing at her. "But he's a good guy, deep down. I thought he was a total jerk when I first met him, but he grows on you."

Sonya let out a short laugh, shaking her head as she headed toward the dining room. "I hope that happens. If I'm around long enough to learn to get along with him."

Jack followed her, the large dining table coming into view. It stretched nearly the entire length of the room, its surface gleaming beneath an oversized chandelier. The table was set with a centerpiece of silver candlesticks and a bowl of fresh fruit.

"You planning on going somewhere?" Jack asked, opening a sideboard to check inside.

"I'm just saying, Fitz doesn't exactly make it easy to stick around," she replied, peeking into a narrow china cabinet. The shelves were lined with delicate porcelain, untouched and pristine.

Jack shrugged. "Nah, he doesn't. But you push him, he pushes back, and eventually, you meet somewhere in the middle."

Sonya arched an eyebrow at him. "That sounds exhausting."

They moved on to the bedrooms. The first was a guest room, tastefully decorated in neutral tones, the bed perfectly made and the closets empty except for a few spare linens. The second was larger, clearly Helene's, with a canopied bed and an antique vanity covered in arranged bottles of perfume and skin care products.

Jack opened the walk-in closet and found it packed with designer clothes, each garment carefully hung and sorted by color. "No sign of a suitcase missing," he said.

Sonya checked the en suite bathroom. "No toothbrush or toiletries missing either. Looks like she didn't plan to leave."

Jack leaned against the doorframe, crossing his arms. "She could just be out. House is clear. Guess we better find Claire."

~

Claire approached cautiously, her hand brushing the shelf aside to reveal the door. It was propped open just enough to let the draft through. Kiko was right behind her.

She pulled the door open further, revealing a narrow tunnel carved into stone. The walls were rough and uneven, patches of moisture glistening in the dim light from her flashlight. The air inside was thick, oppressive, and carried a metallic tang that clung to the back of her throat.

"I don't like this," Kiko said.

"Stay with me," Claire said, continuing down the tunnel. Its floor was uneven and littered with loose gravel that crunched under their boots. Claire moved carefully, the beam of her flashlight casting long shadows that danced along the walls.

The farther they went, the tighter the space became. The walls seemed to close in, the ceiling lowering to the point where she had to duck slightly.

After what felt like an eternity, the tunnel split into three separate branches. Each one stretched into darkness, the ends invisible even in the beam of her light. She crouched, angling her flashlight toward the ground. Faint scuff marks ran along the gravel in the middle branch, as though something—or someone—had recently passed through.

"What do you think, K?"

"I think there's something there, off to the left. I may be turned around but I think straight leads to the water and right dead-ends."

Claire strained her ears, trying to catch even the faintest hint of movement, but there was nothing. Just the sound of her own breathing, shallow and quick. "What I want to know is, why the hell are these tunnels even here?"

She stepped forward into the middle tunnel, her grip tightening on her flashlight, every muscle in her body on edge. A cold silence filled the tunnels, and the sweat on the back of her neck gave her a chill.

Then she heard a sound.

CHAPTER TWENTY-THREE

FOOTSTEPS ON GRAVEL.

Claire's pulse quickened. The sound wasn't coming from ahead. It was behind her—behind Kiko.

She spun around, her flashlight slicing through the dim space she had just come from. The beam landed squarely on Helene, who stood no more than ten feet away. For a moment, both women froze, their eyes locking. Helene's expression was a mix of surprise and calculation.

Without a word, Helene kicked up a spray of gravel toward them and bolted back down the tunnel.

Claire staggered, but didn't hesitate. She raised her arm to shield her eyes and launched herself past Kiko, who had slid up against the wall. Racing after Helene, Claire's boots skidded against the uneven floor. "Kiko! Right behind me!" she shouted, her voice echoing off the walls.

Kiko was only a few steps behind, her flashlight bouncing as she sprinted forward. She moved in sync with Claire, their footsteps pounding in unison as they pursued Helene. The tunnel walls seemed to close in tighter, forcing both women to duck slightly as they pushed forward.

Helene was fast—faster than Claire expected—but the narrowness of the space worked to Claire and Kiko's advantage. Helene had nowhere to go except forward. Claire pushed harder, her breath echoing in the confined space, Kiko staying close behind.

Suddenly, Claire's foot slipped on an incline in the tunnel. She twisted her ankle and went down hard, her cheek slamming into the gravel-strewn floor. The impact sent a sharp sting radiating across her face, and her flashlight skittered out of her hand, spinning wildly before coming to a stop a few feet away.

"Claire!" Kiko shouted, skidding to a halt beside her.

Cursing under her breath, Claire pressed herself up, her palm stinging against the rough ground. She snapped her head toward the passage Helene had disappeared down.

"The left branch," Claire rasped, lunging for her flashlight.

Kiko nodded, her own flashlight trained ahead. "I'll go ahead, catch up when you can," she said, her voice tense but steady. She darted forward, her beam cutting through the darkness as she disappeared down the left branch.

She pushed herself forward, ignoring the throbbing pain in her cheek and the metallic taste in her mouth. Her flashlight's beam illuminated the uneven walls as she closed the distance.

Just ahead, Helene's silhouette stilled, her shoulders rising and falling as if she were calculating her next move. Kiko's light flickered at the edge of Claire's vision, catching up to Helene.

Then Helene turned slowly, raising her hands, fingers spread wide. There was no panic in her expression—only something measured, as though she'd made a decision and accepted its weight.

"I can explain everything," Helene said.

Claire stopped just short of her, angling the flashlight slightly to avoid blinding Helene while keeping it trained enough not to lose sight of her face.

Kiko came to a stop beside Claire, her flashlight bouncing off the walls. "You okay?" she asked, her eyes flicking between Claire and Helene.

Claire nodded, her gaze never leaving Helene. "Let's hear it then," she said.

Helene didn't look like someone caught in a frantic escape. She looked poised, ready to set the terms of whatever came next. "Like I said, I can explain everything."

CHAPTER TWENTY-FOUR

CLAIRE RUBBED at the bandage on her cheek and glanced down at the brace on her wrist. It wasn't broken, but the sprain from her fall throbbed with a dull insistence.

The three ibuprofen she'd taken hadn't kicked in yet. She clenched her hand experimentally, noting the twinge of pain, and focused her attention back on Helene.

"Helene Marquez, you understand you're entitled to an attorney, correct?" Claire asked.

Helene looked up, her face blank, her tone controlled. "I understand. That won't be necessary. At least for now."

To Claire's right, Jack stood with his arms folded, his stance subtly imposing. Fitz loomed to her left, hands resting on his hips, his expression even more focused than usual. Sonya sat just to Helene's right, close enough to be in her personal space but not encroaching. Together, they formed a wall of authority in the sterile confines of the FBI interrogation room.

Despite this, Helene looked anything but cowed.

"Do you understand why we brought you in?" Claire asked, leaning forward just enough to press the question.

"I believe so," Helene said, her tone devoid of inflection.

Claire nodded. "Can you explain why you fled down those secret tunnels?"

"I can, but I don't have to," Helene interjected coolly.

"That's true," Fitz said, his voice slipping into a wry, almost conversational tone. "But it would sure make our jobs a lot easier." He smiled, a grin meant to disarm, but Helene didn't take the bait. Her face remained as stoic as stone.

"You've heard, I'm sure," Fitz continued, "how your ex-husband was killed. The *details*, I mean? The kind of poison?"

Helene gave the faintest of nods, her gaze unwavering.

"I wonder," Fitz continued, "when we check those tunnels thoroughly, will we find any aconitine?"

"Absolutely not." Helene paused, as though making a calculation in her head. "What you will find are documents. Journals, documenting Vincent's abuse of me during our marriage. They're in a storage container."

"Abuse?" Claire asked. This wasn't what she was expecting.

"It was never physical, but, well, it happened." She sighed. "He was controlling, withheld money, and criticized constantly. Belittled me. Gaslit me." She let out a slow breath. "I was down there to find them. Stashed them there over a decade ago. I'd planned to use them to make him give me back control of the app."

"Sounds like another motive," Fitz said.

"Not at all," Helene said. "It's proof I didn't do it. I was going to blackmail him, while he was alive, by threatening to release my diaries, get him *canceled*, as they say. If I was going to do that, why the hell would I also kill him?"

Claire caught Fitz's eye. If the diaries were real, they could be important.

But they had another angle planned for the interrogation of Helene.

"There's something we'd like to show you," Fitz said. He crossed to the door, opening it for Violet. She stepped inside, her laptop balanced carefully in both hands. She moved with purpose, her eyes flicking briefly toward Helene before settling on the center of the room.

Claire leaned back, watching closely.

Helene's blank stare didn't falter.

Violet set her laptop on the table, opened it with a flick, and connected it to the wall-mounted flat screen. Within seconds, the screen came to life, filling the room with the sharp, slightly grainy footage from various surveillance cameras.

Claire glanced at Helene, whose expression remained unreadable. The woman sat with her hands clasped in her lap, her gaze fixed on the screen as the footage began to play.

Violet cleared her throat. "This is a composite of the footage Suzanne gave us from the night of Vincent Blackwood's birthday party," she said clinically. "We've sequenced it to follow key events leading up to his death."

The first clip showed the sweeping driveway, filled with a procession of luxury cars pulling up to the estate. Guests in formal attire stepped out, greeted by staff who escorted them inside. The next clip jumped to the grand foyer, where servers in uniforms offered glasses of champagne as guests mingled. The sound was muted, but Claire could almost hear the polite laughter and clinking glasses as the scene unfolded.

The video shifted again, this time to the expansive patio overlooking the water. Strings of white lights crisscrossed above, casting a soft glow over the well-heeled crowd. In the background, a small orchestra played.

"We're establishing context here," Violet explained. "You'll see the relevant footage soon."

As the clips continued, Claire's gaze shifted toward Helene. She was a master at masking her emotions, but there was a stiffness in her shoulders now, a tension in the way she held herself.

The footage transitioned to the dining room. A server wheeled a gleaming silver cart across the floor, stopping just in front of Geoffrey Osgood. Geoffrey exchanged a few words with the server, then lifted the rare bottle of Scotch from the cart with both hands, holding it aloft like a trophy before setting it on a silver tray. Even on the grainy footage, the bottle gleamed under the light.

"This is Geoffrey Osgood, the Blackwood house manager, receiving the Scotch," Violet said. The video paused briefly, the frame frozen on Geoffrey's face, his expression almost reverent. "At 7 PM, roughly an hour before Vincent died, Geoffrey took the bottle into this room." She tapped a key, and the video resumed, showing Geoffrey disappearing through a side door. "Unfortunately, there are no cameras inside."

The next clip made Claire sit up a little straighter. Helene appeared on the screen holding a glass of red wine, stepping into the same room at 7:12 PM. She was dressed impeccably, her hair swept back, her movements refined.

"This is you entering the same room, roughly twelve minutes after Geoffrey left the bottle there," Violet said.

The footage continued, showing Helene exiting the room fifteen minutes later. She walked briskly, a glass in her hand, pausing briefly in the hallway before turning a corner and disappearing from view.

"That's all the footage we have of the room," Violet said, leaning back in her chair. "As you can see, there's no one else entering or exiting between Geoffrey and Helene."

The screen went dark, and Violet closed her laptop.

Claire leaned forward, her elbows resting on the table. "Helene, you had access to the bottle. You were alone with it. You had time. Do you deny that?"

Helene's eyes shifted to Claire, her face impassive. "No, I don't deny that. But having access isn't proof of anything, is it?"

"It's not," Fitz interjected. "But it's an awfully big coincidence. Not to mention, you just told us Vincent was abusive, and that you'd planned to blackmail him. Plus, I don't believe in coincidences. I believe in love, and the lengths to which love—both unrequited and the kind that can turn into cold hatred during a divorce—can make us go."

Helene folded her hands tighter. "I had my reasons for being in that room, none of which have anything to do with Vincent's death."

"Then why don't you tell us what those reasons are?" Claire pressed.

Helene's lips parted slightly as if she were about to speak, but then she closed her mouth.

"Yes?" Fitz prompted.

Helene's lips tightened before she finally spoke. "There's another door into that room. A secret door."

Violet frowned. "No, there isn't. I've reviewed the house schematics. There's no record of any other door."

Helene gave her a sharp look. "It's a *secret* door. Do you think those show up on blueprints?"

Fitz raised an eyebrow. "A hidden bookcase passage? Really? That's straight out of a bad movie."

"Yes," Helene replied, her voice clipped. "And like most bad movies, it's effective. Who cares if it's been done before?"

Claire pressed her hands flat onto the table. "Who else was in the room with you? No one else was seen entering or leaving during that time."

Helene hesitated, then said, "Brentley Flemming."

"The tennis pro from the club?" Claire asked, glancing at Fitz.

"Yes," Helene said simply. "He and I... we've had a bit of a flirtation. As you know, I too am a widow, and it gets lonely sometimes. He was always welcome at the Blackwood house, and he knew about the passage."

Fitz folded his arms. "Did *he* poison the Scotch?"

"Not as far as I know," Helene said. "But I wasn't in there long. For all I know, someone else could have come in after I left."

"Was he still in the room when you left?" Claire asked.

She nodded slightly. "Yes, but why on earth would he kill Vincent?"

Claire stared at her for a long moment, searching for any cracks in her story. She glanced at Violet, who nodded as though reading Claire's mind. She'd have to go back to the footage.

Claire turned toward the others. They had walked in hoping for clarity and left with another layer of questions. They were right back where they started. "Fitz, Jack, Sonya. Hallway." She nodded toward the door. "Helene, I'm going to ask you to sit tight for a moment."

CHAPTER TWENTY-FIVE

CLAIRE CLOSED the door to the interrogation room behind her and stepped into the hallway. She glanced at Fitz, standing with his arms crossed, his expression tense, and Sonya, whose rigid stance and piercing gaze all but dared him to start something.

Jack stood behind them, arms folded casually.

Fitz didn't waste any time. "We need to go after Helene through Hailey. She's the weak spot. There's enough to suggest Hailey could have been involved in Vincent's death. Even if she wasn't, Helene doesn't know that. She'll fold."

Sonya was incredulous. "You want to use her *daughter* as leverage? That's not just a bad idea—it's cruel. We're FBI, Fitz. Not mercenaries."

Fitz rolled his eyes. "Cruel? You think it's cruel to push a suspect who's lied, misled, and manipulated us at every turn? She's sitting in there playing us, and you're worried about her feelings?"

"I'm worried about our integrity," Sonya shot back. "You're suggesting something underhanded and unethical. A child isn't a tool to pressure someone into confessing."

"It's not unethical," Fitz said, his tone rising. "It's practical. Helene's hiding something, and this will get her to talk."

"Practical?" Sonya stepped closer. "You think weaponizing someone's child is practical? What's next, Fitz? Should we hold a family member hostage? Threaten a dog?"

Fitz scoffed. "Oh, come off it. You're exaggerating because you don't like me. Admit it. This isn't about protocol; this is about us."

Sonya's eyes narrowed. "You think this is personal? Fine, I'll admit it. I don't like you. But that doesn't change the fact that what you're proposing is wrong."

Claire started to intervene, but before she could, two agents turned the corner, chatting as they approached. The argument ceased instantly. The agents glanced at them as they passed, their conversation slowing momentarily before they moved on, their voices fading down the corridor.

Claire looked between Fitz and Sonya, the tension still palpable. She rubbed her temple, tired of constantly refereeing their clashes. Part of her job had always felt like babysitting Fitz—brilliant, reckless Fitz—but this ongoing feud with Sonya was wearing her down. Sonya wasn't a loose cannon like Fitz, but she wasn't easy to manage either. Their constant clashing was becoming just another problem Claire didn't have time to solve.

"Can we stop pretending this is about the case and admit you just don't like each other?" Claire asked, her voice cutting. "It's exhausting."

Neither of them responded. Fitz tapped his fingers against the wall, while Sonya stared straight ahead, her jaw clenched.

"Alright," Claire continued. "Fitz, you want to try the Hailey angle? Fine. But you don't push too hard. Helene isn't just some random suspect. She's powerful and connected. One misstep, and this blows up in all our faces."

Fitz gave a curt nod, though his posture remained defiant. "Understood."

Claire turned to Sonya. "I know you hate this. I get it. But I'm making the call. He'll handle it carefully."

Sonya met Claire's gaze, her tone cold. "I'm not participating. If you're going to let him do this, fine. But I'll be outside. Don't expect me to be a part of it." She spun on her heel and strode down the hallway. She paused and turned back. "Claire, do I have permission to get in touch with Flemming, the tennis pro, to verify her story?"

Claire nodded, and Sonya turned the corner.

As the sound of her steps faded, Fitz sighed and leaned against the wall, his earlier fire dimmed. "I hope I'm right about this," he said quietly. "Because if I'm not, it's going to blow up in our faces."

Claire exhaled slowly, her gaze lingering on the spot where Sonya had disappeared. "I hope so, too."

CHAPTER TWENTY-SIX

"LET'S TALK ABOUT HAILEY," Fitz began.

Claire watched as Fitz took a seat across from Helene. His tone was light, almost conversational, but Claire recognized the rhythm. Fitz always started like this: planting seeds, softening the ground before the questions turned harsh.

Fitz leaned back slightly, his hands resting casually on the table. "She seems... *spirited.* Driving her Porsche into a yoga studio—now *that's* a statement."

Helene ran a finger along the edge of the table, as if grounding herself. "She's my daughter," she said quietly. "She's passionate. Maybe dramatic, yes. But she's not a bad person."

"I'm not suggesting she is," Fitz replied. "Sometimes, though, that kind of passion can get the better of us. Especially when we're young and dealing with the weight of the world."

Helene exhaled, her shoulders slumping slightly. "I made mistakes with her. I tried to shield her, but... I didn't always know how. Vincent was hard on her, and I overcompensated. Gave her too much, when what she needed was—" She stopped and shook her head, her expression clouding. "Well, that's my failure."

Claire noted the flicker of vulnerability on Helene's face. There was regret there, a rawness that felt real.

Fitz leaned into it, his voice softening just enough to keep her talking. "It's clear you love her," he said. "But being cut out of the will... I imagine that must have hit her hard. Sometimes, in the heat of the moment, people make choices they can't take back."

Helene's head snapped up, her eyes narrowing. "What are you trying to say?"

Fitz didn't blink. "I'm saying it's possible Hailey felt betrayed. Hurt. Angry. Maybe she acted on that. She told us she only found out she'd been cut out of the will *after* Vincent was killed, but, well... young women sometimes lie, don't they?"

Helene stiffened, her hands resting on the table like weights. "No!" she said with force, like she was trying to rock Fitz back in his chair. "Hailey *wouldn't* do something like that. She's reckless, yes. Emotional. But she wouldn't—she couldn't."

Fitz leaned forward, his elbows brushing the table's edge. "If it wasn't her, then who was it? Was it you, Helene? Or do you know who it was?"

Helene's gaze darted to the wall behind Fitz, as if searching for something. She didn't answer, but her throat bobbed with a hard swallow. Claire studied her, noting the flush creeping up her neck and the slight tremble in her right hand as it hovered near her lap.

"Help us," Fitz pressed. "If it wasn't Hailey, and it wasn't you, then who? Because right now, Helene, everything points to you. You worked hard on an app that was supposed to unite people. He bought it, bought *you*, and promised it would be a partnership. Then he changed it to monetize the anger of a bunch of twenty-something man-bros who live in their parents' basements. How did that feel?"

Helene's breath quickened, but she didn't speak. Claire glanced at Jack, who stood silently, watching Fitz work. His face gave nothing away, but the tension in the room was thick enough to press against Claire's chest.

Helene finally looked at Fitz, her lips parting as if to respond, but she hesitated, her shoulders pulling back as though bracing for something.

When Helene said nothing, Fitz continued. "So, Brentley Flemming? The tennis pro?" He raised an eyebrow.

Helene seemed caught off guard.

"You said you two had a flirtation. I noticed when we were at the club," Fitz said, "that he seemed to be flirting not only with you but also with Suzanne. And quite a few other women, from what I saw."

Helene's lips tightened, but she answered evenly. "He's known to be a bit of a flirt. It's part of his job."

"Were you sleeping with him?" Jack's voice startled Claire, and she turned toward him.

Helene's head snapped up, her eyes blazing. "How dare you? That's my personal business."

"As inappropriate as that question might have been," Fitz said, "I noticed you didn't answer it." He stood and took a slow lap around the table, hands in his pockets. Claire's eyes flicked to him, noticing the crispness of his blue blazer, a sharp contrast to the rumpled brown one he used to wear like a uniform.

He stopped behind Helene, close enough to loom, but she didn't turn to look at him.

"If you didn't do it," Fitz said, his voice calm, "and Hailey didn't do it, who do you think killed your ex-husband? Who do you think killed Vincent Blackwood?"

Helene looked straight ahead. "I wish I knew," she said.

For the next ten minutes, Claire watched, her frustration building as Fitz chased one dead end after another. His questions became increasingly circuitous, yielding nothing but clipped, one-word answers from Helene. She sat firm, and Claire could see in her expression that Helene knew she had the upper hand.

Fitz was grasping, and he knew it, too.

When the door creaked open, Claire turned, grateful for the interruption. Sonya stood in the doorway, motioning her into the hallway. Claire rose and followed, letting the door shut behind her with a soft click.

"Did you watch any of that?" Claire asked, crossing her arms.

"You mean did I watch Fitz fail?" Sonya smirked. "A little, but mostly I was on the phone with Brentley Flemming and working with Violet. She's downloading some footage right now."

"What footage?" Claire asked, confused. She'd been under the impression that Violet already had all the footage from the party.

"You know those glasses that Meta keeps trying to sell everyone?"

"No," Claire said. "I don't."

"They're smart glasses. They've got AI built into them, can record video, post to Facebook, all that cutting-edge nonsense."

"Okay," Claire said. "So what's the deal?"

Sonya leaned in slightly, her voice lowering. "He was *wearing* them. Flemming admitted right away that he was in the room with Helene, that he'd taken the secret passage. He didn't even think it was a secret, just a shortcut—figured everyone knew about it. He says he has footage from inside the room that proves Helene didn't touch the Scotch."

Claire stared at Sonya, processing. "So, what? This clears her?"

"Not entirely," Sonya replied. "But it proves she didn't do it the way we've been trying to pin it."

Claire exhaled, the tension in her shoulders releasing slightly, though her irritation remained. It was progress, yes, but it meant recalibrating their entire approach. "Fine," she said. "Good work. Let's look at that footage. And then we let Helene go before we piss her off enough to get us shut down."

CHAPTER TWENTY-SEVEN

THE HEAVY GLASS doors of the bank clicked open with a muted thud, a sound that seemed incongruous with the imposing weight of the material. A man in a tailored suit, his silver tie gleaming under the recessed lights, greeted her with a nod and a faint smile that didn't reach his eyes.

He didn't use her name—he never did.

"Your box is ready," he said, gesturing toward the hallway behind him.

"Thank you for accommodating me after hours," she replied. Her voice was polite, almost warm, but carried a weight that brooked no refusal.

The man inclined his head slightly. "Anything for you. The business you've brought to the bank has been... transformative."

He stepped aside, letting her pass, his spicy cologne lingering in the air. The hallway was lined with black marble, polished to a mirror finish, and the faint hum of air conditioning filled the space. Her heels tapped against the floor, the sound sharp, as though each step was a punctuation mark.

At the end of the hall, another set of doors waited—vaulted steel, gleaming and imposing. The man keyed in a code before pressing his thumb to a scanner. With a low hiss, the doors parted.

Inside, the vault was unnervingly quiet. Rows of polished metal boxes lined the walls, each one identical except for the small brass numbers etched onto their surfaces, giving the vault a sterile and oppressive atmosphere.

He led her to a box in the far corner, one she knew well.

"Take all the time you need," he said, stepping back but not leaving entirely. He positioned himself discreetly near the entrance, just far enough to offer the illusion of privacy.

She turned the key and slid the box out of its slot. Carrying it to the small table in the center of the room, she opened it carefully. Inside were the items she'd always hoped she would never need.

A necklace of emeralds and diamonds, the stones glittering under the recessed lights. A set of bearer bonds, the kind no one issued anymore but that still carried immense value. A slim stack of crisp hundred-dollar bills. And a passport. Her backup identity.

She ran a finger over its embossed cover. It was real, of course. She'd paid enough to ensure that. The woman in the photograph wasn't her exactly, but close enough to pass. She'd hoped she'd never need it. Yet here she was.

As she examined the items, her mind drifted again to middle school.

She had been twelve when the boys first started calling her "Fridge." It wasn't until weeks later, after a particularly cruel classmate laughed in her face, that she understood the insult.

"Because you're so cold," he'd sneered. "No one wants to touch you."

The nickname stuck, following her from one grade to the

next. By high school, she had grown accustomed to the whispers, the sideways glances. She stopped trying to dress like the other girls, to wear her hair the way the magazines suggested. It never mattered. The boys always found something to mock, and the girls, eager to avoid becoming targets themselves, joined in.

She snapped the lid shut on the box, as if closing it might seal away the memories. Sliding the box back into its slot, she turned the key again and stepped away.

The banker approached immediately, taking the key from her without a word.

"Have a good evening," he said with a slight bow.

She didn't reply, her heels clicking once more as she exited the vault.

Outside, the streets of Medina were nearly silent at this hour, the kind of quiet that came with obscene wealth and meticulous city planning. The distant trickle of a fountain added to the eerie stillness. She walked to her car, a sleek black sedan, and slid into the driver's seat.

She placed the emerald necklace and the passport into the glove compartment, locking it with a key she slipped into her pocket. As she started the engine, her mind wandered again.

She'd asked a boy to prom once. He'd laughed at her. The sound still echoed in her memory. He'd said something about how he'd "rather go with a mop." The words were etched into her mind, though she hadn't thought about them in years.

She pulled out of the lot and onto the empty streets, her thoughts quiet but far from calm. The cash, the necklace, the documents—they were all part of the plan. A plan she hadn't wanted to enact.

But now, there was no other choice.

CHAPTER TWENTY-EIGHT

CLAIRE SQUINTED AT THE SCREEN. "Hello? Are you there?"

The video call sharpened as the connection stabilized. Diego Vega appeared on the screen, his face tanned and weathered but strikingly youthful. His smile was easy and confident, hinting at a sharp sense of humor and perhaps a bit of charm he still liked to flex. He wore a collared shirt, unbuttoned just enough to suggest he'd been relaxing moments before the call.

"Agent Anderson," Diego said, leaning back in his chair. "Or is it just Claire now?"

"Claire's fine," she said. "And thanks for agreeing to this. It must be late on the East Coast."

He chuckled, shaking his head. "Not quite. I'm actually in San Diego."

"Oh." Claire took a sip of wine, adjusting her position. "I assumed you'd be based in D.C. or something."

"Used to be. These days, I'm all over the place. Full-time traveler now. Just got back from Barcelona, actually."

Claire's eyebrows rose. "Barcelona? My daughters are

there right now—summer abroad between their junior and senior years of college."

"Well, you've raised them right. Barcelona's incredible. I assume they're taking in all the sights, eating too much paella?"

"Knowing them, they're probably trying to figure out how to move there permanently," Claire said with a small laugh. "But they'll be home soon, thank God. I miss them, even if the house is quieter."

Diego nodded. "Quieter isn't always better, is it?"

"No, it's not." Claire found herself smiling. He had an easy way of talking that put her at ease, though she wasn't entirely sure that was a good thing. She set her glass down. "Simone said you were the person to talk to about... the case."

Diego's expression shifted, his smile fading into something more thoughtful. "So, you're the one who lived?"

Claire's stomach twisted, a discomfort she hadn't anticipated. She shifted in her chair. "That's one way to put it."

He held up a hand. "Sorry, poor choice of words. I didn't mean anything by it. I was just an intern at the time. Barely eighteen."

Claire did the math. If he was eighteen then, and it had been more than forty years ago, that put him around sixty now. He didn't look it. "You don't seem old enough to have worked that case," she said, slightly deflecting her unease.

Diego grinned, leaning closer to the camera. "I'll take that as a compliment. Good genes, lots of sunscreen."

Claire let out a soft laugh, then grew serious. "Simone said there was a lot that got left out of the official report. About what happened to my parents. And all the others who died that day."

Diego's smile thinned. He looked off to the side, his jaw tightening slightly. "Simone said that, huh?"

"She did," Claire said carefully. "Is it true?"

Diego sighed, leaning back in his chair and rubbing a hand over his face. "There were things... that didn't make it into the final version, yes. But I'd prefer not to talk about it over the phone. Or the computer."

"Why not?"

"Some things deserve face-to-face conversations," Diego said, his voice firm but not unkind. "Besides..." He flashed her a mischievous smile, the kind that probably got him into trouble in his younger years. "I've never been up to the Pacific Northwest."

"Uhh..." Was he flirting with her? Claire tilted her head, studying him. "You're not just stalling, are you?"

"Not at all," he said, holding up both hands in mock surrender. "Tell you what. You pick the place, I'll make the time. Coffee, dinner, a walk in the park—whatever works for you. And I'll tell you *everything*."

She hesitated, her fingers brushing the edge of her wineglass. There was something disarming about him, but she couldn't decide if that was a good or bad thing.

"Okay," she said finally. "But don't think I'll let you off the hook if you try to backpedal."

Diego chuckled. "Noted. Just tell me when and where."

"Come up next week," she said without thinking.

"Done," he said. "Looking forward to it. And Claire? Take care of yourself until then."

She ended the call, her reflection staring back at her on the darkened laptop screen. Something told her she'd agreed to more than a casual meeting.

She just wasn't sure what.

~

Fitz pulled the car up to the curb outside his duplex, cutting the engine. The headlights dimmed, leaving the porch light to cast a soft yellow glow over the driveway. The car smelled of lemongrass, chili, and basil from the Thai takeout they'd picked up on the way home. He glanced at Margaret in the passenger seat, her dark hair falling in loose waves over her shoulder as she twisted to look at the boxes stacked behind them.

"I think we overdid it," she said with a smirk, motioning toward the precariously balanced boxes in the backseat.

"Nonsense," Fitz replied, his smile soft. "You're moving in. It's supposed to look like chaos."

He still couldn't believe it. Ten weeks ago, he was working late nights, eating frozen dinners, and telling himself he didn't have the time—or the physique—for dating apps. Now, here he was—ten weeks in and utterly besotted, with Margaret moving into his home and a baby on the way. The disbelief was still there, but it was the good kind, the kind that made him feel like maybe, just maybe, he hadn't screwed up *every* aspect of his life.

Margaret opened her door, shaking her head. "If one of those boxes spills, you're cleaning up."

"Yes, dear," Fitz called after her, grinning as he stepped out and grabbed the nearest box from the backseat. "Remind me again why you're moving into my place and not the other way around?"

"Because your place has a yard," Margaret said over her shoulder. "And I'm not raising a baby in an apartment without a yard."

He followed her up the driveway, a box balanced against his hip. "Fair point. But don't go blaming me when the kid decides they like chasing squirrels more than staying indoors."

Margaret laughed, the sound light and easy, and Fitz felt

his chest tighten. He couldn't remember the last time someone had made him feel this way—like he was enough, like he wasn't just tolerable but actually worth sticking around for.

Inside, the duplex was sparsely furnished. Fitz had never been one for decorating, and the only nods to personal taste were the towering bookshelves in the living room, stuffed with true crime books and thick psychology tomes. Margaret set her box down by the door and looked around, hands on her hips.

"You know," she said, "if I'm moving in, we're going to have to do something about the dishes."

Fitz was already heading back out for another box. "What's wrong with my dishes?"

"You don't *have* any," Margaret called after him. "You have mismatched plates you stole from cheap restaurants."

He laughed, grabbing another box from the car. "They're not stolen. They're just... borrowed indefinitely."

When he returned, she was pulling paper plates from a kitchen drawer, setting them on the counter next to the takeout bags. "Well, consider this the start of our new life together. First stop: real dishes."

"Fine by me," Fitz said, dropping the box and cracking open a container of pad see ew. "As long as I get a say in the color."

"Oh, you'll get a say," Margaret said, pulling a plastic fork out of the bag. "But I'm vetoing anything plaid or neon."

Fitz laughed again, watching her as she leaned against the counter. She was radiant, even in the dim kitchen light, even with the boxes and paper plates and the faint hum of the fridge in the background. Ten years younger than him, confident in ways he knew he'd never be, she was everything he hadn't thought he deserved.

"Stop staring," she said, a teasing smile on her lips.

"Can't help it," Fitz replied. "You're beautiful."

Margaret rolled her eyes, but her smile stayed. She nudged his plate toward him. "Eat your noodles, Fitz."

They sat at the small kitchen table, the only sound the occasional scratch of plastic forks against paper plates. Fitz felt the quiet settle over him like a blanket, warm and comforting. He wanted this. He wanted her.

Margaret looked up, catching his gaze. For a moment, he thought her smile faltered. Just the slightest flicker. Then it was back, bright and steady, as if it had never wavered at all.

"Here's to us," she said, raising her water glass.

"To us," Fitz echoed, clinking his glass against hers.

As they ate, Fitz's mind wandered briefly to the case he'd left behind earlier that evening. The puzzle of Vincent Blackwood's death loomed large in his mind, but for now, he pushed it aside.

Margaret was here. They were building something together.

CHAPTER TWENTY-NINE

THE NEXT MORNING, the entire crew gathered in the Boiler Room, and Claire felt as though her task force had a collective hangover. She rubbed her temple, scanning the room, noting the strange tension hanging over the group.

Jack and Kiko seemed locked in a quiet, simmering glare, though neither had said a word. Claire was more convinced than ever that whatever had happened between them, while maybe on pause, wasn't over. Violet had arrived late, her hood pulled up around her black hair, settling silently in the back with a blank, unreadable expression. Sonya, probably still miffed about losing the battle with Fitz yesterday—even if she'd won the war—scrolled on her phone with deliberate disinterest.

Only Fitz and Ranger seemed at ease. Fitz had been there when Claire arrived, tossing Ranger little bacon treats from a baggie, a relaxed smile on his face as he spoke softly to the dog, clearly enjoying the moment. Now Ranger sat by Fitz's side, wagging his tail and looking thoroughly pleased with himself. Claire hadn't asked Fitz why he was in such a good mood—she suspected she already knew. He was dating. That would explain the cleaner clothes, the visible effort he'd put into his appearance lately, and the noticeable weight loss. Whatever was going on in his life, he seemed happy.

Good for him, she thought, though a small part of her couldn't help but brace for some future fallout. As long as Fitz was doing his job—and so far, he had been—she didn't much care what he did in his private life.

She looked over her notes and took a deep breath before stepping to the center of the room. "All right," she said, her voice cutting through the silence. "Let's start with a summary of where we are. Medina PD has pending charges on Hailey Marquez Blackwood. We're not going to get attempted murder or anything like that, but it's not really our problem. With her money and her family's money, this will take a while to figure out." She paused, scanning the room. "Helene Marquez," Claire continued. "I still don't know what to make of her. She *did* volunteer those journals, though. And they seem to confirm what she said. Then we've got Lena Quan, Suzanne Blackwood, and now this tennis pro, Brentley Flemming. Violet, what did you find on the video overnight? Please tell me you found a new suspect and a smoking gun."

Violet didn't look up from her keyboard. Instead, her fingers tapped out a quick sequence, and the video monitor on the wall flickered to life.

"I didn't," Violet said. "But I do have something of interest. This was recorded on Brentley Flemming's glasses—smart glasses that connect to the internet. They've got a crappy AI system built in, but they can record decent video." She gestured toward the screen, where the footage began playing.

Claire leaned forward, squinting at the display. "Is there audio?"

"There isn't," Violet replied without hesitation. "But

there could've been. Flemming says he doesn't record audio because it takes up too much space."

Claire sighed, folding her arms. On the monitor, the video shifted as if Flemming had turned his head, capturing a sweeping view of the extravagant party. The glittering chandeliers, the polished hardwood floors, the guests dressed to the nines—it all seemed pointless. The camera's point of view tracked Flemming's interactions, showing brief moments of him talking to Helene Marquez, then moving through clusters of partygoers.

After a minute, the screen displayed the rare Scotch bottle sitting untouched on the bar, framed by crystal tumblers and a line of unopened bottles. Violet sped up the video as minutes passed with the bottle coming in and out of view as Flemming chatted with Helene.

No one approached it. No one tampered with it.

Claire glanced at Violet. "That's it? Nothing?"

"Pretty much," Violet said. "There's no evidence that anyone did anything to the Scotch. As far as we can tell, it's just Flemming walking around the party, talking to people. And yes," she added before anyone could interrupt, "this is only partial footage. He says he wasn't wearing the glasses all night."

Jack spoke up. "If this is only partial, then we need to bring him in. He's holding out on us. We should ask him directly if he knows anything else."

"I agree," Kiko added from across the room. "If he's got more footage, we need it. Especially if it fills in the gaps."

Claire hesitated, glancing at the screen again. The video had looped back to the beginning, playing the same uneventful scenes of the party. Her mind worked through the possibilities. If Flemming had more footage, he could be sitting on something crucial—or he could be wasting their time. Either way, they wouldn't know unless they pushed.

"Fine," she said finally. "Kiko, Jack, go and try to bring him in for an interview. And take Sonya with you," she added, looking toward the profiler, who had been quietly scrolling on her phone. "In case he needs some convincing."

Sonya raised an eyebrow but said nothing, tucking her phone into her pocket and giving a slight nod.

"Don't spook him," Claire warned. "Just get him here. If he's got more footage, we need it yesterday."

Jack gave her a half-smile. "Don't worry, boss. We'll bring him in nice and polite."

"Sure you will," Claire muttered, rubbing her temple. She turned back to Violet, who had already started pulling up something else on her screen. "Let me know if anything else turns up."

Violet gave her a curt nod. "Will do."

As Kiko, Jack, and Sonya left the room, Claire leaned back in her chair, her gaze lingering on the video.

When Violet excused herself to grab another energy drink, Claire took the opportunity to stretch her legs. She walked a lap around the tables, her gaze scanning the scattered files and monitors.

Stopping in front of Fitz, she crossed her arms. "You said you have a whole new life," she said. It wasn't a statement; it was a question.

"I was wondering when you'd ask," Fitz replied, leaning back in his chair with a faint smile. "What do you want to know, Claire, my dear?"

Claire tilted her head. "I like the new jacket."

Fitz stood, brushing the back of his hand casually along the sleeve as though polishing the fabric. "Not bad, huh? And, for the record, I'm down to a size fifty-two."

"Is that good?" Claire asked.

"Well, I used to be a fifty-eight, so yeah, not bad for me." He grinned. "Margaret has me working out."

"Margaret?" Claire repeated, arching an eyebrow.

"Do I detect a hint of jealousy, Agent Anderson?"

Claire waved him off, shaking her head. "Not at all. Just... curious. She must be something to get you to clean up your act."

They exchanged a long stare, tension thickening between them as Claire tried to read Fitz's expression—a mix of defiance and something softer, almost vulnerable.

The moment was broken by Violet swinging the door open.

"Oh my God," she said, her voice cutting through the room. "Fitz!"

Fitz turned, startled. "What is it?"

"You're going to be a dad?" Violet blurted, wide-eyed.

Claire froze, her gaze snapping to Violet, then to Fitz, and back to Violet. She'd never seen Violet look so genuinely surprised.

Fitz stood, both hands raised as though warding off an accusation. "How did you—I mean, what?" Then a smile broke across his face. "Margaret... Margie. Is she here?"

"I ran into her," Violet said, stepping farther into the room. "She was up at the security booth by the café, trying to convince them to call down to you. Said she has some emergency with her car. She recognized me and waved me over. We got to talking."

"How did she recognize you?" Claire asked.

"I showed Margie pictures of the whole team," Fitz answered. "She and I share *everything* about our lives."

This didn't sound like Fitz, Claire thought, but she was too hung up on what Violet said to pursue anything else. "A dad?"

"It's true," Violet said, "I noticed she kept holding her hand around her belly, even though she's really not showing yet. Anyway, she had this *glow*. I just asked her outright. You know me—I don't have a filter."

Fitz groaned, running a hand over his face, but then his smile widened. "Margie told you?"

"Not exactly," Violet said with a shrug. "She smiled and said something about needing you to answer your phone. That's when I put two and two together."

Fitz pulled out his phone and glanced at the screen. "Oh, I had it on silent. I'll head up there."

"Wait, wait," Claire said, holding up a hand. "What?"

Fitz grinned as he walked to the door. "It's true, Claire-bear, my dear. Margie is pregnant. I'm going to be a dad."

And with that, he walked out, leaving Claire staring at the empty doorway in silence. She didn't know how long she sat there, listening to Violet tapping away at her keyboard, but she only came to when her phone buzzed on the table. It was Jack, and she answered right away.

"Brentley Flemming is in the wind." Jack's voice came over the line like staccato gunshots.

"What do you mean?" Claire asked, her tone sharp.

"Well, we're out front of his house," Jack replied. "We called on the way over, and he said he'd be here, said he'd be happy to come in and chat with us if we picked him up. Got here, and now there's no answer."

Claire frowned. "I think it's time for a wellness check," she said. "You know what to do."

CHAPTER THIRTY

KIKO FOLLOWED Jack into the house, sunlight streaming through the windows and illuminating the tidy interior. It wasn't ostentatious, just a well-kept suburban home with polished hardwood floors, neutral walls, and enough personal touches to feel lived in. A coffee mug sat next to a French press on the kitchen counter, and a pair of running shoes rested neatly by the door.

Sonya waited outside, keeping watch as Jack and Kiko moved inside.

Jack moved purposefully, clearing each room quickly. "Kitchen's clear," he said, heading toward the living room.

Kiko lingered for a moment, glancing at the mug before following him. "Feels good to be working with you again," she said as they stepped into the living room.

Jack paused, turning to look at her. "Not now," he said, though his tone was softer than the words. After a beat, he added, "I've missed you too."

Kiko smiled faintly, then glanced at a wall covered with framed photos. "You know, I've been dating," she said, trying to sound casual.

Jack raised an eyebrow but kept his focus on the room as he scanned it. "Yeah? Me too."

There was a brief, awkward silence before Kiko cleared her throat. "Living room's clear," she said, nodding toward the photos.

The wall was practically a shrine to Brentley Flemming. Photos of him shaking hands at charity galas, posing on tennis courts, and receiving awards filled the space. A large trophy sat on the mantel, engraved with his name and a tournament date from the early 2000s.

"Guy really loves himself," Kiko muttered, studying a photo of Brentley shirtless on a beach, holding a surfboard.

Jack smirked. "Looks like his glory days are well-documented."

They moved down the hallway, clearing a guest room and an office. The office had even more photos—Brentley with various women, some famous, some clearly enamored. One showed him in a suit at what looked like a charity auction, holding a paddle and grinning.

"Guess he wasn't shy about being the center of attention," Kiko said.

Jack opened a cabinet, finding it empty except for a stack of tennis magazines. "Not much of a private guy, either."

Finally, they entered the master bedroom. The bed was unmade, and a suitcase sat open on the floor, half-packed. Jack crouched next to it, rifling through the contents. "Clothes, sneakers... looks like he was planning to leave."

"But if he fled, why did he leave it here?" Kiko opened the drawers of the nightstand, pulling out a framed photo of Brentley with an older man on a tennis court. She flipped it over, reading the inscription aloud: "To my best student, Brentley. Keep reaching for the stars. - Coach D."

They exchanged a brief glance before heading back to the living room. Jack folded his arms, scanning the space one last time. "No sign of him, no sign of trouble. Just a guy who really loves his own reflection."

"Think he skipped town?" Kiko asked.

"Probably," Jack said. "Let's call Claire."

"Sure," Kiko said, "but first, let's see if any of the neighbors have anything to say."

It took twenty minutes before Jack and Kiko found a neighbor who was both willing to talk and knew anything useful. The man's name was Gregory Rousseau, and he stepped out onto his lawn as they approached, adjusting the cuffs of his pale blue button-up shirt.

He looked to be in his late forties, with golden hair cut short but stylish, and a jawline that seemed to be in competition with his well-kept house for sharpness. His faint French accent lent a polished air to his words.

Leading the questioning, Sonya asked. "When was the last time you saw him?"

"Sometime yesterday," Rousseau said, glancing at Flemming's house across the street before his eyes returned to Sonya. "I don't know him very well. But I've taken a few lessons from him. When I first joined the Medina Club."

"What about all the pictures of him at the club?" Jack asked. "Is that from an auction or something?"

Rousseau nodded, his hands tucked casually into the pockets of his trousers. "Yes. He never misses it. I've donated as well. They raise millions of dollars for local charities. People think we're all just a bunch of rich jerks out here, but we do a lot for the community."

Kiko tilted her head. "I'm sure you do."

Rousseau didn't seem to catch the slight sarcasm. "Brentley's a big draw for the auction. He gives away tennis lessons, tickets to matches, that sort of thing."

Jack's eyes flicked toward Flemming's house before settling back on Rousseau. "Any idea where he likes to hang out? We were supposed to meet him here today. Well, not here, but across the street, at his house."

Rousseau tapped his chin thoughtfully. "He likes to eat at that diner—the Greek place down on Springfield Street. I saw him there just last weekend. He's gone keto again, trying to lean up for the auction. Always puts on a few pounds during the year but then tries to cut ten before the event. Wants to look good in the photos."

"That dude is full of himself," Jack muttered.

Kiko raised an eyebrow at Jack, her lips twitching as if fighting a smile. "Maybe we'll check there."

Rousseau offered a polite smile and nodded. "Good luck." Without waiting for a response, he turned and strolled back toward his home, his gait as polished as his manner.

"The diner, huh?" Jack said, already stepping toward the car.

"I'm game for lunch," Sonya said.

"Yeah," Kiko replied, following them to the car. "Let's see if he's ketoing it up with a side of tzatziki."

CHAPTER THIRTY-ONE

"STAKE OUT THE HOUSE," Claire said.

"You just want us to sit here?" Jack asked.

"That's what a stakeout means," Claire replied. "Let me talk to Sonya."

Claire turned the SUV into Suzanne Blackwood's driveway and stopped at the security gate. As she waited, she heard Jack passing the phone to Sonya.

"Claire?" Sonya's voice came through the line. "Wait, are you in the car?"

"Fitz and I decided to go back to Suzanne's," Claire said. "See if we can chat about the tennis pro... and, well, everything else."

"The more I think about it," Sonya said, "the more I'm convinced Brentley Flemming had something to do with this. I know what it's like to be one of the poorest people among these rich folks. It messes with your perspective. By almost any standard, I was raised in affluence. By almost any standard, Flemming is well off. But compared to guys like Vincent Blackwood, he's impoverished. Happiness—or *unhappiness*—has more to do with expectations and comparative judgment than anything else."

Claire could hear the edge in Sonya's voice, sharp but reflective, as she continued.

"In almost any other zip code on Earth, I'd have been the rich kid. Same with Brentley Flemming. Nice house, sure, but one of the smallest in the area. He's essentially a manservant to these rich women. Could his little flirtation with Helene be something more? Could he have done Helene's bidding and killed Vincent? I think he could have."

"Well," Claire said, eyeing the gate ahead, "we're about to ask Suzanne about him —assuming we can get in. You stay at his house with Kiko and Jack. We will check the diner after we talk with Suzanne." She hung up and glanced over at Fitz.

"What do you think?" she asked.

"I think she could be on to something," Fitz said, adjusting the cuffs of his blazer. "As much as I hate to say it."

Claire and Fitz climbed out of the SUV, the midday sun reflecting off the polished stone steps of the Blackwood estate. Fitz adjusted his blazer as they approached the front door, but before they could ring the bell, the door swung open.

Suzanne stood in the doorway, her expression calm but unwelcoming. On either side of her were four attorneys, each impeccably dressed in varying shades of navy and charcoal. They looked like a wall of defense, sharp-eyed and ready for battle.

Claire raised an eyebrow. They must be multiplying, she thought. She hadn't seen this many lawyers in one place since a corporate fraud investigation years ago.

"Agent Anderson, Agent Fitzpatrick," Suzanne said evenly, her voice carrying the smooth cadence of someone who'd been rehearsing. "I'm afraid I won't be able to speak with you today."

"And why is that?" Fitz asked, stepping forward with a touch too much swagger.

"We're just here to ask a few questions. You know, about the murder of your husband."

One of the lawyers—a tall man with a graying beard and a pinstripe suit—raised a hand. "Mrs. Blackwood has already provided extensive cooperation with your investigation. She has no further obligation to subject herself to questioning without proper legal processes in place."

Fitz frowned. "You mean she won't talk unless we get a court order?"

"That's correct," another lawyer, a younger woman with severe glasses and a no nonsense tone, replied. "And given the conduct of your task force, I'd say that's the least you can do."

Claire crossed her arms. "What conduct, exactly?"

"The stunt at the club, for one," the woman said. "Also, the leaks. I'm sure you've seen the headlines, Agent Anderson. Details of this investigation appearing in the press, speculative accusations painting our client in a damaging light. It's clear that this has become less about solving a crime and more about a... witch hunt."

Claire held her ground. "Suzanne has been cooperative," she said. "But if there's more she knows, we have a duty to follow up. And, for the record, none of those leaks were from us. Medina PD has its skin in this game, too. Check with them about leaks."

One of the lawyers, a droopy-eyed man with a suit that hung loose on his thin frame, stepped forward, lowering his voice enough to make the words sting. "Agent Anderson, I'd tread carefully if I were you. S.W.O.R.D. is still a fledgling initiative, isn't it? Plenty of chatter in Olympia about whether it's worth the expense. I happen to know several senators, and the Deputy Governor has been quite vocal about reallocating funds to more 'pressing' needs. It would be a shame if this investigation ended up being the reason your task force was deemed *unnecessary*."

The gray-bearded lawyer stepped in again. "Agents, Mrs. Blackwood has already done everything in her power to assist. She's answered your questions, provided access to her home, and even supplied contacts who might be relevant to your investigation. And yet, here you are, on her doorstep again. She's not a suspect, and yet you treat her as one."

"No one said she's a suspect," Fitz countered, bristling. "But we both know how this works. If you don't have anything to hide, why—"

"That's enough," Suzanne interjected, her voice slicing through the tension. "I have been more than patient, more than accommodating, but this ends now. If you need anything else, bring a court order. Otherwise, leave me alone."

Claire could feel the heat rising in her chest, a mix of frustration and resignation. Fitz opened his mouth as though to argue, but she shot him a look that said, *Not here, not now*.

She forced a tight smile. "Understood. Thank you for your time, Mrs. Blackwood."

The lawyers stood firm, watching as Claire and Fitz turned and walked back to the SUV. As they climbed in and shut the doors, Fitz muttered, "Four lawyers? Really? It's like they were waiting for us."

Claire sighed, gripping the steering wheel. "It's what I'd do if I had their kind of money and the FBI kept showing up."

Fitz leaned back in his seat, shaking his head. "Doesn't mean she's innocent."

"No," Claire agreed, starting the engine. "But it doesn't mean she's guilty either."

CHAPTER THIRTY-TWO

AFTER A QUICK CALL TO JACK, Claire decided the diner was worth a shot. Flemming probably wouldn't be there, but if it was a regular haunt, someone might know something. She swung the SUV out of Suzanne Blackwood's driveway and turned onto the winding streets of Medina, the residential opulence giving way to a quieter commercial area.

The drive was brief but scenic, the kind that might be idyllic under different circumstances. The towering evergreens stood along the clean, winding roads, and the wide lawns gave way to small clusters of boutique shops, a yoga studio, and a deli with a line already forming out front.

Claire barely noticed the picturesque surroundings, though. Her mind was on Flemming and the stubborn brick wall Suzanne's lawyers had thrown up.

Fitz sat silently in the passenger seat, tapping idly at his phone. Claire glanced at him when the SUV came to a stop at a light. "So," she said, breaking the silence. "How are you feeling about being a father?"

Fitz looked up, startled, his thumb hovering mid-scroll. "Didn't think you'd follow up on that one."

"I hadn't planned to," Claire admitted. "Least not until this case was done. But you're practically glowing these days. It's hard not to notice."

Fitz huffed a small laugh and leaned back against the headrest. "Glowing, eh? Like a bloody firefly." He was quiet for a moment, watching the trees pass as Claire drove on. "Truth is, Claire... I'm terrified."

She glanced at him, surprised by the candor. "Terrified? You don't seem it."

"Practice," he said dryly, then sighed. "I've been a cock-up most of my life, you know that. Kicked out of three universities, squandered my inheritance like an idiot, and burned through what little goodwill my family had left. Moving here to America was as much an escape as it was a new start."

"I remember the pills," Claire said softly, not as an accusation but a reminder of how far he'd come.

"Pills, drink, bad decisions. Take your pick." Fitz gave a self-deprecating smile. "This whole fatherhood business... it feels like my second chance. Or maybe my *last*. I've got this one shot to not completely muck it up. To be the man I've always told myself I could be but never quite managed to live up to."

Claire considered that as she turned into a small lot behind the diner. "You're not the same man you were a year ago, Fitz. And you seem different even than a couple months ago. I'm sure Margaret sees that, or she wouldn't be with you."

Claire wasn't entirely sure she believed what she was saying, but Fitz was going to be a father, and he needed all the confidence he could get.

Fitz rubbed a hand over his jaw. "I hope you're right. I just don't want the kid—my kid—to ever look at me and think, *What a bloody disappointment*." His voice was quieter now. "I want them to have better."

"You'll give them better," Claire said firmly. "That's who you are now."

Fitz nodded, his gaze distant. "Let's hope so, Claire. Let's bloody hope so."

The moment lingered as the SUV idled in the parking lot. Then Claire shut off the engine and reached for the door. "Come on, Dad-to-be. Let's see what this place has to offer."

The bell above the diner's door jingled as Claire and Fitz entered. The smell of grilled meat, warm pita, and tangy tzatziki filled the air, mingling with the faint clatter of plates and silverware. The Greek diner was small but cozy, with booths along the windows and a long counter lined with spinning stools. Behind the counter, a middle-aged man with a thick mustache and a sweat-stained apron worked briskly, flipping through order slips and calling out to the cook in the back.

"Be with you in a sec!" he called without looking up, his voice carrying a faint Greek accent.

Claire and Fitz walked to the counter, waiting as the man finished tallying a check for a customer. When he turned to them, wiping his hands on his apron, his eyes widened slightly. "Well, you're not my regulars. What can I get you?"

"We're not here to eat," Claire said, pulling out her badge. "FBI. We're hoping you can help us."

The man's expression didn't change much—just a slight raising of his eyebrows.

"FBI, huh? What's this about?"

"We're looking into someone we think might come here regularly," Claire said, glancing around the diner. A few patrons were watching curiously but quickly returned to their meals. "Brentley Flemming. Do you know him?"

The man chuckled, shaking his head. "Know him? He's in here at least three times a week. Always orders either the falafel or the souvlaki. Lately, though, he's been skipping the rice and bread—extra vegetables on the side."

"Trying to slim down?" Fitz asked.

The man grinned. "For the charity ball. He says he has to look good in his tux for all the photos. We donated a gift certificate to it ourselves—dinner for two, a little PR for the diner."

Fitz nodded. "What kind of guy is he?"

The man began wiping down the counter with a rag. "Brentley? He's a ladies' man, that's for sure. Always in here with different women. Mostly casual—women he's coaching, I think. Young, athletic types. You know the deal."

Claire reached into her bag and pulled out her phone. She brought up a picture of Helene Marquez and turned the screen toward him. "Have you ever seen him in here with her?"

He squinted at the photo, then shook his head. "Nope. Can't say I have."

Claire frowned slightly. Thinking quickly, she scrolled through her photo gallery and pulled up a picture of Suzanne Blackwood. She turned the screen back toward the man. "What about her?"

His face brightened immediately. "Oh, yeah. Her, I've seen. All the time. Brentley and her come in together a lot. Not lately, though. Haven't seen her in a couple of weeks."

Claire exchanged a glance with Fitz. "Did they seem... close?" she asked carefully.

The man shrugged. "They seemed friendly. She's older, but Brentley's good at charming anyone. Lot of rich widows around here looking for love. I didn't think much of it."

Claire nodded, tucking her phone back into her bag. "Thanks. That's helpful."

"No problem," he said, moving to refill a customer's coffee. "Good luck with... whatever it is you're looking into."

As they walked back out to the SUV, Fitz whistled low. "Well, that complicates things, doesn't it?"

Claire climbed into the driver's seat. "Sure as hell does. If Brentley and Suzanne were having an affair, well..."

"Then either they killed him together, or he freelanced it, hoping to get a little *alone time* with her, so to speak." Fitz leaned back against the passenger seat, his hands resting on his thighs. "What are you thinking?"

Claire stared out through the windshield, watching the steady trickle of people passing by on the sidewalk outside the diner. She tapped her fingers on the steering wheel, her thoughts coalescing. "I knew there was a reason I was holding Kiko back from meeting any of these people," she said finally.

Fitz raised an eyebrow. "The charity ball? It's tomorrow, right?"

"Exactly." Claire's voice was firm. "We need to see these people on their own turf. The layers of this case keep shifting, but they all seem to lead back to that circle of people." She glanced at Fitz. "I feel more confused than ever about this case," she admitted. "But somehow, I think we're closer than ever to breaking it wide open."

CHAPTER THIRTY-THREE

BY 6 PM the following night, they were no closer to solving the case, but at least they had a plan.

Claire sipped her coffee inside the van parked discreetly down the block from the Medina Country Club. The mug was warm in her hands, but the caffeine didn't seem to touch her exhaustion. She glanced at Jack, who sat across from her with headphones on, his gaze fixed on the monitor in front of him.

"Are you sure we shouldn't have sent her in with someone else?" Jack asked, his voice concerned.

"She knows what she's doing," Claire replied. Kiko had volunteered, insisting she could blend in better than anyone else on the team. And Claire trusted her—she had to.

Back at the Boiler Room, Fitz, Violet, and Sonya were monitoring everything in real time, connected to both Claire and Jack via headsets. The entire team was also tied into Kiko, who was inside the charity ball, posing as a bartender. It had taken some serious convincing, but Claire had managed to persuade the catering company to add Kiko to their staff for the night. Officially, it was a favor to the FBI.

Unofficially, Claire knew it was the promise of a government contract that had sealed the deal.

"She's a quick study," Claire added, more for herself than Jack. "And she's spent the past twelve hours memorizing every name and face in that crowd. She'll be fine."

Jack adjusted the dial on the console in front of him, bringing up a clearer feed of Kiko's bodycam. The image jittered slightly as Kiko moved behind the long marble topped bar. They couldn't see her body, just her hands as she arranged glasses and wiped down surfaces. The clink of ice against crystal and the hum of conversation filled the background.

On the screen, Kiko's voice came through the earpiece. "Well, this is fancy. I don't think I've ever seen a bar with a chandelier over it. And who drinks champagne out of crystal flutes anymore? Do they know it tastes the same in a regular glass?"

Jack smirked. "Stay focused, Kiko. You're not there to critique their glassware."

"I'm just saying," Kiko replied, her voice light. "Anyway, no sign of Suzanne yet. Or Helene. Or anyone else interesting. Just a lot of people who smell like money."

Claire leaned closer to the screen, watching as Kiko poured a martini like she was a pro.

It was hard not to feel the tension building in her chest. They had a plan, sure, but plans rarely survived contact with reality. Still, this was their best chance to observe the key players in the case interacting in their natural habitat.

"Keep an eye out for Flemming too," Claire said into the headset. "If he shows, we need to know who he's talking to."

Kiko's response was instant. "Copy that. Oh, wait. Hold on. I think—yeah, Helene just walked in. She's wearing red, because of course she is."

"Stay sharp," Claire said. "And keep the chatter to a minimum. We don't want the guests thinking the bartender is talking with herself all night."

She turned to Jack. "Get Sonya on the line. If Helene's here, Suzanne won't be far behind."

Jack nodded, already switching channels on the comms. Claire sat back and took another sip of her coffee, trying to focus on the screen.

CHAPTER THIRTY-FOUR

KIKO SLID a fresh tray of champagne flutes onto the bar, her hands moving efficiently as she scanned the room. The ballroom was alive with glittering dresses, tailored tuxedos, and the unmistakable hum of wealth and influence. She'd always been good at reading a room, slipping into roles like a second skin.

Tonight, she was in her element.

She adjusted her vest and straightened the white shirt beneath it, her eyes roving over the crowd. There was Suzanne Blackwood, stepping into the room with the poise of someone who knew all eyes would eventually be on her. She was wearing a deep green gown that seemed to flaunt its price tag with every shimmer of its fabric.

Close by, Helene Marquez moved with purpose, her sharp gaze skimming the crowd like she was cataloging who mattered and who didn't.

Hailey Blackwood, on the other hand, lingered near the edges, her black cocktail dress slightly askew as though she'd resisted the urge to smooth it out. Lena Quan flitted through the throng, her gestures animated as she spoke to a group of people who seemed half-interested and half-trying to excuse themselves.

Kiko made a mental note of all of them, their movements and interactions, while she adjusted her focus back to the bar. One of the catering staff, a young guy with a slightly wrinkled bow tie, sidled up next to her with a tray of empty glasses.

"Busy night, huh?" he said, setting the tray down with a clatter.

"Tell me about it," Kiko replied, her voice light. "You'd think people who spend this much on tickets would be more careful with their glassware."

The guy laughed. "No kidding. I've already cleaned up three spilled drinks and it's barely seven. New here?"

"Last minute thing. I usually work with the Tacoma crew."

The young man nodded and Kiko smiled, but her attention snagged on a small movement across the room. Helene's gaze landed on Suzanne for a split second before she turned and moved toward a server with a tray of hors d'oeuvres.

The look was quick, but loaded. Kiko filed it away.

A guest approached the bar, drawing her focus back. A woman in a silver dress held out her empty glass with the faintest hint of impatience.

"Another champagne?" Kiko asked, already reaching for the bottle.

"Yes," the woman said, barely looking at her before returning to her conversation with a man in a black suit.

Kiko poured the drink and handed it over, letting her smile linger just long enough to appear genuine but not intrusive. She shifted down the bar to another guest, a young woman clutching her phone in one hand and a half-empty gin and tonic in the other.

"Refill?" Kiko asked.

"Oh, no, I'm good," the woman replied distractedly, her eyes glued to the screen. "Thanks."

Kiko nodded and moved on, catching snippets of conversations as she worked. Most of it was dull—real estate deals, vacation plans, compliments about jewelry. She poured a vodka soda, stirred a Manhattan, and handed over a glass of chardonnay before finally spotting her mark.

"Hey there, darling," a man said.

He was seated at the far end of the bar, leaning back on the stool as though he owned it. Late sixties, maybe early seventies, with perfectly white hair and a classic navy suit. His cheeks were flushed, and the empty martini glass in front of him suggested he was well into enjoying the evening. He caught her eye and smiled, his expression warm and tinged with the confidence of a man who wasn't used to hearing the word *no*.

Kiko grabbed the cocktail shaker and walked over.

"Another martini?" she asked, tilting her head just slightly as she spoke.

"Why not?" he replied, his smile widening. "Make it *extra dirty*, darling."

"Coming right up," Kiko said, spinning the shaker with a bit more flair than necessary. She mixed the drink, poured it, and slid it in front of him, giving him her most charming smile. "Here you go. Hope it's dirty enough for you."

He chuckled, lifting the glass and taking a sip. "Perfect. You're a natural at this."

"Well, I've had some practice," Kiko said, leaning her forearms on the bar. "But you seem like the kind of man who knows his way around a good drink."

"Guilty as charged," he said, raising his glass. "Name's Holden, by the way."

"Caulfield? Wow, I loved you in *Catcher in the Rye*."

He chuckled. "You're a bit young to be throwing around Salinger references."

"I'm more experienced than I look."

He raised an eyebrow. "It's Holden Southers."

"Nice to meet you, Holden," Kiko said. "I'm Kara." She always used a variation of her real name when undercover—it made it easier to respond naturally.

"So, Kara," Holden said, his tone shifting into something flirtatious, "what's a charming woman like you doing behind the bar tonight? Surely you've got better things to do than serve drinks to a room full of old snobs."

"Old snobs like you?" Kiko teased lightly, earning another laugh. She leaned in, keeping her tone casual. "Honestly, it's a great gig. You get to meet all kinds of interesting people."

Holden tilted his head, clearly enjoying the attention. "Interesting people, huh? Well, you've found one right here. I've got stories, darling. Just ask me anything."

Kiko smiled, letting the silence stretch for a beat before speaking. "Okay, here's one. A little birdie told me this whole thing tonight is in honor of Vincent Blackwood. You must've known him, right?"

Holden's smile faltered for just a moment, so brief most people wouldn't have caught it. But Kiko did. She watched as he took a sip of his martini, the glass hovering near his lips for just a second too long before he set it down.

"Oh, sure," he said, his voice quieter now. "Everyone here knew Vincent. This is an annual event, but since he was the biggest donor, yeah. It's dedicated to him this year. Big presence, that guy."

"Yeah?" Kiko said, keeping her tone light. "What was he like?"

Holden shrugged, leaning back again. "Smart, successful. A little intense, maybe. But, you know, he had to be. Running an empire isn't for the faint of heart."

Kiko nodded as she wiped the bar with a clean cloth. "Sounds like quite a guy. Must've been a real shock when he passed."

Holden's eyes flicked toward the room behind her, where Suzanne was laughing softly with a group of well-dressed men. "Yeah. A shock. That wife of his... what a... well... I shouldn't go on." He cleared his throat as he stood. "Hope I see you again, darling."

Kiko leaned across the bar, pulling him in with her eyes. "I'll be here all night."

CHAPTER THIRTY-FIVE

KIKO HAD BEEN WATCHING the ebb and flow of the ballroom crowd for the past half hour, her movements behind the bar fluid and calculated. She kept her interactions light, serving drinks with just the right amount of charm and attentiveness to encourage loose lips. She knew the game well—keep them talking, keep them comfortable, and eventually, they'd tell her what she needed to know.

Holden returned, this time holding a half-empty bottle of beer. His gait was looser now, his tie slightly askew, and his eyes brighter with the unmistakable glaze of a man who'd had one too many. He leaned against the bar, grinning at her.

"Kara," he said, dragging her fake name out like it was a melody. "I had to come back. Couldn't leave the most beautiful bartender in the room without a little company."

Kiko gave him a patient smile, pouring a soda for a nearby guest while keeping one ear tuned to Holden. "Flattery will get you far," she said lightly. "But not a free drink."

He laughed, the sound too loud for the space. "I don't need free drinks. Just a little conversation with you is all I'm after."

She turned to him, folding her arms and leaning against the counter. "Well, you've got my attention. What's on your mind?"

Holden took a swig from his bottle, then glanced over his shoulder toward the crowd. "You asked me about Vincent Blackwood earlier," he said, lowering his voice slightly. "But you know who's the real story? *Suzanne*. That woman... let me tell you, she's something else."

Kiko tilted her head, feigning casual curiosity. "What do you mean?"

He leaned closer, the sour tang of beer and alcohol on his breath. "She's been through three husbands. Three. And every single one of them ended up dead." He gave a dry chuckle. "If I were number four, I'd be looking over my shoulder."

Kiko's stomach tightened, but she kept her expression neutral. "That's... tragic," she said carefully. "What happened to the second one? I heard it was a boating accident?"

Holden nodded, his grin fading slightly. "Yeah, that's the story. Poor bastard. His body was all mangled, half-eaten by sharks when they found it. But you know what they don't tell you?" He leaned in closer, spraying a fine mist of spittle as he whispered. "His business was sinking faster than a lead weight. I know. My firm handled the books."

Kiko resisted the urge to wipe her face. "Really?" she asked. "What kind of trouble was he in?"

Holden took another swig of beer. "Oh, it was bad. Debts piling up. Vendors unpaid. He was weeks away from bankruptcy. The kind of collapse that takes down a whole family with it." He smirked. "And Suzanne? She would've been left with nothing. Not a dime."

Kiko's heart raced, but she kept her voice steady. "So, what happened?"

Holden's smirk widened, his voice dropping even further.

"Here's the thing. After he died, the creditors backed off. The insurance money came through—a big, fat payout. And then she sold the company's assets, struck a deal with one of the competitors. They took on the debts in exchange for the patents, equipment, and some contracts. She walked away with enough cash to set herself up for life. Pretty damn convenient, huh?"

Kiko felt a chill creep up her spine, but she forced a laugh. "That's quite a story, Holden."

"Oh, it's more than a story, darling," he said, wagging a finger at her. "It's the truth. I saw the numbers. I saw how everything changed after he was gone. Suzanne's not just lucky—she's smart. Real smart."

Kiko gave him an indulgent smile, her mind racing. "Well, thanks for the insight," she said, swapping out his beer with a fresh one. "You've definitely given me something to think about."

Holden raised his bottle in a mock toast. "Anytime, Kara. Anytime."

Suddenly his eyes got aggressive and he reached and grabbed her wrist. "Meet me in the men's room in five minutes."

Casually, but with a good amount of force, Kiko shook her wrist free. She leaned in close, so close she could smell his expensive cologne. "Touch me again and I'll break your face."

As Holden stumbled away, Kiko heard Fitz in her headset. "Nice work, Kiko. Another Oscar is on your way. But can you move around the space a bit? Sonya and I are trying to get more of a lay of the land."

Kiko grabbed a tray of champagne flutes and moved through the crowded ballroom. The soft clink of glass accompanied her steps, mingling with the hum of polite laughter and the notes of a string quartet tucked into a corner. Around her, the glittering auction tables stretched in neat rows, each item displayed under carefully angled lights.

This was no PTA raffle. A sleek robot dog, still in its pristine packaging, caught her eye. Its glossy exterior boasted the latest AI capabilities, promising companionship and clever tricks for its future owner. A photo of a gleaming yacht stood propped on an easel nearby, the starting bid scrawled in bold: $50,000 for a one-day trip. Jewelry, custom art pieces, exclusive vacations—it was a playground for the absurdly wealthy.

"Who donated the robot dog?" Fitz's voice crackled in her ear.

Kiko didn't break stride as she scanned the small card beside it. "Suzanne Blackwood," she said.

"Not Suzanne and *Vincent* Blackwood?" Fitz pressed.

"No," Kiko confirmed. "Just Suzanne Blackwood."

Fitz was silent for a beat before asking, "Anything there tied to Vincent Blackwood?"

Kiko slowed her pace, her eyes darting over the tables as she walked. She passed intricate crystal sculptures, bottles of vintage wine, and exclusive spa packages, but nothing bore Vincent Blackwood's name.

She adjusted her grip on the tray and murmured, "No, nothing from Vincent."

"Huh," Fitz said. "Interesting."

CHAPTER THIRTY-SIX

FITZ PACED THE BOILER ROOM, his blazer flaring slightly with each turn. He spun on Sonya, who was seated at the large desk. "Could you stop tapping the desk with that infernal pen?"

She tapped it a few more times, then tossed it at his head.

He dodged, the pen hitting the wall behind him.

"I'm just saying, it's *odd*," Fitz said, ignoring the attempted assault. "Why wouldn't Suzanne have donated something on Vincent's behalf this year? She's handled the charity donations for years, hasn't she?"

Sonya barely glanced up from her laptop, where she was cross-referencing the donor lists from previous charity balls. "Why would she? He's dead, Fitz. She doesn't owe anyone a sentimental gesture."

Fitz stopped pacing and fixed her with a pointed look. "Exactly. He's dead. Which is why she *should* have. It would be the perfect way to keep his memory alive, to show the community that she's still honoring him. People like Suzanne—rich, powerful, image-conscious—they thrive on appearances."

Sonya leaned back, crossing her arms. "Maybe she didn't want to draw more attention to herself. Or maybe she thought donating something in his name would look opportunistic, like she was milking the tragedy for goodwill."

Fitz snorted. "Come off it. Assuming Suzanne did all the donating, each year she put something in Vincent's name. A trip to Tuscany one year. A diamond necklace another. Always something high-profile, something splashy. And this year? Nothing. Zilch. She donated an expensive robot dog, but only in *her* name."

"He's *dead*," Sonya said slowly, emphasizing the word like she was talking to a child.

"No," Fitz countered, his voice rising. "It doesn't add up. Suzanne's meticulous, isn't she? She'd have planned this charity ball down to the last canapé. Weeks ago, months ago. If she's managing the donations—and she is—she'd have known how it would look not to include something from Vincent. The omission is glaring."

Sonya frowned, her fingers stilling on the keyboard. "You're assuming she even cares about appearances. Maybe she's grieving."

"Or maybe," Fitz said, stepping closer, "she didn't include anything from Vincent because she knew there wouldn't be a Vincent Blackwood this year."

Sonya blinked. "You think she knew he'd be dead before this charity ball even came around?"

Fitz nodded. "Think about it. She's involved in every detail of these events, year after year. If she skipped over adding his name this time, it wasn't a mistake. It was deliberate. She knew."

Sonya's gaze dropped back to her screen, her lips pursed in thought. "It's a stretch," she said, though her voice had lost its earlier sharpness.

"Is it?" Fitz asked, sitting down across from her. "Or is it the crack we've been looking for?"

For a long moment, neither of them spoke, the hum of computers filling the silence. Finally, Sonya sighed and pushed the keyboard toward him. "Fine. Let's work this angle. But don't think for a second I'm buying into your gut instinct over hard evidence."

"You should be happy. If I'm right, you may just win our little bet after all."

Jack sat on the swivel-mounted seat bolted to the floor of the surveillance van, his knees brushing the metal console as he tossed his headset onto the table in frustration. "We shouldn't have let her go in there alone with these vultures," he said.

Claire sat across from him on a bench seat, her laptop balanced on her knees. "She can hold her own," she said. "You know that."

"That's not the point," Jack muttered, leaning his elbows on his thighs. "She shouldn't have to."

Claire looked up from her screen, her gaze narrowing. "Why are you focusing on that instead of what she just got out of Holden? He practically handed us a motive for Suzanne's second husband's death. Maybe we should have been on that one all along."

Jack straightened, avoiding her eyes as he turned his attention to the grainy live feed from Kiko's hidden camera. The tension in his shoulders, the way he shifted in his seat—it all pointed to something deeper than professional concern.

Claire studied him. They'd both admitted to the affair months ago, swearing it was over. It was awkward, painful even, but necessary for the sake of their team. And yet, watching him now, Claire couldn't help but wonder if those old embers hadn't been entirely extinguished, if Jack's protectiveness over Kiko went beyond what was appropriate. She hoped she was wrong.

"Jack," she said carefully, her tone firm, "focus. She's doing what she does best, and she's gotten us a lead. Don't lose sight of that."

Jack exhaled through his nose, sitting back and gripping the armrests of his seat. "You're right. I just... I don't like the idea of her dealing with guys like that. Not alone."

"She's not alone," Claire said. "We're here. She's got us in her ear, and she knows exactly what she's doing. Trust her."

Jack gave a reluctant nod but stayed silent, his gaze on the screen. Claire turned her attention back to her laptop, but her mind churned with thoughts about Suzanne Blackwood. The information Kiko had pried from Holden was another thread in the web they were trying to untangle. If Suzanne really had benefited from her second husband's death, it could change everything.

The van's comm system crackled to life, breaking the tension. Claire glanced at the console as a familiar voice came through. "Boiler Room to field team," Fitz said. "Claire, we've got something. Call us back."

Claire closed her laptop with a snap. "Fitz," she said to Jack. "Maybe they've got a breakthrough."

CHAPTER THIRTY-SEVEN

CLAIRE TAPPED her headset as the van's console lit up. Fitz and Sonya's voices came through at the same time, overlapping in a burst of chaotic urgency.

"Claire, just hear me out—" Fitz began.

"We need to focus on this—" Sonya interrupted.

"Stop interrupting!" Fitz snapped.

"Then get to the point!" Sonya fired back.

"Enough!" Claire's voice cut through the noise, commanding. "One at a time. Fitz, go."

There was a pause and Claire could almost picture Fitz shooting Sonya a look before he spoke. "Here's the thing. Every year, Vincent Blackwood donated something significant to the charity auction. We're talking showpieces—yachts, diamonds, exclusive trips. Stuff that made headlines. We're assuming that Suzanne arranged it all, did it in his name as she was the master of the house."

"And this year?" Claire asked, already sensing where he was headed.

"This year," Sonya cut in, "there's nothing from him. Not one item with his name attached. The only contribution from the Blackwood household is the robot dog, and it's listed solely under Suzanne's name."

"A robot dog?" Claire repeated, more to buy herself a moment than because she needed clarification.

"Exactly," Fitz said. "Like the one she had at her house. And the one Geoffery had as well."

Claire frowned. "So you think Suzanne handled the donations, and the omission wasn't an accident?"

"Precisely," Fitz replied. "Think about it. If she knew he wouldn't be alive by the time of the auction, why would she bother pretending he'd donated something? She wouldn't."

Sonya's voice came back on the line. "It lines up with what Kiko got from Holden at the ball. He said Suzanne's second husband was about to take their family business under. And then suddenly, a 'boating accident' solved everything. That wasn't luck, Claire. That was a plan."

Claire's mind flickered back to photos she'd seen a few days earlier—the second husband's mangled body, half-eaten by sharks. And now she had an image of Suzanne, pushing him overboard. She shivered involuntarily. "But if she's as careful and calculating as you're suggesting, why would she make such a glaring mistake now? Not putting Vincent's name on anything—it's careless."

"It's not careless," Fitz said, his voice gaining momentum. "It's arrogance. The kind that grows over time. Suzanne killed her first husband in self-defense—no one's disputing that. I looked at the file, and Violet went over it with a fine toothed comb. But with the second one, she saw what killing could do. She saw it could save her. Solve her problems. And she got away with it."

"And that rewires a person," Sonya added. "She's used to people buying her performance. The grieving widow act, the innocent benefactor. By now, she doesn't just think she can fool us—she thinks she's untouchable."

Fitz jumped back in. "Exactly. She's not sloppy; she's overconfident. She's done this before, and each time, it's worked. She doesn't even see this as risky anymore. She thinks she's above suspicion."

Claire leaned back, staring at the faint glow of the monitors in the van. If Fitz and Sonya were right—and the evidence pointed that way—then Suzanne wasn't just a killer. She was a master manipulator.

Claire turned toward Jack. "Get Kiko on the line."

Jack didn't hesitate, slipping his headphones back on and flipping the switch to connect with her. "Kiko, this is Jack. Do you copy?"

Static crackled faintly through the van, but no response came.

Jack frowned, adjusting the dial. "Kiko, it's Jack. Are you there?"

Claire's stomach tightened. "Try again. Switch channels."

Jack flipped through frequencies, his movements growing sharper. "Kiko, this is Jack. Come in. Do you copy?"

Nothing.

"Still nothing?" Claire's voice rose just slightly, her eyes narrowing as she watched the concern bloom across Jack's face.

He shook his head. "No comms. I don't like this." As Jack reached to adjust the monitor displaying Kiko's video feed, the screen flickered—and then went completely black.

Claire felt the air in the van shift, a subtle charge that sent a ripple of unease down her spine. She leaned forward, her voice sharper now. "What the hell just happened?"

When Jack didn't reply immediately, she said, "Can you still get Violet?"

He switched to the Boiler Room channel. "Violet?"

"I'm here." Violet's voice came through the speakers in the van. "And I'm already working on it."

CHAPTER THIRTY-EIGHT

KIKO HANDED off her last champagne flute, letting the tray rest against her hip with ease. She moved toward the bar, her focus drifting for just a moment—until something pulled her attention.

Suzanne Blackwood had approached the auction tables, her movements slow and careful. Slowly, Kiko moved to within a few yards of her, standing in the corner as Suzanne surveyed the auction items.

"Yeah, we got these three dogs." A man in a sharp tuxedo and his impeccably dressed wife had stopped in front of the robot dog next to Suzanne.

His tone was casual but tinged with pride. "One for us, two for the kids. So we always know what they're up to."

The woman beside him chuckled, swirling her wine glass. "Barry has practically turned us into gods."

Barry grinned at Suzanne. "You can set them up to link with your e-glasses too. We're all-seeing, all-knowing. Basically, the kids think we've got eyes in the backs of our heads. They think we're psychic."

"More like paranoid," the wife muttered, though there was no real bite to her words.

He laughed. "Best million we ever spent. Hell, it was cheaper than my last divorce."

His wife nudged him with her elbow. "Don't give me any ideas." She turned suddenly. "Oh, Barry, there are the Pendleton's, let's go schmooze them a little." She reached out and touched Suzanne's arm. "We'll catch up later."

Kiko forced a polite smile as Holden walked by her with a woman she assumed was his wife, turning the exchange over and over in her mind. Three dogs. All seeing. All-knowing.

She glanced at the auction table where the box had once been displayed, now conspicuously absent. Finding Suzanne, Kiko's mouth dropped open slightly. She'd removed the box holding the robot dog and was carrying it toward the front entrance.

Kiko tilted her head, her mind clicking into gear. Suzanne's casual demeanor didn't match the action. She placed her tray on the bar and followed, weaving through the clusters of guests still milling about. As she passed through the doors into the cool night air, her steps became quieter, more measured.

Outside, Suzanne stopped beneath an elegant awning. The soft light from a hanging lantern illuminated her as she adjusted her grip on the box. Kiko slowed, slipping behind a column to stay out of view. She was deciding her next move when a sharp voice interrupted the stillness.

"No, Brentley isn't here," a woman said. "But I think I know where he is."

Kiko shifted her position just enough to see Lena Quan pacing near the edge of the building, her phone pressed tightly to her ear. Lena's free hand gestured sharply, punctuating her words with frustration. The conversation had a charge to it, like it was leading somewhere important.

Kiko's instincts pulled her in two directions. Lena could be a lead—a real one—but Suzanne was still moving, the box clutched to her chest. Whatever this was, it felt... off. After a beat, Kiko chose Suzanne, slipping back into the shadows and trailing her down a narrow path.

As Suzanne made her way past the tennis courts and toward the pond, Kiko followed, her steps quiet against the gravel, her movements blending with the night. She crouched behind a low hedge as Suzanne stopped by the water's edge beneath the drooping branches of a willow tree.

Kiko leaned forward, eyes narrowing as she watched Suzanne open the box and pull out the sleek, polished form of the AI robot dog. Suzanne cradled it for a moment, her expression unreadable, before kneeling by the pond.

The first dip was gentle, like testing the water's surface. Then, with an unhurried, murderous certainty, Suzanne submerged the robot completely, holding it under. The ripples spread outward in widening circles, catching the faint glow of the moonlight.

She was drowning the robot dog.

Inside the van, Claire sipped her coffee nervously as Jack leaned forward in his swivel chair, perched on the edge of it like he might launch himself into action at any second. His elbows pressed into his knees, his hands tightly clasped together.

"Here's my best guess," Violet said, her voice filling the van over the comms system. "The comms were working perfectly until they weren't. No gradual drop-off, no static buildup, just a clean break. That rules out most equipment failures on our side."

Claire's eyes flicked to Jack. The lines around his mouth had deepened, and his shoulders were tense enough to snap.

"Which leaves environmental factors," Violet continued. "Something external had to have cut the connection. The most likely culprit? Signal jamming."

Jack muttered something under his breath—something Claire couldn't catch but didn't need to.

"But here's the problem," Violet went on. "Jamming leaves a trace—disruption spikes, interference patterns, things you can see even after the fact. I don't see that here. What I'm seeing is... clean. Something at the venue—a power source, a badly shielded device, or even a weird frequency from their internal security system—could be blanketing the comms. It wouldn't even have to be intentional. It could be as innocent as an industrial microwave in the wrong spot."

Jack leaned back but only for a moment. His jaw was so tight Claire could see the muscles jumping near his temples.

"It could be intentional," Violet said. "Something subtle—an automated jammer or a misused device designed to target frequencies like ours. Hell, it could even be some amateur trying to mask a hotspot and getting lucky."

Claire let out a breath through her nose, watching Jack, who was already inching toward the door. "Fine," Claire said, "but we can't wait much longer."

"I'll dig deeper," Violet continued.

Jack didn't wait. He was up in an instant, the chair spinning behind him. He yanked open the van's door without a word, the night air rushing in.

"Jack, hold on!" Claire called after him, but he was already halfway across the street.

She sat back for a second, the van suddenly feeling larger without him in it. This wasn't just about protocol or even Kiko's safety, Claire realized as she stared after him.

Jack wasn't just worried—he was something else entirely.

Kiko froze, the surreal nature of the scene rooting her in place. Suzanne pushed the robot deeper into the water, her movements methodical.

Kiko crouched lower. What kind of person drowns a machine like this—an item worth a quarter of a million dollars?

She stiffened at the sound of footsteps approaching along the gravel path.

She turned, her instincts sharp, but the shadows obscured her view until it was too late. A man surged forward, sweeping her legs out from under her with a force that sent her crashing to the ground, the breath jolting from her lungs.

Before she could recover, another figure lunged, pinning her shoulders with crushing weight. Kiko's mind raced, her body twisting instinctively against the hold, but they had the advantage—and they knew it.

PART 3

FOR LOVE OR MONEY

CHAPTER THIRTY-NINE

JACK SPRINTED ACROSS THE LAWN, his heart pounding with a fury that matched his speed. The world blurred around him—the soft glow of lanterns lining the pathways, the murmur of distant conversations from the ball, and the hum of crickets that seemed to mock the chaos unfolding.

He didn't stop to flash his badge at the security guards flanking the entrance. Instead, he barreled past them, ignoring their startled shouts.

Ahead, he saw the tennis courts illuminated by overhead lights and, just beyond, the glint of water from the pond. Two figures moved near the edge, their postures aggressive. Jack's pulse spiked as he recognized Kiko pinned beneath one of them, her body struggling against the weight.

A white-hot anger surged through him, obliterating reason. "Get off her!" he bellowed, his voice carrying across the grounds like a crack of thunder.

One of the men barely had time to turn before Jack smashed into him with the force of a freight train, sending the man sprawling onto the grass. The second guard froze, his hand hovering near his belt. Jack's weapon was out before the man could think twice, the muzzle steady and aimed.

"Move away," Jack ordered, his voice sharp, his eyes locked on the man.

The guard hesitated, then slowly raised his hands and backed away, muttering apologies. Lena Quan appeared at the edge of the scene, her heels clicking against the pavement as she approached.

"What the hell is going on here?" Jack demanded, turning his weapon toward her instinctively before lowering it when she raised her hands in surrender.

"This was a misunderstanding," Lena said, her voice calm but her expression rattled. "I saw her—that bartender—following Suzanne. I didn't know who she was. I sent security to handle it."

"You sent them to assault her?" Jack shot back.

"They weren't supposed to—" Lena began, but Jack cut her off with a glare.

Kiko rose to her feet, brushing herself off. "She said she knows where Flemming is. I heard her."

Jack looked at Lena. "Is that true?"

"I said I *think* I know where he is," Lena corrected. "And it was a *joke*. My friend Tammy and I always joke that he's sleeping with Brenda, the other tennis pro here."

Suzanne Blackwood stood nearby, having wandered up the hill from the pond.

"What about her?" Jack asked, jerking his chin toward Suzanne.

Lena hesitated. "I... I don't know why she's here."

Susan looked detached, her gown trailing in the grass. "Please leave," she said.

Jack turned back to Kiko. "Are you okay?"

Kiko nodded. "I'm fine."

Jack glanced at the guards. “You two better hope we don’t press charges for assaulting a federal agent.”

One of the guards stammered an apology, but Jack had already turned to Kiko. He grabbed her arm—not roughly, but with enough force to make his point clear.

“We’re done here,” he said.

The guards protested, saying they needed to stay until management arrived, but Jack’s glare silenced them.

“Screw that,” he said, his voice dangerous. “We’re leaving.”

He didn’t look back as he guided Kiko toward the path leading out of the chaos.

CHAPTER FORTY

IT WAS past midnight by the time Kiko was allowed to see people, and Claire was already on her second crappy hospital cappuccino. For the last hour, she'd waited with the rest of the S.W.O.R.D. team in the lobby.

Kiko had pretended not to be injured, but it turned out she'd broken a rib when she was smashed to the ground by the security guard.

Claire spent much of the time in the hospital going over the case with Fitz, Jack, and Sonya. They'd all agreed that Suzanne's actions were at the very least suspicious and, at the most, evidence that she was the killer. However, drowning a robot dog wasn't a crime. That's why Violet was back at the Boiler Room doing what Claire assumed was the first-ever autopsy on a quarter-million-dollar artificial intelligence dog.

"Claire, we need to talk."

She looked up. It was Gerald Hightower, her boss, and he did not look pleased.

Hightower sighed heavily. His usually commanding presence seemed deflated, his shoulders slumping slightly as he stepped closer to Claire. She could smell the faint scent of aftershave, mingled with stress.

"Claire, I feel like hell even saying this," he began wearily. "But I'm close—*so close*—to pulling the plug on the entire S.W.O.R.D. task force. That is, if I even have a job anymore."

Claire straightened, the words jolting through her exhaustion. She opened her mouth to respond, but he held up a hand.

"Don't. Just listen." He exhaled again, his tone heavy. "That stunt at the charity ball? Sending Kiko undercover like that without proper authorization? It's making waves, Claire. Big ones. I've got senators calling my office. The Deputy Governor's breathing down my neck. They're all saying the same thing: stop harassing the rich people—by which they mean, *the political donors*—in Medina."

Claire set down her cup, the bitter taste of the hospital cappuccino still lingering in her mouth. "Gerald, you know—"

"I know," he cut in sharply, his eyes meeting hers. "I *know* you're just doing your job, and you're damn good at it. Better than anyone I've got. But this case—" He gestured vaguely, as if trying to gather his thoughts. "This case has stirred up a hornet's nest. And these aren't just any hornets. They've got deep pockets and friends in high places." He lowered his voice. "I'm with you, Claire. You know I am. But this? This is political now. And if we don't bring this thing home in the next day or two..." He trailed off, his mouth tightening as though the thought itself was too frustrating to articulate. "I don't know what happens after that," he finished quietly, shaking his head. "Just... figure it out, Claire. Fast. I can't protect you from these people. Hell, I may not even be able to protect myself."

"But Hightower, I—"

He held up a hand. "I didn't used to believe this, Claire,

and I still don't *want* to, but here's the damn truth: This world runs on money, not justice."

Without waiting for a response, he turned and walked away, leaving Claire to stare at the empty doorway, the weight of his command settling over her.

As he disappeared down the corridor, Claire slumped back against the wall. Before she could fully process his words, the elevator doors slid open, and Kiko emerged, wheeled out by a nurse.

"Look who's back," Jack said, stepping forward with a grin that didn't quite mask his concern. He crouched, meeting Kiko's eyes. "How's the rib?"

"Hurts like hell," she admitted, managing a smile as the team gathered around her. Fitz stood with his arms crossed, trying not to look too relieved, while Sonya hovered nearby, her expression unreadable.

"Don't let her fool you," Jack said, straightening. "She's tougher than she looks."

"Not that tough," Kiko replied, rubbing her side gently. She turned to Claire. "I heard something interesting while they were patching me up."

"What's that?" Claire asked, stepping closer.

"Jack said Violet was doing an autopsy on the robot dog. I want to know the results."

Sonya tapped her phone, her voice dry. "She's probably neck-deep in circuits and sensors right now. If there's anything to find, she'll find it."

"Good," Kiko said. "Because if that thing holds any answers, I want to know before I go back out there." She looked at Claire, her expression steady despite the exhaustion in her eyes. "Whatever's happening here, Suzanne's at the center of it. I can feel it."

Claire nodded, glancing around at the team. "Tomorrow

morning. Early. By then, Violet should be ready to share the results. Time's not exactly on our side."

She didn't say it, but Hightower's words still rang in her ears: *This world runs on money, not justice.*

~

The group lingered near the hospital's front doors, the sliding glass panels opening and closing with a faint whoosh every time someone entered or exited. Jack exchanged a few quiet words with Kiko before pushing her wheelchair toward the exit. Sonya followed close behind, her phone glowing in her hand.

"I'll drop them both off," Jack said. He glanced at Claire and Fitz. "You two get some rest. It's been a hell of a night."

Claire nodded. "Thanks, Jack." She raised a hand as they rolled out through the sliding doors, the night air carrying their voices away. Turning back to Fitz, she adjusted her coat. "Heading home?"

Fitz nodded distractedly. "Yes, I suppose."

Claire gave him a sidelong glance. "Seeing Margaret tonight?"

He hesitated. "No. She's busy. We're having breakfast tomorrow."

They lingered for a moment in the lobby, the quiet of the late hour wrapping around them. Just as they were about to head out, Fitz stopped midstep, his gaze fixed on the sliding glass doors.

"Margaret?" he murmured.

Claire followed his line of sight. A woman had just walked in, arm hooked through the elbow of another man. The man, younger than Fitz—perhaps late thirties—walked with an easy confidence. His tailored peacoat hung perfectly on his frame, and his stride carried a casual arrogance that set

Claire's teeth on edge. The two were laughing softly as they turned down the hallway toward the maternity ward.

"Fitz..." Claire began, but the word caught in her throat. "Is that..."

Fitz stood frozen, his chest rising and falling sharply.

Margaret looked radiant, her face flushed, her free hand resting lightly on the man's arm. As they neared the hallway's bend, the man glanced back and spotted Fitz. He stopped, then slowly, Margaret turned as well.

Fitz stepped forward. "Margie? What's—"

"So you're the douchebag she's been squeezing for coins," the man said suddenly, his voice venomous.

Fitz staggered back a step, his shoulders slumping under the weight of the words.

Margaret looked at Fitz, mouthed *I'm sorry*, then turned and pulled the man away.

Fitz's eyes, wide and unfocused, shimmered with tears.

Claire reached out instinctively, her hand brushing his arm. "Fitz..." she said softly, but he shook his head, jerking away from her touch.

Tears spilled over as he turned, his face contorted with a pain Claire had never seen in him before. He strode toward the front doors, his movements almost frantic.

"Wait!" Claire called after him, stepping forward.

But he raised a hand, his fingers trembling, as if to hold her back.

He pushed through the sliding doors and disappeared into the night, leaving Claire standing in the hospital hallway, the fluorescent lights buzzing faintly above her.

CHAPTER FORTY-ONE

"WELL," Claire said, leaning against the edge of the table as everyone dug into the muffins, pastries, and coffees she'd brought for them the next morning, "the robot dog autopsy came up empty. Violet, explain."

Between bites of a blueberry muffin, Violet set down her coffee and gestured toward the laptop open in front of her. "I ran a full teardown on the thing," she began, crumbs sprinkling the table as she spoke. "It was a pain to access—these Littermates robots are built like Fort Knox. But once I cracked it open, here's what I found: nothing."

"Nothing?" Fitz asked, raising an eyebrow. He'd been in the office when Claire arrived, and she'd avoided any mention of what happened at the hospital.

"Exactly. A little water damage, but not much. Still gained access and got a bunch of factory-sealed nothing." Violet tapped a few keys, and a schematic of the robot dog's internal systems appeared on the screen. "The operating system had no data logs, no user settings, no registered pairing with any e-glasses or external devices. The firmware was untouched. In fact, there wasn't even a boot sequence recorded."

Jack frowned. "What does that mean?"

"It means it was fresh out of the box," Violet said. "Never powered on, never configured. The hardware was pristine, and the AI cores hadn't even been initialized."

Kiko leaned forward. "So, basically, it was completely empty?"

"Brand spanking new," Violet confirmed. "Like it came straight off the production line and into Suzanne Blackwood's hands. For the life of me, I can't figure out why she'd bother drowning the thing."

"It had no incriminating data?" Claire clarified.

"None. I even checked for physical modifications—hidden compartments, added hardware, you name it. But it's exactly what it looks like: an untouched quarter-million dollar robot dog with zero evidence or intel to offer." Violet shook her head, popping the last bit of muffin into her mouth. "Honestly, I'm stumped."

Claire sighed. "So, we still have no idea why Suzanne would try to destroy something that, by all accounts, didn't hold any secrets."

"It makes no sense," Jack said, flipping through his notebook.

Claire folded her arms, scanning the team. "Here's what we *do* know. Suzanne and Vincent bought the three-pack of Littermates—these robot dogs. One was at Geoffrey's house, another at Suzanne's, and the third was the one she tried to destroy. It wasn't much, but it was enough to get us a warrant overnight for the other two."

Jack sighed. "Kiko and I already served the warrant at Geoffrey Osgood's house this morning."

Claire's eyebrows rose. "And?"

"It's gone," Jack said flatly. "He claimed it was stolen. Said it vanished overnight."

Violet made a noise of disbelief around a sip of her coffee. "Convenient."

"Too convenient," Kiko added. "He didn't even seem fazed. Just gave us that polished shrug, said it must've been taken, and offered us tea like it was no big deal."

"Which means," Claire said, pushing off the table, "the only one left is the one at Suzanne's house."

"What if," Kiko said, "she *thought* there could be data on one she drowned? I mean, she doesn't exactly seem like a tech wizard, and the couple she was speaking with said they could all be connected right before she snatched it. So maybe she had already disappeared the ones at her house and Geoffrey's, then realized, 'Oh crap, I have to get rid of this one I'd donated in case it, too, carries incriminating evidence.'"

"I'm sold." Fitz glanced at his watch. "When are we heading over?"

"No need to head over," Claire said. "She and her gaggle of lawyers are on the way over *here*. Voluntary cooperation, though I don't think she'll be especially cooperative."

"And she's bringing the dog?" Jack asked.

"When I told him we had a warrant, the lawyer assured me he'd have Suzanne bring it."

The FBI conference room was tense as Claire glanced around the long table at her team. The slideshow continued its silent loop on the monitors: Vincent Blackwood's face, the Littermates robot dogs, Brentley Flemming in his tennis whites.

Jack tapped his pen steadily against the table. Fitz fiddled with his watch, his focus split between the screens and the door.

Violet, hunched over her laptop, seemed more interested in her second muffin than the slideshow. Kiko, seated slightly away from the others, cradled her injured side, though she tried to look nonchalant. Sonya sat like a statue.

The door slid open, and Suzanne Blackwood walked in, flanked by six lawyers. Dressed impeccably in a cream suit and pearls, she looked every bit the grieving widow who had nothing to hide. Her lawyers fanned out, taking up seats at strategic points along the table. Suzanne settled at the head, smoothing her skirt as she crossed her legs.

"Mrs. Blackwood," Claire began, keeping her tone measured, "thank you for coming in. We appreciate your cooperation."

"Of course," Suzanne replied, her voice light. "I'm happy to help. Though I must say, it's becoming increasingly clear that you're fixated on me rather than solving my husband's murder."

Claire ignored the jab. "Let's start with the robot dog. You were supposed to bring it in this morning."

Suzanne raised an eyebrow, her lawyers shifting slightly. "Unfortunately, I can't do that. It was stolen from my home last night."

Fitz straightened. "Stolen?"

"Yes," Suzanne said. "I woke up this morning to find my security system tampered with and the dog missing. I've already reported it to the Medina police."

"That's interesting timing, Mrs. Blackwood," Claire said. "First the dog you tried to destroy, and now the one from your house is gone. Plus, the one you gifted to Geoffrey disappeared as well. Odd."

Suzanne's expression didn't waver. "Interesting, perhaps. But surely you're not implying I orchestrated a theft of my own property."

"We're not implying anything," Claire said. "But this does seem convenient."

One of Suzanne's lawyers leaned in. "Agents, if you have evidence to suggest my client is involved in any wrongdoing, present it. Otherwise, these baseless accusations are wasting everyone's time."

Claire turned her focus back to Suzanne. "Let's talk about the dog you drowned."

Suzanne sighed softly, as if the question pained her. "First of all, it was a machine, not a real dog. But it reminded me of Vincent. Seeing it was unbearable."

Fitz leaned forward. "Why not sell it? Donate it? Throw it away? Why go to the trouble of drowning it?"

"Yeah," Jack said. "It was set to be auctioned off that night. You never had to see it again."

Suzanne's fingers drummed on the table. "It was cathartic. And frankly, I don't see why this is relevant. The dog was mine to do with as I pleased."

"Cathartic enough to destroy a quarter-million-dollar robot dog?" Jack asked, his skepticism clear.

"Grief doesn't always make sense," Suzanne replied. "I've lost my husband. If destroying a meaningless object brought me even a sliver of relief, who are you to question it?"

"Meaningless object?" Fitz pressed. "It was part of the Littermates set. A gift you and your husband bought together."

Suzanne's jaw tightened, the first crack in her polished demeanor. "Vincent handled the purchase. It meant nothing to me."

Claire's eyes narrowed. "Did it mean anything to Brentley Flemming?"

Suzanne tilted her head, her expression unreadable. "What does Brentley have to do with this?"

Fitz answered before Claire could. "You tell us. Do you know where he is?"

Suzanne shook her head "No, I don't. But if you're suggesting he stole the dogs, I wouldn't be surprised. He was always... ambitious."

"Ambitious enough to kill?" Fitz asked. "Kill for a woman he loved? We have reason to believe you and he may have been... *involved*."

One of the lawyers snapped, "This is absurd. You're fishing, and it's disrespectful."

"I'm asking a question," Fitz said, his eyes locked on Suzanne. "Do you believe Brentley killed your husband?"

Suzanne shrugged, her calm demeanor back. "I don't believe anything. But you're the investigators, aren't you? Maybe those glasses of his captured something. You should look into that."

"And why were you trying to destroy the robot dog?" Claire asked. "If Brentley's the killer, wouldn't you want us to have every piece of evidence?"

The lawyers spoke up in unison, their objections drowning out Suzanne's voice.

"We're done here," one of them said firmly, standing. "My client has cooperated more than enough."

"Sit down," Claire said. "We have something else. Violet?"

CHAPTER FORTY-TWO

VIOLET CLICKED A REMOTE, and the screen at the front of the room came alive with a stark white background and a series of technical schematics. She stood confidently, a laser pointer in hand, and began her explanation.

"This," Violet said, circling a small metallic module in the schematic, "is the data core of the Littermates robot dog. It's essentially the dog's brain, capable of processing and storing massive amounts of information."

Claire sat back, watching Suzanne's expression carefully. The widow's face was calm, but her hands rested a little too tightly on the table.

"Now, when I say this dog was full of data, I mean *full*," Violet continued. "The dog was wirelessly linked to the other two in the Littermates set: one at Suzanne's house and one supposedly at Geoffrey's house. These three units communicate constantly, syncing and sharing data through an encrypted cloud system. So, while Suzanne was drowning one dog, it had already uploaded and stored data to the other two, and vice versa." Suzanne's lawyers exchanged glances, but none of them interrupted.

"I was able to extract terabytes of data from the dog, including logs of its GPS location, audio recordings, and even visual data captured by its camera sensors. It's essentially a roaming surveillance device. These dogs weren't just toys—they were a high-tech monitoring system."

Claire watched Suzanne's expression darken, but stayed silent, letting Violet finish.

"We're still combing through it," Violet said, switching to a slide showing timestamps and encrypted files, "but I can tell you that the preliminary data places this dog—and by extension, Suzanne's set—near Vincent Blackwood on the night he died." The room fell silent.

"And," Violet added, "it's going to show more. I'd bet my career on it."

One of Suzanne's lawyers, a middle-aged man with an expensive suit and a cutting tone, finally spoke. "This is preposterous. You expect us to believe that this so-called autopsy revealed all of this? Conveniently tying my client to her husband's death? Via a dog that my client says was *never even turned on*? It's absurd."

"It's data," Violet replied sharply. "It doesn't lie."

"Well," the lawyer said, standing, "we don't believe you. And frankly, we're done entertaining these baseless accusations. Let's go, Suzanne."

Suzanne rose gracefully, smoothing her skirt as her lawyers gathered their things. Her movements were slow and precise, as if to signal that she had already won.

She walked out without another word, her entourage trailing behind her like shadows.

In the Boiler Room, the atmosphere was thick with frustration.

Fitz leaned back in his chair, tossing a stress ball up and down in his hand. "Well," he said with a sigh, "that failed miserably."

"Sorry, everyone," Violet said, spinning slightly in her chair, her voice carrying a tone of guilt. "I really tried."

Fitz stopped tossing the ball and leaned forward. "Sometimes when you bluff, the lawyers call you on it. They smelled weakness and went for it."

"I BS'd as hard as I could. I thought—"

"We know," Claire interrupted gently, walking over to stand beside her. "We all know you did your best."

Violet exhaled heavily, rubbing her temples.

Jack, standing by the coffee machine, let out a low groan. "So we've got nothing?"

"No, I—wait." Violet's tone shifted and she swiveled quickly back to her screens, her fingers flying across the keyboard. "Holy crap."

Claire immediately moved to her side. "What is it?" she demanded, leaning over to look at the monitors.

"I just got a ping from the second robot dog," Violet said, her voice rising with urgency. "The one from Geoffrey's house."

"Where is it?" Claire asked, her pulse quickening.

"It's... it's on Suzanne's property," Violet said, her eyes darting between several data streams. "But it's not in the house. It's somewhere... outside. The signal is weak, but it's definitely there."

"In the yard?" Jack asked, moving closer.

"Or maybe *under* the yard," Violet murmured, frowning at the data. "It's hard to tell."

"The tunnels?" Kiko said, her voice cutting through the room like a spark. "Does Suzanne's house have tunnels like Helene's?"

"Maybe, but.. no it's... it looks like the house next door. One of the guest houses or whatever."

"That's where Hailey and Daniel Blackwood are staying."

Everyone froze for half a second, the realization sinking in. Then Claire barked, "Let's move!"

Chairs scraped and monitors flickered as the team bolted for the door, the Boiler Room suddenly alive with purpose.

CHAPTER FORTY-THREE

CLAIRE STEPPED out of the SUV, the cool late afternoon air brushing against her face as she led Jack and Sonya toward the Blackwood estate's dual guest houses. The sprawling grounds were quiet, save for the faint rustle of leaves and the distant sound of waves lapping at the shore.

The guest houses loomed ahead, elegant structures that seemed less like secondary residences and more like retreats for the wealthy.

She glanced over her shoulder and saw Fitz and Kiko hanging back by the SUV. Fitz leaned casually against the hood, chatting with her as if they were on a coffee break instead of investigating a case that was teetering on unraveling. Claire turned her attention back to the task at hand as she approached the guest house door.

Without hesitation, she knocked firmly. The sound echoed in the stillness, and after a few moments, the door opened. Daniel Blackwood stood there, his surprise evident. He was dressed in a crisp button-down and slacks, his salt-and-pepper hair neatly combed. He blinked at the trio of agents.

"Claire Anderson," he said, his tone wary. "To what do I owe this unexpected visit? Or, if you're looking for Hailey, she's next door." He smirked slightly. "Meeting with her lawyers."

"We're here about the robot dogs," Claire said without preamble.

Daniel blinked again, a confused laugh escaping his lips. "The robot dogs? Are you serious?"

"Yes," Sonya interjected, her voice steady. "We've tracked one of them to this property. Care to explain?"

Daniel stepped back, rubbing the back of his neck. "I didn't realize the FBI cared so much about household gadgets."

Jack crossed his arms. "Why don't you tell us why it's here?"

Daniel hesitated, then shrugged. "Look, Suzanne told me to get rid of them. All of them. The one from her house, the one from Geoffrey's, and this one. She said they were... I don't know, compromised or something."

Fitz reached into his pocket and pulled out a pack of mints, offering one to Kiko, who stood nearby, arms crossed and scanning the estate grounds.

"Ever hear the history of the boozey tunnels?" Fitz asked. His eyes flicked to the massive modern mansion in the distance. Its sleek design, all glass and steel, contrasted starkly with the surrounding greenery.

Kiko shook her head, glancing at him. "What about the tunnels?"

"The ones you were in. With Helene and Claire," Fitz said, popping a mint into his mouth. "Underneath these grand old estates in Medina. They're a relic of prohibition.

Back in the 1920s and early '30s, this area wasn't just a playground for the wealthy—it was also a hub for some rather clever bootleggers. The laws may have banned alcohol, but you know how it goes. People with means find their way around inconveniences like legality."

Kiko smirked, leaning her shoulder against the SUV. "And these people had plenty of means."

"Precisely." Fitz gestured toward the mansion, though his gaze lingered on the guest house. "The tunnels were dug discreetly beneath the properties, connecting basements to hidden entrances at the shoreline. Boats would pull up under cover of darkness, unload crates of Canadian whiskey or rum from the Caribbean, and the alcohol would disappear into the estates without a trace."

Kiko raised an eyebrow. "How do you know all this?"

Fitz tapped the side of his head. "British, remember? We're obsessed with history. Besides, one of the books I read years ago mentioned that Medina's wealth wasn't just from tech tycoons. The old money here—bankers, industrialists—they funded quite a bit of it with illicit liquor."

"So, Suzanne's place could have a tunnel," Kiko said, turning to eye the mansion. "Like Helene's?"

"Could?" Fitz gave a quiet laugh. "I'd wager it does. These newer homes have obliterated much of the old charm, but no one fills in a good tunnel. Too useful."

"Compromised?" Claire raised an eyebrow.

"Yeah, something like that," Daniel said. "She was insistent, said it needed to be destroyed. But come on, do you know how much those things are worth? Quarter million dollars' worth of tech? I'm not just going to toss it into a dumpster."

"Do you have proof Suzanne asked you to dispose of it?" Claire asked.

Daniel shifted uncomfortably, pulling his phone from his pocket. "Yeah, she texted me. Hold on."

As he scrolled through his messages, Claire studied him. His unease seemed genuine, but she wasn't about to let her guard down. When he handed her the phone, the text was there, clear as day. Suzanne's instructions to "take care of the dog at Geoffrey's" were vague but damning.

"Keep that thing here," Claire commanded, handing the phone back to him. "It's evidence now. Is Suzanne home?"

Now that they had the second one, she desperately wanted to see what the third one had recorded.

Daniel glanced toward the main house. "She's inside, far as I know. But if you're planning to question her, good luck. She's not exactly in a chatty mood these days."

Fitz tilted his head, studying the mansion's mirrored windows and the way the sunlight reflected off the polished glass. It revealed nothing of what was happening inside. "She could be sitting in there right now, sipping tea and thumbing her nose at us. Or, knowing her, she's already out the back door, plotting her next move. My guess is she knows we're close and is prepping to disappear to some small European country with no extradition treaty with the U.S."

Kiko pushed off the SUV, stretching her arms. "You always assume the worst of people, don't you?"

"It's not the worst," Fitz said. "It's just a pattern. When someone builds a life on secrets, they rarely stop adding to them."

Kiko opened her mouth to respond, but a loud creak interrupted her. She turned to see the door of the guest house swing open, Claire stepping out first, followed by Jack and Sonya.

"Any action over there?" Claire called as she approached, her gaze flicking between the SUV and the mansion beyond.

Fitz shook his head. "Quiet as a graveyard."

Claire glanced at Kiko. "Daniel has proof Suzanne asked her to dispose of the dogs. That means we have her on a lie, and on disposing evidence she'd been ordered to hand over."

"She's fleeing," Jack said. "I'd bet anything on it."

"Agreed," Sonya said.

Fitz spoke up. "What about the tunnels?"

Claire turned to him, brow furrowed. "The ones under Helene's? What about them?"

Fitz gestured toward the mansion. "They're all over Medina. From back in the Prohibition days. These properties are riddled with them. And Helene's house is nearby. My guess is they all have them and they all connect."

Jack frowned. "You think Suzanne's using them now?"

"Wouldn't be the craziest idea," Fitz replied. "Comes back from our office with her army of lawyers, they warn her we're getting close, she decides to disappear through the tunnels, meet up with a boat, head to a private plane. That's what I'd do if I had unlimited money."

"So the tunnels always come out at the lake," Claire asked.

Fitz nodded. "Yup, that's how they brought the booze in."

"But we don't even know if there *are* tunnels at this house," Jack said. "And even if there are, we don't know where they are."

"Leave that to me," Fitz said, already on his way over to Suzanne's house.

CHAPTER FORTY-FOUR

THE AIR in the stone room was heavy, damp, and reeked faintly of mildew. Suzanne Blackwood struck a match, the flare of light illuminating her elegant fingers. She touched the flame to the wick of a thick candle, its flickering glow casting distorted shadows across the rough walls.

Brentley Flemming sat slumped on a decrepit wooden chair in the corner, his once perfect posture broken, his confidence eroded. His eyes darted toward the flame, then to Suzanne's face, filled with a strange mix of hope and desperation.

He'd been in this dungeon-like room for two full days.

"Is it time?" he asked, his voice cracking. "Can we finally leave together?"

Suzanne smiled and walked toward him, the candlelight catching on her flawless cheekbones, making her appear ghostly in the dim room. "Leave together?" she repeated, her tone dripping with mockery. "Brentley, darling, that sounds so... romantic."

He straightened in his chair, his brows furrowing. "You promised. You said we'd be free of all this. The lawyers, the cops, the media. All of it. I did everything you asked. Got the aconitine for you and—"

"You did fine, Brent." She tilted her head, watching him like a scientist observing a particularly dull specimen. "But did I really promise that?" Her voice was soft, teasing. "You know how I am with promises. So easy to make, so... flexible in interpretation."

His face twisted in confusion and a hint of anger. "You said—"

"Oh, Brentley." She sighed, placing the candle on a small, uneven shelf along the wall. "You're sweet, really. A touch dim, but sweet. I suppose that's what made you so easy to work with. So easy to *work*."

It felt good having this power over a man. After being mocked and teased through school. After being dumped by her first husband for being too "ambitious." After being abused by her second husband for years before finally finding the courage to push him down those stairs. And after watching her third husband screw up his businesses so badly that she'd to put him out of his misery to save her own fortune.

Brentley's jaw dropped slightly, but no words came. Suzanne watched him for a moment, almost amused by his dawning realization. She felt a flicker of pity for him, a brief pang of something that might have been guilt in a weaker person. But she had spent decades building walls around her emotions. Pity was just a passing feeling, like hunger or thirst. Easily ignored.

Pushing her second husband down the stairs had started her down a new path. He'd had it coming, sure, but it hadn't been pre-meditated. Drugging her third husband and pushing him off the boat had solidified her love of killing men.

Then, when Vincent stole Helene's app and began

turning it into a breeding ground for sexist incels and toxic masculinity, she'd decided to go all the way. To make an example out of him by killing him in the most brazen way possible. She didn't think she'd get caught, but she'd come up with a backup plan, just in case.

"You used me," Brentley said, his voice shaking.

She laughed softly, a sound devoid of warmth. "Used you? That's such an unkind way to put it. You were a tool, Brentley. A useful one, but a tool nonetheless."

His face contorted with a mix of betrayal and fear. "So what now?" he asked. "You just leave me here to rot?"

She gave a thoughtful tilt of her head. "Something like that."

He lunged to his feet, his body trembling. "You can't do this. You can't just—"

Before he could finish, Suzanne reached into her coat, her movements precise and unhurried. The gun was small, elegant, but its weight felt good in her hand. She raised it and pulled the trigger without a second's hesitation.

The shot echoed sharply in the confined space, the sound reverberating off the stone walls. Brentley stumbled back, clutching his stomach, his expression frozen in shock and pain as he crumpled to the floor.

Suzanne stepped over his writhing form, her shoes clicking softly against the stone. She didn't look down, didn't give him the satisfaction of her gaze. Instead, she reached for the heavy wooden door, stepped into the tunnel, and carefully closed it behind her.

She slid the iron bolt into place, the metallic scrape loud in the silence. He was locked in.

As she stood there, her hand resting on the door, she allowed herself a small, satisfied smile. Brentley didn't deserve this. Not exactly. Sure he was a smarmy womanizer who'd been easily seduced by Suzanne's promises of wealth beyond belief. At his core, though, he was too weak to do any real damage.

But, she thought, sometimes one man had to pay for the crimes of so many others.

"Goodbye, Brentley," she said.

And with that, Suzanne walked away, the faint glow of the candle inside flickering weakly through the cracks in the door.

CHAPTER FORTY-FIVE

FITZ LED Jack along the sleek, glassy exterior of Suzanne's mansion, his eyes scanning the ground where the polished walls met the trimmed lawn. The contrast between the ultra-modern architecture and the landscaped yard was seamless—almost too seamless.

"This is all new," Fitz murmured, gesturing toward the foundation. "But there's something odd about how the house meets the earth here. It's like they built over the original structure rather than tearing it all down."

Jack raised an eyebrow, crossing his arms. "You're saying this fancy glass box might be hiding something old?"

"Precisely." Fitz crouched low, running his fingers along the ground. Then he spotted it—a faint seam in the concrete, partially concealed by the landscaping. A narrow staircase, made of older stone, descended a few feet down to what looked like a metal door.

"See this?" Fitz said, standing and brushing off his hands. "This is part of the original foundation. Likely the basement of the old property before the remodel. And that—" he pointed to the door "—isn't part of any modern blueprint."

Jack leaned in for a closer look, his lips twisting into a smile. "Well, you're the brains. Let's see if it opens."

Fitz grabbed the handle and tugged, but it didn't budge. The door was thick, solid metal, with an ancient lock hanging just below the latch. "No surprise it's locked," Fitz said, stepping back. "This thing's been here for decades, maybe longer."

Jack moved forward. "Step aside."

Fitz barely had time to comply before Jack lifted his boot and slammed it against the lock. The old mechanism gave way with a metallic crunch, and the door creaked open, revealing a dark staircase descending into the earth.

"Subtle," Fitz remarked, but Jack only grinned.

They both stepped cautiously inside, Jack leading the way as Fitz scanned the walls with a wary eye. The staircase was steep, made of aged stone that seemed to absorb the faint light from outside. The air grew cooler as they descended, the smell of damp earth and mildew curling up from below.

At the bottom of the stairs, a narrow tunnel stretched out into the darkness, the ceiling low and reinforced with wooden beams that looked decades old. Jack pulled a flashlight from his jacket and flicked it on, the beam cutting through the gloom.

"After you," Fitz said with a dry smile, though he stayed close behind.

Jack stepped forward, the echo of his boots swallowed by the oppressive quiet. The tunnel yawned before them, shadowed and unwelcoming.

"Do you smell something?" Fitz asked, heading deeper into the tunnel.

"Lavender. Spice."

"Bingo," Fitz said. "It's Suzanne's perfume."

CHAPTER FORTY-SIX

JACK LED the way through the tunnel, his flashlight beam bouncing off the rough stone walls as they walked. Fitz stayed close behind him.

They reached a three-way intersection, the tunnels splitting off in three directions. Jack stopped, scanning the options. "Left, right, or straight?" he asked, sweeping the flashlight over each option. "We're guessing here."

Fitz furrowed his brow, his mind racing. "Left," he said firmly.

Jack shook his head. "No, it makes more sense to go straight. If she's running, she'll take the shortest path toward the water."

"That's an assumption," Fitz said. "These tunnels were built for smuggling. Left might lead to the water, too."

Jack hesitated for a moment, then nodded. "Fine. Left it is. But if this is wrong..."

"Let's just go," Fitz interrupted, already moving.

They hurried down the left tunnel, the uneven floor making every step an effort. Fitz's mind was a tangle of thoughts, replaying everything he'd ever read about tunnel systems like these, imagining where Suzanne might be heading.

A faint sound caught his attention, and he froze, holding out a hand to stop Jack. "Did you hear that?"

Jack tilted his head, listening. Another faint noise echoed through the tunnel—a low, agonized cry.

"This way," Fitz said, quickening his pace.

At the end of the tunnel, they found a heavy wooden door. Fitz pushed against it, but it wouldn't budge.

"Try unlocking it first," Jack said sarcastically, shining his light on the bolt.

"Right, right." Fitz reached up, unbolted it, and pushed the door open.

Inside, the faint glow of candlelight illuminated a small, dank room. Brentley Fleming lay sprawled on the floor, his hand pressed against his stomach, blood seeping through his fingers. His face was pale, his breaths shallow and ragged.

"Bloody hell," Fitz muttered, stepping aside to let Jack take the lead.

Jack crouched beside Brentley, pulling a handkerchief from his pocket and pressing it against the wound. "Hold this," he said, guiding Brentley's hand to the makeshift bandage. "Keep the pressure steady."

Brentley's eyes fluttered open, his gaze unfocused. "Suzanne," he whispered, his voice weak and pained.

"Where is she?" Fitz asked, crouching down beside him. "Brentley, focus. Which way did she go?"

Brentley's lips moved, his words faint. "Toward... the water. She has a boat... we were supposed to go... together."

Fitz exchanged a look with Jack, who was still working to staunch the bleeding.

"I've got him," Jack said. "You go."

Fitz hesitated for a fraction of a second, then nodded. He stood and turned toward the tunnel, his pulse pounding in his ears. "Hold on, Brentley," he called over his shoulder as he sprinted down the tunnel. "We'll get her."

The faint cries of Brentley and Jack's steady voice faded behind him as Fitz pushed forward, the promise of an end to this chase driving him faster into the darkness.

CHAPTER FORTY-SEVEN

CLAIRE'S PHONE buzzed in her pocket as she stood on the gravel path outside Suzanne's mansion. The stillness of the property grated on her nerves—no sign of Suzanne, no motion in the house.

Jack's voice came through, sharp and urgent. "We found the tunnels under her house. I'd bet anything she headed down there when we arrived, or when Daniel told her we'd found the dog. She's likely heading toward the water. Fitz and I are in pursuit through the tunnels. Check if there's a dock or anything leading to the lake."

Claire snapped her fingers at Kiko and Sonya, who were already alert. "Move!"

The three of them sprinted to the SUV. Claire climbed into the driver's seat as Sonya slammed the passenger door and Kiko jumped into the back. Without hesitation, Claire threw the vehicle into gear, veering off the driveway and across the lawn.

The SUV jolted and bounced over uneven ground, crushing flower beds and leaving deep ruts in the manicured grass. A wrought-iron trellis toppled under the wheels with a metallic clatter. Sonya braced herself against the dashboard while Kiko gripped the handle above her head.

"Claire—" Sonya started, but Claire cut her off.

"She wants the water? Let's not give her time to get there."

The vehicle tore through a row of hydrangeas before slamming back onto a gravel path that snaked toward the shoreline.

In the distance, the glimmer of the lake reflected bright sunlight into Claire's eyes. She tightened her focus on the narrow path ahead, her heart pounding as they raced to cut Suzanne off.

Fitz burst from the tunnel, his breath ragged as he staggered into the daylight. The transition from the dark, damp passage to the open brilliance of the lakeshore made him squint, but he didn't stop moving. The ground sloped up sharply, the rocky terrain causing him to trip multiple times. Then he spotted her.

Suzanne stood on the deck of a sleek, impossibly expensive speedboat, the kind meant to impress more than anything else. Its polished white hull glinted in the sun, the engine idling with a predatory hum. She was already untying the rope. Slowly, carefully, as if time were on her side.

The boat began inching away from the dock.

Fitz didn't think—he just ran.

He pushed his body harder than he thought possible, his legs burning as he sprinted down the incline. The world around him blurred; there was only the boat, only Suzanne. Her head turned at the sound of his approach, her expression flickering with surprise before settling into a cold mask.

With a final, desperate lunge, Fitz reached the edge of the

dock and vaulted onto the boat. The impact sent a shudder through the craft, and for a split second, everything was still.

Then chaos erupted.

A man—broad, muscle-bound, and clearly a bodyguard—emerged from the cabin. Fitz barely had time to register him before a punch landed squarely on his jaw, sending him reeling. He stumbled, but recovered quickly, throwing a wild punch that connected with the man's ribs. The bodyguard grunted but barely flinched, his sheer size absorbing the blow like it was nothing.

Fitz ducked as another punch whistled past his head, surprising himself with his own dexterity. He jabbed again, this time catching the man on the chin, and followed with an elbow to the gut. For a moment, he had the upper hand, his desperation fueling his strikes.

But the bodyguard was relentless. A knee drove into Fitz's stomach, knocking the wind out of him. Fitz staggered, his vision swimming as the man's fist came down hard against the side of his head. The world tilted, and Fitz hit the deck, the impact reverberating through his skull.

Darkness encroached as he fought to stay conscious, Suzanne's calm figure the last thing he saw before everything faded to black.

Claire slammed the brakes, the SUV skidding wildly as the tires tore up the lawn, flinging dirt and grass into the air. The shoreline loomed closer than she'd realized, and the vehicle came to a bone-jarring halt just as the front wheels kissed the edge of the water.

"Out!" Claire yelled, her voice mostly drowned out by the sound of the engine.

Sonya flung her door open first, hitting the ground

running as Kiko scrambled from the backseat, nearly colliding with her. Kiko leapt out, the force of her movement rocking the SUV. Claire barely had time to register the sudden shift in weight before the back end tilted, dragging the vehicle forward.

"Wait—" she began, but it was too late.

The SUV tipped, plunging nose-first into the dark water of Lake Washington. The windshield cracked on impact, and the icy water surged in, engulfing Claire in seconds.

She clawed for the door handle, but the force of the sinking vehicle pinned her for a terrifying moment. Her body froze in the frigid rush, her breath stolen as she struggled to think.

Sonya leapt onto the sleek boat, her boots skidding on the polished deck. She drew her firearm in one fluid motion as she regained her balance, leveling it at the man standing over Fitz's crumpled body.

"Hands up!" she barked.

The bodyguard froze mid-step, his eyes darting between her and the pistol trained on him. Slowly, he raised his hands, his lips pressed into a line.

"Cut the engine!" Sonya snapped, glancing briefly toward the controls.

Suzanne, standing rigid at the helm, hesitated before finally reaching for the throttle. The boat's rumble softened to an idle, the water lapping gently against the hull.

Sonya kept her weapon locked on the bodyguard as she crouched beside Fitz. Blood trickled from his temple, matting his hair, but his chest rose and fell steadily.

She pressed two fingers against his neck, feeling the reassuring thrum of his pulse. "You'll be okay," she muttered under her breath.

As she turned, Suzanne's facade cracked. Tears streamed down her face as she sat motionless, gripping the edge of the console. "It wasn't supposed to be like this," Suzanne whispered, her voice trembling. "None of it was supposed to go this far."

"Save it," Sonya growled, not taking her eyes off the bodyguard. "You've got plenty of time to talk once we're back onshore."

The man shifted slightly, as though weighing his options, but Sonya's firearm didn't waver. "Don't even think about it," she warned, her tone as deadly as she could make it.

Claire hadn't been wearing her seatbelt—thank God. Twisting against the pressure, she braced her foot on the center console and shoved. The door gave with a groan, swinging open just enough for her to wriggle out. Her lungs screamed for air as she kicked furiously, her hands reaching for the surface.

Bursting out of the water, she gasped, choking on the cool air as she swam for the shore.

Kiko was already there, shouting her name, her face searching. "Claire!" Kiko waded into the water, arms outstretched.

"I'm fine!" Claire sputtered, coughing as Kiko grabbed her arm, hauling her onto the muddy bank.

She collapsed onto the ground, water dripping from her hair and clothes as she stared up at the sky.

CHAPTER FORTY-EIGHT

THE LAWN of Suzanne's sprawling mansion was a mess of trampled flowerbeds, churned-up grass, and the chaotic remnants of the drama. The sun hung high now, bathing the scene in a harsh, midday light.

Claire sat on a stone bench, a towel draped over her shoulders as she watched Brentley Flemming being loaded onto a stretcher across the lawn.

Medics moved quickly but not urgently, their movements confident.

Jack and Kiko stood a few feet away from the ambulance, Jack's hands on his hips as he watched Flemming be loaded in. Kiko's posture was slightly hunched, her arm wrapped protectively around her midsection.

Spotting Claire, they strolled over.

"How're you holding up?" Jack asked.

Claire shrugged, wiping at her damp hair with the towel. "I've been better. How's Brentley?"

"He'll live," Jack said. He glanced back at the ambulance. "Tougher than he looks, I'll give him that. Was actually talking. Gut wounds are the worst, but I managed to stop the bleeding long enough for the medics to take over."

Claire nodded, her eyes drifting back to Brentley as the medics closed the ambulance doors. Sonya joined them, a satisfied smirk on her face as she approached.

"Well, we've got her," Sonya said, folding her arms. "Attempted murder of Brentley Flemming. That'll keep Suzanne locked up for a long time."

Claire let out a breath. "I don't know if we'll ever be able to pin her for her husbands' murders, but this? This is something. We've got her, at least partially."

Kiko snorted, shaking her head. "Partially? You mean the sleazy douchebag she shot in the gut? He asked me out. Can you believe that?"

Sonya raised an eyebrow. "You're kidding."

"I wish," Kiko said, rolling her eyes. "Jack saw it. I'm standing there, and this dude—twenty-five years older than me, mind you—has the nerve to ask if I'm free Friday night. As he's bleeding out!"

"Not gonna lie," Jack said. "I was a little jealous."

Claire decided to let that one go. She was too cold and too wet to worry about those two right now.

The next morning, Claire shuffled into the Boiler Room, nursing her second cappuccino of the day. The air smelled faintly of burnt wires and stale takeout, a sure sign Violet had been up all night.

Her suspicions were confirmed when she found Violet slouched in her chair, eyes red-rimmed but sparkling with mischief. On the large table before her sat the three AI robot dogs, their sleek metallic bodies gleaming under the fluorescent lights. After catching Suzanne, they'd found the second one in another hidden passage in the tunnels, and they'd gotten the third from Daniel in the guest house.

Before Claire could ask, Violet said, "Not a single shred of evidence on them. At the party, Hailey was with Suzanne's all night, trying to train it to fetch her champagne and pouting when it wouldn't. The one at Geoffrey's house hadn't even been set up fully. No video or audio recorded."

"So Suzanne thought they might have incriminating evidence, but they had none?"

"Exactly," Violet said. "Not a surprise, really. Rich people buy all sorts of tech they don't understand. I mean, not just rich people. You think Fitz understands how to use his iPhone?"

"Good point." Claire frowned, noticing that all three of the robot dogs were turned on and seemed to be listening. "Please tell me you didn't reprogram those things for fun."

Violet grinned, clearly proud of herself. "Fun? Claire, this is *art.* Watch."

She tapped a few keys, and the first dog, the one formerly known as Suzanne's, sprang to life. Its head swiveled, its glassy eyes glowing blue. "Ah, Claire!" it said in a perfect imitation of Fitz's clipped British accent. "Finally graced us with your presence, have you? Thought you might sleep through the apocalypse."

Claire blinked, utterly stunned, as the second dog chimed in, its voice an identical match. "Apocalypse, my metallic rear end. The real tragedy is Manchester United's midfield lineup. Utterly embarrassing."

The third dog piped up, its tone full of disdain. "Oh, give it a rest, you pint-pouring troglodyte. The beauty of a well-drawn pint of lager is leagues beyond your overpriced craft ales."

Claire set her coffee down slowly, afraid she might drop it. "Violet. What. Did. You. Do?"

"I taught them a trick," Violet said, beaming. "Now they're all Fitz. Triple the wit, triple the charm. Isn't it great?"

One of the dogs, now trotting in a tight circle, huffed. "Great? I'm surrounded by amateurs. Lager versus ale? Try debating the finer points of Kierkegaard versus Nietzsche, you philistines."

"Nietzsche was a blowhard," snapped another dog, its ears twitching. "And you wouldn't know Kierkegaard if he smacked you with *Fear and Trembling*."

"Don't drag Kierkegaard into this, you pompous keg of bolts," retorted the third dog. "Now, back to the matter of importance—who in their right mind prefers lager over a proper English ale?"

Claire pinched the bridge of her nose, but she couldn't stop the smile creeping across her face. "Violet, do you realize the trouble you've just invited into our lives?"

"Oh, relax," Violet said, waving a hand. "They're hilarious. And educational. You've got three Fitzes, each with his own philosophical hot takes. I'm calling it... *FitzBot 3000*."

One of the dogs climbed down onto a chair, turning its glowing eyes toward Claire. "Claire, my dear, don't listen to her. This isn't about amusement. It's about elevating the intellectual discourse of this team. Would you care to debate the metaphysical implications of crime-solving?"

The others barked in protest, devolving into a full-on argument about whether the existence of free will could justify premeditated murder. Claire leaned back in her chair, sipping her coffee as she watched the chaos unfold.

"I'm going to regret asking," she said. "But... can you make them stop?"

"Sure," Violet said, but she didn't move a muscle. Instead, she leaned back with a grin, watching the robot dogs bicker like an old British sitcom come to life.

Claire shook her head, laughing despite herself. "This is insane."

The first FitzBot turned to her, its metallic ears perking up. "Insane? No, Claire, this is genius. Now, lager or ale? Do *try* to keep up."

The door to the Boiler Room swung open, and Fitz strolled in with Sonya close behind. Despite a black eye and a limp, Fitz looked unusually polished, his shirt crisp for once, while Sonya had her jacket slung over her shoulder, her stride easy and more relaxed than it had been in days. Claire sipped her coffee, her gaze flicking between them.

Something was different. There was a rhythm to their movements, a silent conversation that hadn't been there before.

"Morning," Fitz said, his eyes narrowing on the table where the robot dogs sat in eerie stillness. "What's this? A yard sale?"

"You don't want to know," Claire said flatly, setting down her mug.

"Oh, come on, of course he does," Violet said, swiveling in her chair to face Fitz. The gleam in her eyes made Claire's stomach tighten. Violet was about to cause trouble.

"Not yet, Violet," Claire interjected quickly. "We've got other things to discuss."

Fitz turned toward Sonya. "What's this? Claire keeping secrets now?"

Before Sonya could reply, Claire cut in again, redirecting. "Sonya, I hear Quantico is calling your name?"

Sonya leaned against the table, arms loosely crossed. "It is. I've decided I'm not staying."

Jack and Kiko, who had just walked in, froze mid-step. Jack frowned, while Kiko raised an eyebrow, a quizzical look aimed at Sonya.

"You're leaving?" Claire asked, trying to mask her

surprise. Hightower had told her that Sonya had been offered a position, but Claire hadn't believed she'd quit the team so quickly. She rested her hand on the back of her chair, waiting for an explanation.

"Fitz is your guy," Sonya said with a shrug. "I can see that now. Plus, I've been offered a top position at Quantico. Too good to pass up."

Jack leaned against the wall. "Quantico, huh? Big leagues."

"Exactly," Sonya said with a small, deliberate nod. "No offense, but I'm not sticking around here when I could be training the future FBI elite."

Fitz tilted his head, feigning insult. "So we're not good enough for you? Our little crew doesn't meet your high standards?"

"You said it, not me," Sonya replied, her mouth twitching into what might have been a smirk.

Jack let out a short laugh, shaking his head. "Well, you're leaving us for a bunch of rookies, so maybe you're not that smart after all."

"Don't ruin the moment, Jack," Sonya quipped, though her tone carried no bite.

Claire watched the exchange, noting how at ease Sonya and Fitz seemed now. Just as they'd become friendly, Sonya was leaving.

Violet clapped her hands. "Enough sentimentality. Fitz, you have to see this."

"Violet—" Claire warned, stepping forward.

Violet ignored her, reaching for her keyboard. "I've been working on something brilliant."

"Violet, no," Claire repeated.

Too late. Violet hit a key, and the robot dogs sprang to life. Their blue eyes lit up, and they stood in unison, their movements unnervingly precise.

The first one cocked its head, its voice unmistakably Fitz's. "Alright then, let's talk Nietzsche. Or perhaps the tragic state of British football. Your pick."

The second chimed in, "Nietzsche is for amateurs. Lager versus ale, Fitz. The debate of our time."

And the third, with a mocking tilt of its head, said, "The answer is clearly ale. Anyone who says otherwise should root for Spurs and call it a day."

Fitz froze, his mouth falling open as he stared at the robotic trio. Around him, the room erupted in laughter.

Claire rubbed her temple, muttering, "I told you."

Fitz pointed at the dogs, his voice half an octave higher than usual. "Violet. What in the name of all things holy is this?"

"Your legacy," Violet declared with a flourish. "*FitzBot 3000*—three versions, less brooding, more entertaining."

"You're fired," Fitz said flatly, which only made the others laugh harder.

CHAPTER FORTY-NINE

Three Days Later

CLAIRE STOOD near the baggage carousel, her hands brushing nervously against the smooth fabric of her blazer. Her daughters had insisted this was the perfect outfit—light cream slacks, a pale blue blouse tucked neatly, and a tailored navy blazer that accentuated her figure. A delicate gold chain hung just above the blouse's neckline, a compromise between professional and approachable.

She glanced down at her shoes—low, block-heeled pumps in a neutral tone—and wondered if the whole look leaned too much toward "job interview" rather than "casual meeting."

Casual. That was the goal. Casual but significant.

Diego Vega was flying in for this. The man who had been on the task force investigating her parents' deaths, the man who had hinted he had something explosive to share about the case, was coming here. To her. Not because this was a date—absolutely not—but because they shared a mutual desire for the truth.

And yet, as Claire stood there waiting, smoothing nonexistent wrinkles in her blazer, she couldn't ignore the butterflies in her stomach. She mentally chastised herself. Silly schoolgirl, she thought. You're here for answers, not wine and candlelight.

The crowd thinned around the carousel as bags were claimed and passengers filtered out. His flight had landed twenty minutes ago, and most of the luggage was already gone.

Claire checked her phone. No new messages. She typed out a quick text: *Diego, I'm at baggage claim. Are you here?*

No reply.

She bit her lip, scanning the remaining bags. A navy duffel circled lazily on the belt. Diego's? She frowned and shifted her weight, glancing toward the terminal doors. This wasn't like him, was it? Their conversations had been brief but purposeful, his demeanor moving easily between professional and flirtatious. He wouldn't just vanish.

Another five minutes passed. Claire's unease sharpened. She dialed his number. It rang once, then went straight to voicemail.

"Diego, it's Claire. Just checking in. I'm at baggage claim. Call me when you get this."

The moment she hung up, a wave of irrational embarrassment washed over her. Had she been stood up? No, that didn't make sense. Diego wasn't coming here for dinner. He was coming with information. Critical information. Information he had insisted could not be shared over the phone.

Claire opened Facebook and searched for his name. His profile came up instantly, his easy smile and dark eyes staring back at her. She scrolled through his recent posts—nothing for the last forty-eight hours. Odd.

Then she saw the tags.

Her chest tightened as her thumb hovered over the words: *Rest in peace, Diego Vega.* Her breathing quickened as she tapped the tag and saw a flood of tributes: *You were taken too soon. Such a tragedy. Can't believe you're gone.*

Claire's pulse pounded in her ears. Her vision blurred as she stumbled across a link in one of the comments. An article.

She clicked it, her heart pounding as her eyes scanned the headline:

Retired FBI Agent Diego Vega Killed in Car Bombing Outside San Diego Apartment Complex

The ground felt like it had shifted beneath her feet. Her grip tightened on her phone as she read on. The explosion occurred forty-eight hours ago, only hours after their last phone call. Diego Vega, the man she was here to meet, was gone.

Her phone buzzed in her trembling hand. A text. But it wasn't from Diego.

It was from Fitz: *You okay?*

She stared at the screen for a long moment before replying. *No.*

CHAPTER FIFTY

A Week Later

FITZ STOOD at the edge of the dumpster, balancing the last box of Margaret's things on the rim before letting it tumble inside with a hollow thud. The box landed atop a heap of crumpled paper and discarded takeout containers, its contents spilling slightly—her yoga blocks, an old scarf, a paperback she'd left half-read on his couch.

He lingered there for a moment, hands resting on the lip of the dumpster. The cool evening air nipped at his face. For the first time in days, he let himself feel the absurdity of it all. Here he was, finally rid of Margaret, and yet he couldn't shake the strange hollowness that came with the silence.

As he turned back toward his building, he noticed the way his shirt hung looser against his frame, the slight ease in his step. He was in better shape now—that was one good thing that had come out of the relationship. She'd pushed him to exercise, to stretch, to eat better. Even if the push had been more about her than him—another one of her manipulations—the results were undeniable.

But it wasn't enough to dull the sting. Fitz had always prided himself on being the smartest person in the room, the one who saw through every lie and read between every line.

And yet, when it came to love, he was a bloody fool. He could admit that now.

After the hospital—after seeing Margaret hand in hand with the man he'd thought was her *ex*-boyfriend—he'd done what he did best: research. A deep dive through social media, text logs, and old photos revealed the truth in unflinching detail. They hadn't been truly broken up, not in the way she'd led Fitz to believe. Maybe there had been a brief falling out, but they were clearly back together now, as close as ever. And Fitz? He'd been the stopgap, the fool with just enough disposable income to float her through tough times.

The kid wasn't his. That much he knew for certain now. It was the final nail in the coffin, the proof that everything between them had been a farce. Margaret and her partner were broke, but Fitz had been an easy mark—generous, distracted, and, despite his self-perception, painfully naive.

"Idiot," he muttered to himself as he climbed the stairs to his apartment. "Absolute bloody idiot."

Inside, the dim light of his living room greeted him. The space was emptier now, stripped of her things and her presence. His yoga mat sat neatly rolled up in the corner, next to a set of weights he'd started using more frequently. The mat had been a gift from her, a token from the days when she'd seemed so invested in his wellbeing. He'd almost thrown it out with the last box, but something had stopped him.

Fitz unrolled the mat and stood over it, hands on his hips. He wasn't much for sentiment, but he couldn't help thinking that maybe he owed himself this one small act of care. For five minutes, he stretched. Nothing too ambitious—just a slow loosening of stiff muscles.

As he finished, he sat cross-legged on the mat, staring at

the blank wall ahead of him. The apartment felt quiet, but it wasn't oppressive. He could feel a shift, faint but unmistakable, like a crack of light edging its way into a dark room.

For the first time in days, Fitz allowed himself to smile.

Melancholy, yes. But hopeful.

~

Claire leaned against the doorframe of Benny's room, watching as her son animatedly explained *Scribble Sight* to Jacqueline and Caroline. They had barely set down their bags from Barcelona before Benny had roped them into testing his app. She already knew all about it, but she stayed silent, letting him have his moment with his sisters.

"It's called *Scribble Sight*," Benny said, practically bouncing in his chair. "You draw something—anything—and the app uses AI to analyze it. Based on the patterns, pressure, and how much space you fill, it gives you a psychological profile. It's like a personality test, but way smarter."

Jacqueline leaned in, eyebrows raised skeptically. "So, it's going to tell me I have deep-seated trust issues because I drew a dog?"

Benny grinned. "It's not that literal. It's more about what your drawing says about how you think. Like, if you use jagged lines, you're stressed. If you leave blank space, maybe you're hesitant. It's all rooted in psychology. Try it."

Caroline grabbed the stylus first, shrugging. "I'll bite. What do I draw?"

"Anything," Benny said. "Something simple."

She started sketching—a quick, clean image of a book. Benny hit a button, and Scribble Sight spun for a moment before displaying its interpretation.

"'You're methodical, curious, and goal-oriented,'" Benny read aloud. "'You approach problems with a logical mindset, but you can sometimes miss emotional cues.' Sound familiar?"

Caroline tilted her head, impressed but trying not to show it. "Okay, not bad, genius. I'll give you that."

Claire had spent much of the last week dealing with the fallout from the Suzanne Blackwood case. She'd lawyered up immediately and wasn't saying a word. Eventually she'd go to trial for the attempted murder of Brentley Flemming, but Claire was unsure if they'd ever uncover enough evidence to convict her of anything else. Even Flemming himself wasn't talking, despite the fact that she'd shot him in the gut. Though discouraging, there *had* been one new break in the case. Working with a forensic accountant, Violet had discovered that Geoffrey, Suzanne's house manager, had been stealing money from the Blackwood's for years. A thousand bucks here, two grand there. Not enough for them to notice. But it had been enough to bring him in and pressure him into agreeing to testify against Suzanne. As the head of the household, he'd known she was sleeping with Flemming for months.

The rest of the week had been spent pressing every contact she had for details about Diego Vega's death, but the truth remained maddeningly elusive. The local police she'd spoken to admitted they were at a loss. The car bomb, they said, was highly sophisticated—definitely not an accident and not something slapped together by an amateur.

Theories were swirling about possible ties to organized crime or a long-buried connection to the mafia, but so far, there were no leads, no suspects, nothing solid to go on. Claire couldn't shake the feeling that whatever had happened to Diego, it was far more complicated—and far closer to her own past—than anyone knew.

Or, perhaps, than anyone was willing to admit.

Jacqueline took the stylus next, rolling her eyes. "Let's see how deep this thing can go." She drew a loose, messy flower, the lines slightly uneven. *Scribble Sight* processed for a few seconds, then displayed its result.

"'You're a romantic at heart, but you sometimes let self-doubt get in your way,'" Benny read. "'You crave connection but need to stand up for yourself more.'"

Jacqueline snorted. "Crave connection? What is this, a dating app?"

"Don't knock it," Caroline teased. "It's not wrong."

They all laughed, and Claire couldn't help but smile at the moment. It was light, easy—a rare slice of normalcy. But her thoughts drifted, unbidden, to Fitz. How would a brilliant psychologist like him react to an app like *Scribble Sight*? She could almost hear him scoffing, dissecting its methodology, pointing out its reliance on generalized data. Or perhaps his experience with Margaret had humbled him. Perhaps he'd secretly admire Benny's ingenuity, even begrudgingly.

Her mind lingered on Fitz longer than she wanted. She felt a mix of emotions when she thought about how thoroughly Margaret had played him. Part of her was glad—maybe it was a lesson Fitz needed. Even the most arrogant, brilliant people could be felled by love, or what they *thought* was love. But she worried, too. Fitz had been putting his life back together, even if it was all built on lies. Would this tear him apart again? Would he spiral?

Part of her hoped not, but another part wondered whether Fitz needed to have his life in shambles to do good work. After all, over the last few weeks he'd seemed healthier than ever, and yet he'd completely whiffed on Suzanne as the killer, while Sonya had called it right from day one. Maybe Fitz was one of those unfortunate creatures who was at his best when he was at his worst.

"Mom, you want to try it again?" Benny's voice broke through her thoughts.

Claire blinked, shaking her head. "Not today, buddy. You three enjoy."

She walked away as their laughter spilled into the hallway, carrying a bittersweet note. For now, she let herself enjoy the sound.

Moments like these didn't come often enough.

—The End—

If you're enjoying this series, don't miss Book 4: Beneath Hemlock Skies.

A NOTE FROM THE AUTHOR

Thanks for reading!

If you enjoyed this book, I encourage you to check out the whole series of FBI Task Force S.W.O.R.D. novels. Each book can be read as a standalone, although relationships and situations develop from book to book, so they will be more enjoyable if read in order.

And if you're loving S.W.O.R.D., check out my first hit series of fast-paced Pacific Northwest mysteries: the Thomas Austin Crime Thrillers.

I also have an online store, where you can buy signed paperbacks, mugs, t-shirts, and more featuring the S.W.O.R.D. team's lovable golden retriever, Ranger, as well as locations and quotations from all my books. Check that out on my website.

Every day I feel fortunate to be able to wake up and create characters and write stories. And that's all made possible by readers like you. So, again, I extend my heartfelt thanks for checking out my books, and I wish you hundreds of hours of happy reading to come.

D.D. Black

MORE D.D. BLACK NOVELS

The Thomas Austin Crime Thrillers

Book 1: *The Bones at Point No Point*

Book 2: *The Shadows of Pike Place*

Book 3: *The Fallen of Foulweather Bluff*

Book 4: *The Horror at Murden Cove*

Book 5: The Terror in The Emerald City

Book 6: The Drowning at Dyes Inlet

Book 7: The Nightmare at Manhattan Beach

Book 8: The Silence at Mystery Bay

Book 9: The Darkness at Deception Pass

Book 10: The Vanishing at Opal Creek

FBI Task Force S.W.O.R.D.

Book 1: *The Fifth Victim*

Book 2: *We Forget Nothing*

Book 3: Widows of Medina

Book 4: Beneath Hemlock Skies

Standalone Crime Novels

The Things She Stole

ABOUT D.D. BLACK

D.D. Black is the author of the Thomas Austin Crime Thrillers, the FBI Task Force S.W.O.R.D. series, and other Pacific Northwest crime novels. When he's not writing, he can be found strolling the beaches of the Pacific Northwest, cooking dinner for his wife and kids, or throwing a ball for his corgi over and over and over. Find out more at ddblackau thor.com.

facebook.com/ddblackauthor
instagram.com/ddblackauthor
tiktok.com/@d.d.black
amazon.com/D-D-Black/e/B0B6H2XTTP
bookbub.com/profile/d-d-black

Made in the USA
Monee, IL
30 January 2025